The Enemies of Vengeance: Vampire Formula #3

P.A. Ross

SCARLETT THORN

http://www.thornsneedles.com/

Copyright © 2020 By P.A. Ross

Scarlett-Thorn Publishing

1st Edition

This is a work of fiction. Names, characters, businesses, places, events, locales, and incidents are either the products of the author's imagination or used in a fictitious manner. Any resemblance to actual persons, living or dead, or actual events is purely coincidental

All rights reserved.
ISBN-13: 9798606490592

TABLE OF CONTENTS

CHAPTER ONE 1
CHAPTER TWO 8
CHAPTER THREE 14
CHAPTER FOUR 23
CHAPTER FIVE 35
CHAPTER SIX 39
CHAPTER SEVEN 49
CHAPTER EIGHT 61
CHAPTER NINE 72
CHAPTER TEN 79
CHAPTER ELEVEN 92
CHAPTER TWELVE 108
CHAPTER THIRTEEN 117
CHAPTER FOURTEEN 126
CHAPTER FIFTEEN 132
CHAPTER SIXTEEN 139
CHAPTER SEVENTEEN 147
CHAPTER EIGHTEEN 158
CHAPTER NINETEEN 165
CHAPTER TWENTY 170
CHAPTER TWENTY-ONE 180
CHAPTER TWENTY-TWO 189
CHAPTER TWENTY-THREE 205

Chapter One

I looked out from the top of the Eiffel Tower over the sprawl of Paris, the river Seine running alongside it cutting the city in half. The green symmetry of the Champ de Mars gardens leading up to the tower. The garden's walkways filled with tiny figures of people swirling around in chaotic patterns, camera flashes illuminating their figures against the backdrop of the Eiffel Tower.

The city shone from street lights and car headlights; the engines sending a buzz into the air. In the distance, police sirens grabbed my attention as their blue lights squeezed past the frenzied flow of traffic.

A summer's night gentle breeze blew across my face. Behind me, the chatter of other tourist merged into a massive concoction of different languages and accents. The sense of their emotions creating a background of psychic chatter.

Thorn's hand squeezed mine, her thumb rubbing across my golden dragon Union ring. "See, so much better than the fake tower in Vegas. This is the real deal in the city of romance. There is no better place to spend our first week together in Union," she said.

I gazed into her sky blue eyes as her raven hair flickered from the warm breeze. She smiled, and I reciprocated the gesture and smiled back.

"It is better. Shame we had to go through so much to get here," I said, remembering my Dad's murder and my tortures at the hands of the Hunters.

"The journey is important. Without it, the destination isn't the same. I am sorry about your father, but we will have our revenge. They have tried their best to break us and they have failed. We are even stronger than before. We are in Union," Thorn replied and held up her hand with her gold thorn Union ring.

We had destroyed the Hunters and Turned in battle. Then we joined in Union and became Queen and King of the Dragans. The golden dragon scaled ring I wore and the gold thorn ring she wore were symbols of our union. We had put our past, with its arguments and betrayals, behind us and committed to a union to strengthen our bond.

Behind us, the crowds milled around and left a space while everyone else crammed together. "Do they know? Is that why they leave us alone?" I asked.

Thorn looked at the gap left around us, with the tourists squashing in against one another. "Not on a conscious level. But subconsciously, they can detect our Dragan auras. I sense a level of underlying fear from them. They probably can't understand it. But it's enough for their primitive instincts to give us a wide berth."

Although I wasn't entirely Dragan, it was apparently enough to be given some space. I had taken the formula at the time of the Union to consummate it properly, as Dragan to Dragan. The formula would have increased my overall Dragan genetics and decreased my human side.

After the union ceremony, we spent a beautiful couple of days together in her Chateau in the south of France. Once the formula wore off, we travelled north to spend the last of the honeymoon in Paris.

"It's our last night. What shall we do after this?" I asked.

"Well, I am getting hungry. There are a couple of areas where I think a meal might find us."

"Then what?"

"Back to the hotel and say our goodbyes."

I stepped back and stared at her. "Goodbye?"

"Yes. I have some news for you. Kieran O'Keefe is being released from prison. I thought you may want to return home and finish your revenge," she said, and pulled out an envelope from her back pocket and offered it to me. I took it and ripped it up. Inside was a single train ticket for the following morning back to London, England.

"You're not coming with me?"

"No. This is something you should do by yourself. Plus, Cassius has a lead on Cyrus. We are going together to find him."

I was confused and scared. Since my ordeal with the Hunters, I hadn't left her side. I felt safe when together. The phantom torture pains in my body re-ignited. The sight of Patrick's grinning face as he smashed my toes apart. Carmella's seductive offer and my betrayal of Thorn flooded back. She wanted to be rid of me so soon after our Union, to go off with her former lover, to search out another former lover.

"But we should always be together. You promised we wouldn't separate again. This isn't what I expected from our Union," I said.

"We will always be together regardless of distance. I meant our bond holds us to one another. But at times, it makes sense for us to take action apart. There are many things that we must do to win this war against the Hunters and Turned. We must spread our skills as required."

"So you are sending me away while you run off with your ex-lover to find another one of your ex-lovers?"

"Jealous?"

"Yes. Of course I am jealous. You hope that both of them together might solve your infertility problems."

She laughed. "Don't be such a child. You know they were never romantic attachments. I believe the Dragan blood is changing you."

I scowled back and then stared into the night. It was true, the more Dragan I became, the more fiery my temper and I hadn't learnt to control it. "Maybe, but still I don't like it."

"You will have to live with it, as I am trusting you not to do anything wrong. Not to misuse your seductive powers for pleasure."

I knew she was referring to Amber, but I wouldn't respond. "I am not sure I care about Kieran and revenge anymore. I would rather stay with you."

"How sweet, but Cassius and I can move quicker without you. And I am afraid that you will scare off Cyrus."

"Why?"

"He will detect the human part of you."

"But you aren't exactly best friends, anyway. I thought you were enemies. Why will he stick around to talk with you and not just run or attack regardless if I am there?"

"We are enemies, but he will at least know what to expect from me. A human, however, is another matter. From what Max said, Cyrus seems to be ready to talk."

"So how exactly did you and Cyrus try for a baby, considering your feud?"

Thorn raised an eyebrow. "It was before the feud and purely as part of the breeding program."

I gazed back into the night sky. "And Cassius?"

"And Amber and Scarlett? You aren't in the position to hold moral judgement on my previous relationships. My deeds were long before you were even born. However, yours have been while we have been together."

"I don't like it. I should stay with you."

"As my chaperone? In case I get ideas?"

"But you will be with other Dragans. I know that is what you want. I know that is what you desire, as I can only stay in Dragan form for a short time."

"But the formula lasts longer every time and one day it will change you completely."

"I know, but in the meantime, I am a poor substitute for a real Dragan."

She pulled me around to face her and took both my hands in hers. "My god, you are like a petulant child at times. I suppose I got to learn how to control and understand my Dragan side as I grew. It must be difficult to have all those emotions sprung upon you at once. To set the record straight. I enjoy our time together, even when you are only human. I have told you before I have had relationships with humans, and I enjoy it but in a different way. You must know this, as we spend time together in both your forms. There is a different dynamic depending on your state of Human or Dragan."

I bit the inside of my lower lip. I knew what she meant, probably in more detail than she realised. When I was only human, I could detect her emotions in my hybrid form and knew she enjoyed our intimate time together. She loved the fact that I was at her mercy and she could snuff me out in a single blow. Instead, she satisfied herself with a bite and a small sip of blood. However, she enjoyed the absolute power.

I always knew she had the power and ability to end my life, but until I detected her emotions, I hadn't realised how raw those feelings were. They were always on the edge of her mind but forced back by her self-control. How many times had I been moments away from death?

"Yes. I know only too well why you enjoy it."

She frowned back at me. "Pardon?"

"Because of the heightened state between us and my new abilities, I can sense your emotions. I know your desires."

She blushed. I had never seen her do that before. "You think you can shame me, then think again. You know what part you play when we are together. Don't act the innocent, pretending you didn't know your role. Just accept it and enjoy it."

It was my turn to blush. Of course, I knew my place as the weaker partner, but to feel her base desires was another level entirely. But it hadn't stopped me from being with her. It was like plummeting to your death in the arms of your lover. There was no place I would rather be.

"Anyway, we agreed on no mind reading," Thorn said.

"It just sort of happened. I wasn't expecting it."

"You can only use that excuse so often, V. Learn to control your powers. We could do with no more incidents of young women falling in love with you."

I knew she wasn't just referring to Amber and Scarlett, as a few of the waitresses at the hotel had been watching me.

"Sorry, I just forget that I am doing it."

"You enjoy the attention, I think. Remember who you really are."

I nodded.

"So we are agreed, you go to Leeds, and Cassius and I are off to Rome to find Cyrus."

"I could still come but keep in the background."

"No. There is another reason you want to come."

"I just... I just don't want to be alone. Sorry, I'm not the great big powerful King of the Dragans you want."

"You are the King of the Dragans, and you will find your strength. This is why you must take your revenge. You have to find yourself again after what happened with Carmella and the Hunters. I don't need psychic powers to notice you are suffering still."

Carmella. I wish Thorn hadn't mentioned her. The torture was terrible, and I suffered from nightmares. But I also felt guilty about Carmella. Her story of being turned and just wanting a normal life struck a chord as it had parallels to my situation. I felt a tinge of loss when Thorn killed her, even though I realised she was just manipulating me. She was playing good cop to Patrick's bad cop as he tortured me.

"But I don't think I want to kill Kieran. It's beneath me."

"Do whatever you like. But he may seek revenge on your family. You still have an aunt and uncle in the area, and he may even hurt Giles's family. You can make sure they all stay safe by paying him a visit."

She was right. He would look for someone to blame for the death of his dad and younger brother. Liam, Kieran's twin, knew it was me, which may lead Kieran to attack my relatives as revenge by proxy.

"I will go back and make sure he knows to stay away. I will put a little fear in him, and if that doesn't work, I will make him feel some more pain. He has a family as well."

"Good. We could do without the distractions later on."

"Okay. I will go."

"When you are there, I want you to visit Miss Jones first. Make sure Annabel and Lucinda are okay. Also, scout out a new property for us. We need to re-establish a base in England."

"You mean after I gave up the location of the last one?"

"You had to tell them something. I understand. But a new base would be useful. From London, travel up and visit Kieran and his family, and then once you are done, get in touch, and we will arrange a meeting."

"Okay. I am sure I can handle a little house hunting and scaring off a human."

Thorn dropped her small handbag off her shoulder and fished out a box wrapped in wedding wrapping paper. "A gift," she said and handed it to me.

I took it and pulled apart the paper to find a smart watch inside the box. "Thank you," I said and leaned in and kissed her.

"It's a Union present or wedding present if that makes more sense to you. But it is more than just a watch. Read the instructions, and you will find out how to trigger a GPS transmitter."

"Cool," I replied and pulled the watch out of its box and placed it on my left wrist.

"I have installed an app on my phone. If you trigger the transmitter, I will get a notification. So if you get into trouble, you can quickly signal for back up, and I will know where to find you."

I smiled. She understood my fears and had taken measures to help me.

"I have one as well. And I have installed the app on your phone. Likewise, I can always signal for you to come to my rescue."

"As if that will be necessary?"

"You underestimate yourself. The power you exhibited in the warehouse battle was immense. To transform into a part Dragon is more than any of us can manage. To create the scales, talons and Dragon strength makes you almost invincible."

"But I haven't been able to do it again."

"Nor should you. It will probably drain you too much as it did the original Dragans."

"Okay. You have convinced me to go to England. I can tell I won't be able to change your mind."

"Good. You can take the formula with you and the testing kit to indicate when to take it next. According to the last measurement, you have another few days to go before you can transform again. We need to make sure it isn't sooner, else we may not have enough needles to complete the full change to a Dragan."

"You trust me to take the needles?"

"Of course. Take three of them. I will safeguard the others in case of an accident. Three should be enough for a journey to England and back."

"Three should be plenty. I don't plan to stay too long."

"Nor do I want you to. I want you back as soon as possible. Use the communication channels we agreed on to set up our reunion. Remember to see Miss Jones first. The address is in the envelope. I will let her know you are coming."

"Of course. No problem."

"Great, now let's finish off our last night with a bite and a bang," Thorn said and wrapped her arms around my back and squeezed us together.

Her flawless pale face and blood red lips tilted up to mine. Her sky blue eyes diluted with the black of her pupils. She closed her eyes as our lips moved together. I shut my eyes, leaned into the kiss and held her tight in my arms. Our lips pressed against one another while our hands embraced each other's bodies. We kissed passionately, and I heard a few comments from the crowd of tourists but I didn't care. I was with Thorn and the universe had stopped.

Chapter Two

We stood in the middle of the metro train, in a quarter-full carriage, on our way to Montmartre in Paris. The seats lined the sides, with adverts on the walls. In the centre were metal poles and overhead bars where a few people held on. An older couple sat at one end, holding hands.

I held onto a pole in the middle of the carriage near the doors, and Thorn had wrapped her arm around my waist for stability. I had just eaten a burger and fries, and now we were going to find Thorn some food before daylight.

We pulled into the last stop before Montmartre. The doors slid back, and the passengers shuffled in and out of the carriage onto the concrete platform. Two groups of young men entered on either side of us. They ranged from late teens to late twenties and dressed in casual streetwear of jeans and t-shirts. They held onto the poles and overhead bars as the train pulled away from the station. Thorn gripped onto my waist to steady herself against the train's movement.

The groups on either side scanned the carriage and then whispered to one another. The group of four men near the older couple shuffled towards them, asking how their night had been. Thorn coughed and stared at the group talking to the old couple. The men noticed her. Everyone noticed Thorn.

I wrapped my arm around her and pulled her in tight. The two groups waved at each and shouted over the top of us.

"Hey, you left your phone at the restaurant," the tallest guy shouted over.

"Cheers," a man responded, and the two groups walked towards us, with Thorn and I stuck in the middle. I tried to focus my senses to listen to their thoughts, but there were too many people on the train. The two men stood next to us, and the rest of the group moved together, shook each other's hand and patted each other on the back.

"Fancy seeing you here."

"Long time no see."

They all laughed and crowded together, with Thorn and I jammed in the middle. I didn't like it. I was used to people giving us plenty of room, a wide berth. I pushed my elbows out to provide us with some space. Two men pretended to fight one another to great shouts and cheers from the group.

The train jolted and the men jerked into us, squashing our arms into our sides, bashing into our bodies and legs. They knocked us from all sides, and then the train slowed to a halt at Montmartre station and the men moved away.

"Sorry," one of them said to us as they exited.

Thorn grabbed my hand and dragged me from the train. She scowled at me as we marched down the underground platform; her face in a rage.

"What's the matter?"

"What's the matter! Are you blind? They did that on purpose. A couple of them put their hands on me. I have found my meal."

"Excellent."

"Your partner gets touched up, and all you can say is excellent?"

"Sorry. But it is good that we found someone that deserves a beating."

"A beating? I am going to kill them."

"I thought that was against your moral code. Only if they hurt other people."

"They've touched me. You know the rules. I am Thorn. Touch me and you bleed. Anyway, check your wallet."

I padded my hand on my front pocket, but it was empty. "Bastards. I am going to rip their bloody heads off. How dare they? Do they not know who we are?"

"Good. I see you are getting into the spirit of things."

Further down the white-tiled tunnels, two men looked back at us as I shouted and it echoed up. They marched ahead to catch up to the front of the group, and all the men took a moment to glance back as they strode to the exit. Good, they were heading out into the night and we could take our revenge.

The tall man at the front stopped before the barrier and stood to one side. He talked to the others and they chatted to each other. He stared at me and smiled.

I let go of Thorn's hand and walked over. "I think you owe us an apology and my wallet."

"Sorry. Do I know you?" he said and smirked. His followers all laughed.

"Yes. We were on the train when you squashed us together and groped my wife and stole my wallet."

"I am not your wife. I am your partner," Thorn said as she joined my side.

"You can't even keep your little lady under control, let alone your wallet."

"You're right; I can't keep her under control, which will be a shame for you. Let's step outside and she can show you."

"I don't think so. Why don't you go about your business? No need for your night to end any worse."

"You don't understand. We came here for you. We ain't leaving until you step outside the safety of this station and the CCTV above us."

"If you think I did something wrong, why don't you go to the police? There are usually some that patrol around here. But I can tell you now, they won't find anything."

"Hey, mate," one of the younger gang members shouted back from down the tunnelled walkway. He had doubled back. "I just found this wallet on the floor. Is it yours?"

The younger man walked over and handed it to me. I opened it up, but it was empty. "Where are the money and credit cards? I had hundreds of euros inside."

"I don't know. I just found it on the floor. I was just trying to give it back to you."

"Sure. The money just evaporated. You have nothing to do with it," I said.

"I am just trying to help. Why don't you go home? I am sure you are insured."

Thorn laughed. "Are you insured?"

The men shrugged and looked bewildered at each other. "Insured for what?"

"Life insurance."

"Go home tourists while you can," the leader said and stepped forward, so his forehead was against mine, and then he pushed it forward and shoved me back. I noticed a gold watch on his wrist as Thorn dragged me away to the tunnel wall, opposite the men.

"Not here," she said as two policemen walked around the corner. "We get the gang to leave."

"You heard them. They aren't leaving if we are here."

"We make them leave. Give them a reason to follow us," she said and flicked out a claw.

"I can't believe they attacked us. I thought our dark auras would be enough."

"You would think. Must have been a temporary lapse or they couldn't sense it," she said and winked.

"You did this? You blocked our auras and encouraged them."

"Maybe. But it was their choice to attack us. They were looking for a victim on that train. If I hadn't attracted them, they were going for that old couple at the other end. I saved them."

"So you wanted them to grope you?"

"No. I didn't expect that. It was their own idea," she said and her eyes flashed red.

"But why? I am sure we could have found someone else outside the station."

"True, but I wanted you to fight as well. I wanted to give you motivation."

"Why?"

"Part of your training, my young apprentice."

"Drop the star wars dark sith impressions."

"You need to regain your confidence. There is no better way than to dispatch a bunch of lowlife street criminals."

"Have I not fought enough recently, at the warehouse against the Turned and then against the bikers?"

"Both times you were in your Dragan form. You don't need any confidence as a Dragan. But as a human, you are still suffering."

"Suffering from my tortures?"

"Yes. You need to remember how strong you are. Now let's get on with the night's mission. Then we can go back to the hotel, and I can give you extra reasons to miss me on your trip to England."

I smiled and then we smiled over to the gang, and we watched the two policemen walk around the corner and out of sight. The gang leader frowned back. I'm sure things didn't normally happen this way.

With the policemen gone, Thorn strode across and I followed. "Give him his money," she shouted and grabbed hold of the man's coat, trying to go through his pockets. A gang member grabbed her arms from behind, but she kicked back into his shins. He hobbled away and I tripped him over. The leader grabbed her shoulders and tried to shove her back. But she twisted around into the centre of the group.

I followed up. "Leave my wife, I mean partner, alone."

I pushed my way into the group. We wrestled through, out the other side and walked through the barriers.

We stood on the other side and smiled. I held up my hands with cash and credit cards and the leader's gold watch.

"Give me back my watch," he shouted.

"Boss!" one of the gang said and removed his hands from his stomach to show a growing red patch. Another one dropped to the floor with his hands across his groin, blood dripping between his fingers.

"Get them," the boss shouted and hurtled towards us.

"Run," Thorn shouted and bolted down the street. "This way," she said and veered off to the left. I chased after her, but it wasn't difficult; she was going slow enough for the gang to keep up. We ran across the roads, forcing cars to slam on their brakes and blare their horns as the gang pursued. She took us on a few turns until we ran into a dead-end in a dark street.

The gang ran in and slowed up. They spread out, circling around us and a few reached into their pockets for knives. "What's the plan?" I asked.

"We smash them, of course."

"But there are about twelve of them. You only need one for a feed."

"The rest is practice. I go first and take the initial blows and stabs, as I can heal. Follow up in the chaos and take them out. I want the gang leader as my meal."

The gang encircled us and moved in. The gang leader stood at the back. "Who do you think you are? You could have just walked away minus your money."

"But you can't take back your filthy hands on me," Thorn shouted.

"Oh, please. You should be grateful that a real man touched you and not this arrogant boy."

"He is mine," I shouted and charged. Thorn darted in front of me, her weapons at the ready. "No way."

The sight of her red eyes and claws paused the gang's response, and she carved through them. She slashed at the wrists holding the knives, and they dropped them to the floor and applied pressure over the wounds to stop the bleeding. She kicked one in the groin and punched another on the nose. I followed up and roundhouse kicked the two men holding their wrists. They crashed to the floor, uncovering their wounds. The men behind us moved in. I scooped up the knives in each hand and waited for their attack. Thorn finished off her group and chased down the gang leader.

The group of six moved in. I spun the knives around in my hands, holding one pointing up and the other down. The sight of my skills with the blades panicked them. Two of them dashed around the sides and out of the dark street. I threw the knives away. The point of the fight was training, so I decided hand to hand would be best.

The final four all charged at once. I front kicked the first one onto his back and the rest scattered. I side-kicked another one off his feet. Then blocked a punch and jumped in with a head butt into the man's nose. Bones crunched and blood streamed out. The man clutched his nose and stumbled away and crashed to the pavement.

A gang member hit my face but only hurt his hand in the process. He cradled it in his other hand. I stepped in and whipped in an elbow into his cheekbone, dropping him to the floor. The two I kicked to the floor stayed down, pretending to be knocked out.

I spun around to see if Thorn needed my help but only found scattered broken bodies. Thorn was crouched against a wall with the gang leader clasped in her jaws.

I wandered up the alley to keep a lookout while Thorn finished her dinner. After twenty minutes of draining his blood, she strolled up to my side; the blood disappearing into her glowing skin. She grinned. "How do you feel?"

"Much better. You were right. I forgot how superior I am to humans and how good it is to beat up criminals."

"Good. I am glad you enjoyed yourself, so did I. Now we've had dinner, we can move to dessert," she said.

"Back to the hotel?"

"Yes. Back to the hotel for our farewell."

Chapter Three

My toes and fingers were on fire, sweat dripping down my back, my heart beating faster. My eyes popped wide open, and I stared up at the blank white drapes of the four-poster bed while the air conditioning hummed in the background. The duvet rubbed against my agitated body. The phantom pain from the torture still revisited me, along with the nightmares of Patrick inflicting them. I breathed in slowly, trying to calm myself down. I gripped the sheets between my hands and rolled my head to one side to see where I was.

Thorn's pale, serene face greeted me, and my hands released their grip from the sheets and my heart slowed. I was safe; I was with her; I was with my Queen.

With her eyes closed, a hand moved out and touched my shoulder, and then she lightly kissed my cheek. She then rolled around to face the other direction. I was glad that she had noticed my abrupt awakening. Although there were no words of comfort, it was enough to know she was there, as it meant I was safe.

That day, I would have to leave her. She had given me a train ticket to find Kieran and finish my revenge. Even though I didn't want to go, I had to see this through. I had to put my life back together again and stop being scared all the time. It seemed ridiculous to be scared considering the formula could transform me into a Dragan. But the Hunters had proved to me that no one was safe. Any of us could be captured and hurt if the circumstances were right.

I continued staring up at the top of the four-poster bed while focusing on slowing my breathing and heart rate. My body calmed down, and my heart rate restored to normal. I flung the sheets off and slid out of bed. I picked my watch off the side and clicked it on. Last night, I had scanned the instructions and had tested the GPS functionality. If ever in trouble, I could spin the wheel, press a button and a signal would be sent. Thorn's phone would automatically notify her with a map of my location. It provided some comfort for when the Turned and Hunters came for me again.

The time was 9 AM, and I had only been asleep for just a few hours, but as I was awake, so I decided to get the train back to England.

I left the lights off to allow Thorn to sleep. I trudged into the white marbled en-suite, and I flicked on the light. Curved glass sectioned the shower off, and I spun the dial around and a wide circle of water burst into life. I stepped in and washed off the night sweats and then stood under the shower, allowing the water to roll down my body.

I took a moment to contemplate the days ahead and reflect on the wonderful time I had enjoyed with Thorn since our Union ceremony. But I couldn't stay on holiday forever. Life had to go back to normal if you counted being on the run with the Vampire Queen as normal.

After rinsing away the body wash, I grabbed the nearest large white fluffy towel and dried. I brushed my teeth and checked my stubble. For the next few days, I could get away without shaving. I wrapped the towel around my waist and went back into the bedroom to get dressed.

I left the light on in the shower room and left the door ajar to offer some light while gathering my clothes and packing my bag. We were staying in the honeymoon suite in a top hotel. The rest of the room matched the elegance and grandeur of the shower room. The bed was a large four-poster, with drapes that could be pulled around but were left tied to each corner. A leather sofa and a polished oak table and chairs were positioned in the corner. The balcony looked out over Paris. We had spent most early evenings scanning the city and plotting our night's adventures.

I pulled on a clean pair of jeans, suede boots, a T-shirt, and a black fleece. I packed the rest of my stuff in a backpack, grabbed my train ticket and put it in my pocket. Inside my backpack, I also had three of the vampire formula needles. And I had a test kit to ensure I took the formula at the right times.

I was all ready to go, ready to leave Thorn again and ready to venture out by myself. But this time, she knew where I was going and I had her permission. This time, I wasn't abandoning her and running away. Last time I left her, I went out the door without saying a single word and without her knowledge. I would not make the same mistake again.

I placed the backpack by the door, walked over and clambered onto the bed. She rolled around and opened her sleepy eyes. She smiled and flashed her eyelashes.

"I want to make sure I said goodbye properly this time," I said.

"Good. I would have been annoyed if you run off without saying goodbye."

I leaned down, and she put one hand up and wrapped it around the back of my neck, pulling me down to kiss her on the lips. She held me there for a while, savouring our farewell. She let go and lay back in the bed and then rolled around to face away from me again.

I clambered off the bed, walked to the door and picked up my backpack. I opened the door and had one last look back at Thorn lying in bed, her pale back curving down to her hips and her raven hair cascading down her neck. It reminded me of the time I ran from her when on the road from Vegas to Seattle. I said goodbye, this time in the knowledge she knew exactly where I was going.

I looked around the room once more at its plush surroundings and realised I would be roughing it for the next few weeks in comparison. I blew her one last kiss and whispered goodbye. Then I heard her thoughts in my head. '*Good luck. Come back safe. I love you.*' I replied the same, closed the door and marched down the corridor.

I got the lift down to the lobby and walked to the reception desk, where I asked them to get me a taxi to the train station. I took a seat on one of the large leather sofas and waited for my taxi to arrive.

The bellboys pushed luggage trolleys in and out of the hotel; the wheels echoing off the marble floor and terracotta tiled walls. A waitress carried over steaming cups of coffee to guests sitting on the big sofas and at the tables. The guests exchanged conversations in many languages, and the receptionists answered the phones and dealt with a queue of customers.

I listened to their conversation with my enhanced senses and matched them with my psychic abilities to gauge their genuine emotions. A man sat at a table sipping his coffee while watching the spinning hotel doors. He was obviously waiting for someone. I dug into his mind to see the image of a woman and with it came intense desire. He tapped his pocket to check the hotel key, and he wished she wasn't married.

A group of suited men sat on the sofa next to him. They all had a small suitcase and a second small bag for a laptop. They chatted about the conference, but their minds were elsewhere. One man wishing he was at home. Another man was looking forward to a night away from his nagging wife.

The concierge fetched me for my taxi, which dropped me at the front of the Gare du Nord train station. I caught the next train from Paris to London, St Pancras International station via the Channel Tunnel.

I spent the journey making plans for the week ahead. After visiting Miss Jones, I would catch the late train to Yorkshire. I would do the house hunting on my return. I couldn't delay in London as I had to catch Kieran leaving prison.

I knew what time they released Kieran. Once there, I would follow him and wait for a suitable moment to take my revenge. I hadn't booked anywhere to stay in Leeds, as I didn't know how long it would take me to confront Kieran for the last time. I could stay in the city centre, as I had the money to pay over the odds if necessary.

I spent the rest of the journey taking a nap, trying to adjust my body clock. I had spent so much time awake at night with Thorn that I was still feeling tired after our night's exertion. I hoped the sleep on the train would allow me to adjust, so I could get used to being awake during the day and a sleep at night.

I awoke as the train slowed up, and the other passengers grabbed their bags from the overhead shelves and packed away their food and devices. I sat next to the window and left everyone else to fight their way out before leaving through the empty train.

I followed my planned route via the tube stations to get within a twenty-minute walk from the shelter where Miss Jones worked. I climbed out of the underground at the last stop and headed off towards the shelter, using Google maps to navigate my way through the maze of streets. Finally, I got onto the last street, Winchester Street, and headed down the road.

The buildings were broken down and boarded up, and on the street corners, gangs of young men and boys hung about. I kept my eyes focused straight ahead as not to draw any attention to myself. Further on, I walked past some police tape flapping around on the floor and tyre marks on the road.

I saw the homeless shelter up ahead and a group of men outside smoking tiny rolled-up cigarettes. The shelter looked like something that had been built in the seventies. It was a one-level brick building, with looped barbed wire encircling the rooftop and dirty steel heating equipment kicking out steam.

The men stared at me but said nothing. They just continued smoking and talking to each other. I walked past them into a small hallway with a notice board of events. Next, I went into a sleeping area of camp beds laid out in neat rows. The beds already had belongings scattered over them, with people claiming their territory. I walked through the aisle of beds and into an eating area with rows of tables and benches half occupied. I had been told I would find Miss Jones near the kitchen or in the office at the back.

"Who are you?" A man garbled with a mouthful of bread. He stood up from a long table and walked over. "I asked you a question."

The man was obviously a regular attendee of the shelter. Although his clothes were dirty, he looked reasonably clean underneath and not too skinny. His attitude gave away his sense of ownership of the shelter. This was his place, and he clearly knew most people who attended, and I looked out of place.

I stared at the man to let him know I wasn't intimidated. "I am looking for Miss Jones. I believe she runs this place."

"And your business with Marcy is?"

"None of your business. Now tell me where she is?"

The man looked at the tables of others eating. "Boys, we have a problem."

"Yes, Tommy," one of them said and stood up. The rest of the men and a couple of women all pushed back their food, clambered out of the benches and congregated behind him.

Tommy scanned his gang, turned back and smiled, revealing missing and blackened teeth and a foul-smelling breath of stale smoke and whiskey. "It is our business. We are going to protect our own from now on. After what happened to our Mary-Anne and the attack on Marcy the other day, no stranger like you can just wander into this place and start making demands. So I suggest you start talking, sunshine."

I scanned the group of homeless people. I could easily beat this rabble. I would strike Tommy and he would crash into the rest, taking them down. Then I would hit the next nearest and take them out of action. This would probably send the rest into flight mode. But I wasn't here to fight.

"She is expecting me. Tell her Jon is here and that Tracey Horn sends her regards."

Tommy's eyes widened, and he nodded his head frantically in agreement. "Of course, sorry, sorry. I didn't know you were friends with Tracey," he said and turned to the back of the hall and shouted, "Marcy, you have a visitor." The gang of homeless people went straight back to their food, a couple of them arguing over who owned which bowl of soup. Tommy went off to mediate.

From the back of the hall, which joined into the kitchen, an older grey-haired woman walked out. She had a green plastic apron over a long-sleeved red shirt, and she wiped her hands on the back of her jeans. Wrinkles formed around her eyes as she smiled. She walked across the hall and held out a hand. "You must be Jon," she said. I nodded and put my hand in hers and shook. "Tracey gave me a description. And you obviously aren't here to use the shelter."

"Thorn, I mean Tracey told me to come and visit you first."

"Follow me into the back; we can talk properly in there," she said and headed in the direction of the kitchen.

I followed on after her and noticed Tommy keeping an eye on me. We went through the kitchen with the sinks full of dirty bowls and plates, and a pot of tomato soup still simmering on the hob. We headed into a small hallway and then into an office on the left.

Filing cabinets crammed the office and it had one main work desk, a low coffee table and a set of orange plastic chairs. On the wall, there was a montage of photos from the homeless guests that had stayed at the shelter.

She spun around a black chair from the desk and sat down and then offered me one of the orange plastic chairs stacked at the side. I pulled it out and sat opposite her.

I looked past Marcy to the desk and saw three photos on it. The first one was of Thorn, but even though she hadn't aged, I could tell it was from a long time ago. Thorn had blue eye shadow, black bobbed hair, and a black and white chequered mini dress on. It was a sixties' fashion.

The picture next to it was of Annabel and Lucinda, the two girls Thorn and I had rescued from a gang. They looked different from when I last saw them; they were smiling and looked clean. I was glad to see their lives had changed and that I had made a difference.

The last photo was of another woman in her early twenties. She had light brown, mousy hair and blue eyes. She looked like the average girl next door.

"I see you are admiring my photos," Marcy said, as she turned around in the chair to look at them. She picked up the photo of Thorn and passed it to me. "I tell everyone this is a woman called Tessa Horn. She took me off the streets. She became my guardian, and she's the one that helped fund the homeless centre. Whenever Thorn visits, I always tell them it is Tessa's actual daughter, Tracey. We tell everyone that Tessa died some time ago and that the trust fund to run the homeless shelter is now administered by Tracey."

I held the photo and stared down into Thorn's sky blue eyes lined with thick black mascara. "I guess it's an easy way of passing down her wealth, pretending to be her own daughter." I handed the photo back to Marcy.

Marcy took the picture frame and placed it back on the desk. "She has been doing it for generations. Tracey is the latest incarnation of herself, but it is always a T Horn, so it becomes Thorn. There has been a Tracey, a Tessa, Tabatha, a Tilly, and a Tallulah, as far as I know."

"I'm sure there have been many. I didn't know she used this method of passing down her money. She has never told me about her time with you and her identity as Tessa."

"I'm sure she still has lots of secrets from you. But who wouldn't at her age? Having lived so many different lives and in so many different places, it must be hard to remember everything worthwhile repeating."

"And Annabel and Lucinda, are they doing okay?" I asked, looking at their photo.

"Yes, both of them are enrolled in College. Annabel is studying catering, and Lucinda is studying accounting. It took a while to gain their trust, but we are moving in the right direction, thanks to Thorn's help."

"The other woman. Is this your daughter?"

Marcy stared at the photo, picked it up and continued looking at it as she spoke to me. "Not biologically, but I've always thought of her as a daughter. She is someone I helped off the streets, just as Thorn helped me off the streets. Her name is Mary-Anne." Marcy's eyes welled up.

"Is everything okay? Is there anything I can help with? Thorn said there may be some issues." I said.

"Mary-Anne has been in a little bit of trouble recently. I'm sure she can take care of herself. However, the last time she was here, she attacked a gang that had barged their way in. She hurt them badly; she's a martial arts expert. Unfortunately, I think the gang will return to exact revenge, and if Mary-Anne isn't here, they will find others to hurt."

"Let me know if you have any issues, and I will try to scare them off permanently."

"Thank you, Jon. Thorn normally takes care of this for us or hires someone to protect us. Normally we don't stop the gangs if they invade the shelter, but Mary-Anne lost her temper and it's provoked them."

"It will be no problem. Let me give you my phone number," I said and handed over my phone with the number displayed. Marcy grabbed a piece of paper and scribbled it down.

She then pulled out a key from her pocket and placed it in my hand. "You will need this key. It opens a self-storage unit four miles away. I will write the address down. In the storage unit, you will find weapons and money for you to fulfil your mission and do a little house hunting."

I pocketed the key and the piece of paper with the address into my back pocket.

"I best be going if I'm to visit the self-storage and then get the late train to Leeds. But if anything happens, call me straight away. Do as Thorn says and don't engage the people in any conflict. I will take care of them on my return."

"Good luck on your journey, Jon. We will see you on your return."

After saying goodbye, I stood out of the chair and shook her hand. I headed back through the kitchen, dining hall and back onto the street. I waved to Tommy as I left, and he looked away to his gang of followers.

I walked back down Winchester Street, following the route back to the tube station, past the police tape and the boarded-up houses. I looked up the location of the self-storage unit and planned out my journey via the tube. It would only take me half an hour to get there, which would leave me enough time to get the train to Leeds.

I navigated through London's underground and walked the last leg to a big yellow self-storage unit. I went inside, presented my key and credentials to a bright red-haired lady with red glasses. She tore herself away from the TV and pulled out a red book. I signed in. She walked around the desk and set off down the grey corridors, which had rows of yellow locked doors. As we walked, the lights flicked on above and we took several turns to Thorn's locker.

The locker was one of the bigger ones in the warehouse. I waited for the receptionist to leave before putting in my key and opening up, as I wasn't sure of what might be inside. I pulled the door to and switched on the light. Inside were a stack of boxes labelled with different letters on them.

On top of the first set of boxes was an envelope marked V in big black marker pen. I opened it up and poured out the contents. Inside was a map of the boxes, each label referring to its contents. Also, there was a letter from Thorn. She had arranged for this stuff to be put together for our return.

I scanned down the list: weapons, money, clothes, computers and others. The weapons box was marked with a big W. I grabbed it first and ripped off the tape. Inside were three metal cases. I lifted out the first and opened it. A pistol lay encased in foam and two sets of bullet magazines. The next had another handgun the same. The last case had a set of three silver knives. I took one pistol and clunked in the magazine, flicked the safety on and shoved it into the back of my jeans.

I opened the box mark M next. Inside was a large metal tin. I prized off the top and found rolls of cash in different currencies. I took a few rolls of British pounds and a few rolls of Euros. I had money anyway and a credit card if things got desperate, but I preferred to use cash.

I went through each box. I left the computers packaged up as I already had one. I had enough clothes, so I opened the box marked Others. The box had several other boxes and an envelope on the top. I opened it up to find another inventory list: Jewellery, car keys, gold, mobile phones, and first aid kit.

I took the first aid kit and shoved it into my rucksack. I opened the smaller box with car keys written on. Inside was a set of car keys and a folded up piece of paper with a description of the car and its address.

The car was only parked a few miles walk away, so I bundled all the stuff into my bag, locked up, signed out and walked to its location.

The car was in a secure underground garage of an apartment block, and Thorn had rented one of the parking spaces. The car was a black Audi sports Quattro, a good fast car, but not too flashy that it would draw attention.

I triggered the ignition and the engine hummed into life. I typed in Leeds into the inbuilt satnav and fired up the radio. The car purred through the underground garage as I drove out and followed the satnav to the motorway.

I was going back to where this journey began. Back home to take my final revenge on the O'Keefes.

Chapter Four

I drove up the motorway to Leeds, planning to stay in the city centre, but I saw the hotel that I had stopped in on my last visit with Scarlett. I immediately hit the indicator and swung in towards the hotel, having instantly decided to stop there for the night.

The hotel was a member of a large chain. The branding made it look like the other indenti-kit hotels throughout the country, with the half-moon symbol with zzz flowing out of it. I checked in at the reception and got a room.

Thankfully, I wasn't in the same room as before or on the same floor, but just being in the same hotel brought back enough memories. I took my stuff up to the room and dumped it on the double bed with a purple bedspread and sat on it.

Although it was a different room, they all looked very much the same, with purple bed covers, curtains, white walls and brown carpets. I couldn't help but think that Scarlett was next door, just as she had been the last time we visited.

Last time we were here, I had thought our relationship may have been rekindled. I had left Thorn on the road to Seattle after discovering she had lied to me about vampires and her promise to make me like her. I had flown back to England to get answers. First, I visited Scarlett to find out if she had anything to do with the Hunters. I had suspected she was part of the conspiracy, having set me up to take the formula and then trying to capture me at the night club.

I had quizzed her on her involvement and been convinced of her innocence. I asked her to come with me to Leeds to speak with my dad and find out if he was also innocent. She had agreed to help me out, and we had stopped at the hotel the night before I confronted my dad.

That night at the hotel, I had thought about knocking on her door and using my seductive powers. However, I had made a promise to Thorn and I intended to keep it. I was glad now I had stayed away, but I wish I had never asked Scarlett to travel with me.

Since the events at the car park and being captured by the Turned, I hadn't seen Scarlett. The last time I saw her, she had escaped the clutches of a Turned vampire and was running to safety. I had thrown a knife into the back of the chasing vampire, and it evaporated to ash as it grabbed hold of her shoulder. Scarlett had screamed and brushed off the dusted vampire before disappearing into the stairwell. I hoped she managed to get to safety.

Thorn promised to use her contacts to search for her. I doubted if Thorn had really done this, so I had hacked her emails to find the proof that she had employed private detectives to search for her. She had but there were no leads. I just hoped that she was okay. I should have left her in London with her new boyfriend. It was wrong of me to drag her into my dangerous life; none of this was her fault after all.

The next day I woke up early, grabbed a big breakfast and headed off to the prison to wait for Kieran's release. They released the prisoners between nine and ten in the morning, so I planned to get there ten minutes beforehand.

I took the last turn in and drove past the prison's main part, a huge grey stone building. Towers marked each corner of the front of the building and in the centre a large green solid metal-studded gate in between two towers. The towers and prison front had fortified brickwork and arrow loopholes. I noticed newer prison buildings out the back and adjoining new red brick walls to the castle front with looped barbed wire scrolled across the top. The old castle had been converted into a prison, but only the front remained to show signs of its historical past.

I felt uncomfortable near the prison, the layers of security intruding on my thoughts, the barbed wire cutting through my senses. A Union Jack flag fluttered atop of each tower while the grey clouds bore down on the stony walls, forcing the depressive atmosphere further inside. A growing dread emanated from the prison walls, and I could sense the inmates were suffering at the hands of each other.

I was a wanted man in the UK for the killings of the O'Keefes and gang in the park when I first transformed into a Dragan. I could end up in a prison cell, locked behind these fortified walls and barbed wire fences. But if I were unlucky, the Hunters and Turned would get to me first and my fate would be worse than imprisonment.

I swung the car around and reversed into a parking space along the road opposite the green metal gate. I put on a baseball hat and sunglasses to hide. I didn't want Kieran spotting me as he left, as I wanted to pick my time and place to reveal I had come back for him.

On the road opposite the castle front, a blue pickup truck with bull bars on the front wedged itself into a parking space between a blue Nissan Micra and a black saloon car. On the other side of the road was a fenced-off area and one storey modern brick buildings. It looked like the staff parking and offices from the activities of the prison officers inside.

I watched the prison gate, waiting for Kieran to walk out. I still wanted my revenge, if only for the sake of closure. I wanted to get it over and done with as soon as possible, so I could get back to Thorn. I didn't like the idea of her being surrounded by her ex-lovers.

The prison reminded me that Giles's mother was locked up somewhere in Leeds as well. I could have stopped her imprisonment if I hadn't been on the run with Thorn. The thought of Giles's mum suffering inside a similar prison gave my revenge a renewed rigour. I would ensure Kieran suffered.

At 9:30 AM, a little door inside the main green gate opened up and out stepped three men. Behind, the prison guard shut the door and it clunked into place. The first man out of prison was Kieran. His hair was cut short but still greasy. He wore grey trainers and blue jeans. He wore a black t-shirt, showing off his tattoos on both forearms and carried a black leather jacket and a brown paper bag in the other hand.

The doors to the blue Nissan Mirca swung open, and an over-sized woman in a grey tracksuit pushed herself out and held herself up on the door. She puffed with the exertion, reddening her face. Her grey and white hair scruffily tied back.

On the other side of the car, a younger woman got out and pulled down her black mini skirt from where it had hitched up in the car. She wore a leopard skin top, and her bottle-blonde ponytail stuck out to the side of her head.

He spotted them and walked over. The younger blonde woman shuffled around the car in her tight skirt and white high heels. The women stood together, and he held out his arms as he walked towards them. They both hugged him. It was his mother and eldest sister.

He then got into the car's front seat, the mother in the back and his sister got into the driver's seat. She u-turned the car around and drove out of the prison complex, joining the rest of the morning traffic.

I figured if I followed him for long enough, the opportunity would come up for my revenge. I thought Kieran would probably go out for a drink to celebrate his release, at which point I would confront him and take my final vengeance.

I had killed his dad and brother, but I would probably be happy with just giving him a severe beating to make sure he left Giles' and my family alone. I didn't want him seeking any revenge of his own.

I followed them through the city, expecting them to be heading back to their house for a welcome home party, but the car spurred off the main road in another direction. I followed a few cars back as not to give the game away. We reached the edge of the city when the car turned into a cemetery and parked up. I followed in and parked a few rows back.

The car park only had a few cars in it. A hearse and a few other black limousines were parked up nearest to the pathway. Through the gravestones, I could see a gathering of black-clothed people around a grave and a priest in his white cloak.

Kieran, his mum and sister, left the car and walked through the line of graves, skirting around the mourners. I left my car and followed on as a blue pickup truck drove in and parked near the back.

Trees were scattered through the graveyard and a couple of large stone tombs, which I kept concealed behind. The grey clouds had followed us from the prison and raced overhead, blowing the trees' branches and scattering the leaves over the graves.

I followed them on; the wind blowing the women's hair over their heads. They brushed it back as they picked their way through the gravestones. They walked up to two more women in their twenties. Both of them dressed up in party clothes like his sister. Between them, a young man dressed in a black suit sat in a wheelchair in front of two newish headstones. The women were holding wreaths and opened their arms to Kieran as he approached. They all hugged him and kissed him on the cheeks. Kieran knelt down in front of the wheelchair and hugged the young man, who didn't respond but just fidgeted.

It was the rest of his family, his other two sisters, and his twin brother, Liam, who had been paralysed by Giles's mother in the car accident. The incident that had sparked my dark journey.

His sister handed him a wreath, and Kieran went to a grave and placed it on top. His other sister handed over the next wreath, which he put on the next grave. He stood back, in-between them all, and cried. His sisters cried and comforted each other with arms wrapped around one another and tissues being handed out.

I couldn't see the names on the graves, but I knew it was his father and brother, both of whom I had killed. At the time, I felt no remorse for their killing; in fact, I had swelled with satisfaction at their deaths and of my revenge.

Even though I had later considered their deaths a step too far, I had justified it to myself because of their threats of them burying me in a shallow grave in the woods. Although I had gone there intending revenge, I hadn't been certain about killing them until his father had threatened me. I had no choice but to kill them in order to protect myself.

After killing his brother, I had wanted to march up the stairs and kill his sisters and mother. Thorn had stopped me in my bloodlust. As I stared at them crowded around the graves of their father, husband and brother, I felt regret and I was pleased Thorn had prevented my path of destruction.

But I could also remember all the horrible things the O'Keefes had done, including the O'Keefe sisters who had attacked Giles's sister. Also, Kieran had just come out of prison for attacking Giles's father, but murdering them was not the answer. Seeing their grief at the loss of their family made me understand they were just ordinary people, although not very nice people. Because of my changes through the vampire formula, I knew they were more human than me. I had no right to be judge, jury and executioner. I should have only scared them or found a way of bringing them to justice, regular human justice, not paranormal rage.

They had suffered enough, but I had to be sure they would not come after anybody else. I had to make sure they would leave Giles's family alone and any of my relatives who still lived in the area. I could pick my time when to ensure they left my family and friends alone, but now at the graves of their family was not the time or the place. I would give it a day and then find Kieran by himself to make sure he understood.

I was about to leave the O'Keefes to their mourning when I heard a rustling in the leaves. I sniffed at the air and a strange, musky smell wafted through. It was a smell I'd been told to remember in case I ever came across it again.

The first time I had smelt this odour was in Max's diner on the route to Seattle from Las Vegas. It could only mean one thing: a werewolf was nearby. I took in a big breath of the musky air.

I scanned the area looking for the possible source of the odour. It must be blowing from upwind, and the wind was blowing across the graveyard from the car park and towards me. I peeked my head around the tree and saw two men walking across the cemetery.

One man was mid-height, just under 6 foot with brown curly hair. The next man was more slender but taller, about 6 foot with a hoodie pulled up so I couldn't see his face.

They walked towards the O'Keefes, and Liam stopped fidgeting and rocking in his chair. He said something to Kieran, who stepped out to stop the men in their tracks.

The man with the black hoodie stepped forward and shoved Kieran back into his sisters. I decided to get closer to hear what they were saying. I moved between the gravestones, trying to keep covered by the trees and the tombstones. One sister noticed me but said nothing to the others.

Being closer, I could see the detail of the man with the brown curly hair. The man sniffed at the air and glanced around. I ducked back behind the tombstone as he looked over in my direction. I looked back again after a moment. He had a thick forehead and eyebrows that met in the middle and small brown eyes.

I had a flashback to the warehouse fight against the Hunters where Thorn, Max and Cassius had come to my rescue. On that night, Max had battled with another werewolf. I remembered his face and knew he was the same man now talking to the O'Keefes.

The werewolf man was sniffing the air and then grabbed the other man on the shoulder. I was now close enough to hear them.

"There is a vampire nearby," the man said.

Kieran staggered back. "They are real then. We thought, we thought Liam had gone mad."

The man with the hoodie pulled it down and turned to face the curly-haired man. "Is it him?"

"Yes, I remember his smell from when he was held prisoner by the Hunters."

The younger man scouted around. He had short, light brown hair and stubble. I recognised the features, but something didn't seem right. The person I knew was shorter and younger.

I knew from reading the files we had stolen from the Hunter's base that Giles was the apprentice of a werewolf, and he was taking a formula, the original werewolf formula my dad had worked on before moving on to the vampire formula. From that information and the familiarity in the features, I knew it had to be Giles. Although he was much taller and more mature than when I last saw him. But then again, so was I. Sooner or later, we were going to run into one another.

"Jon, show yourself. I know you are here. You have come to finish your revenge, but it is I who shall have revenge today. Not just on you for your cowardice, but also on the O'Keefes. You had no right to kill them. That was my right and my right only. You stole my revenge, and I will make you suffer."

Kieran stepped forward again, his face red and his fists pulled up. "No one will take revenge on us again. I will kill you. I will kill that bastard Jon if he shows his face. I don't believe any of this bullshit about him being a vampire. This is just some sick game the two of you have cooked up."

His sisters grabbed him, but he wrenched free and strutted towards Giles. He threw a punch at Giles's head, but Giles blocked it with ease and counter-punched with enough force to knock Kieran off his feet, landing him on the graves of his brother and father, crushing the wreaths he had laid.

"Stay down, you idiot. Your time will come."

I couldn't decide what to do. Should I confront him and talk him around or get away from this place? Any movement would alert them to my presence. Out in public and during the day, I doubted they would want to fight. I stepped out from behind the tombstone and strode across.

"It's not a game, Kieran. Ask your brother Liam. He saw everything the night I slaughtered your brother and father. I only regret that you weren't there," I said

As I walked across the graveyard, Liam fitted in his wheelchair. His sisters hugged him, trying to settle him down. Kieran scrambled to his feet and charged. He scooped up a brick and chucked it at me. I ducked out of the way and waited until he was upon me with fists swinging. I swayed out the way of a strike, grabbed his arm, and then turned it around, threw him over my shoulder and twisted his arm to hold him still, putting pressure against his joints.

"Kieran, stay still. You are in great danger. I am going to let you go. Then I want you to take your family and get away from here as quickly as possible."

Kieran struggled and pushed against my grip, but I twisted his arm further, sending him into yowling pain. "Kieran, you have to trust me. Giles wants to kill all of you. He's a werewolf."

"You are both bloody mad. I don't believe in any of this. I don't know how either of you are suddenly so big and strong, but I certainly don't believe in things that go bump in the night. You've been taking steroids or some such stuff."

"I don't care if you believe me. You've seen the change in us, and you saw how easily both of us have beaten you. Regardless of what we are, he is going to kill you. He is going to kill your sisters and mother. So do us both a favour. Get up and get the hell out of here."

"Why the heck do you care?"

"I think your family has suffered enough. I took my revenge in the death of your brother and father. That was a step too far. Stop arguing with me and just get up and go."

Giles stomped over. His forehead scowled into his brown eyes and his face redden. His short light brown hair bristled up, and his fists swung at his sides as he marched over the graves. "Jon, let him go. He's mine. I will decide what happens next to him and his family. After all, it was my father he beat up, it was my sister they attacked, and my mother got sent to prison. All that happened to you was a brick through your window. You have no right and no understanding of the hell I have been through."

Giles pulled up his sleeves, laying bare slash marks across his wrists. I remembered my dad saying Giles tried to kill himself in the bath rather than face any more bullying at school. He had been committed to a psychiatric hospital for his own protection.

"Giles, I understand. You had it much worse than me. But after what I saw them do to you and your family, I was terrified the same would happen to me. I know it doesn't make it right. And I am sorry I never made it to your mum's court case. But I got myself into trouble in London, and it was a situation I couldn't get out of."

I let go of Kieran's arm and stood up to face Giles. Kieran skirted around us both and scrambled back to his family.

"I know all about what happened to you in London. I've heard about you releasing the vampire from her prison, stealing the formula, killing the gang, and then your return to Leeds, where you stole my revenge."

Kieran's family moved away from us as I engaged Giles in conversation. I had to keep him talking to let them escape.

"So you understand, as soon as I could come back and put things right, I did."

The werewolf man with Giles blocked the O'Keefe's escape. He snarled at them and Giles spun around. "I never said you could leave, stay. I haven't finished with you yet," he shouted and pointed at them.

"Giles, talk to me, forget them. They are insignificant compared to us."

Giles shoved me back. "Stop trying to save them to keep your revenge to yourself, just like last time." Giles turned back to the werewolf man

"Norris, don't let them go."

The sister with the leopard skin shirt stepped in front of Norris. Her hand was on the furry bobble on her fake Gucci handbag. "Let us pass. I have my hand on a rape alarm. If you stop us, I will pull it, and all those people at that funeral will look over," she said, looking at the group crowded around the graveside, just by the car park. Norris glared at the group of mourners and back to Giles. "We can't attract attention to ourselves attacking a grieving family. There will be plenty of time for you to take your revenge."

Giles nodded to Norris and then turned back to me. The O'Keefe family skirted past Norris and into the car park.

"Are you happy they got away? It makes no difference. I know where they live. Just as you do. But for now, I shall satisfy myself by taking my revenge on you. Just two blokes fighting won't cause the same attention as a rape alarm from a young woman. You traitor, you coward, you bastard!"

I held my hands up to appease Giles. "I am sorry for what happened to us when we were at school. I'm sorry I never came to the court case. But I am not sorry I took revenge on the O'Keefes, as I did it in your name. I am sorry I killed them but not the intent of the revenge. They left me no choice."

"But you denied me my revenge. I wanted to see Patrick's face when I took his life. It was always him that made our lives a misery. It was my revenge, not yours."

"I said I was sorry. But how was I to know that you had hooked up with the Hunters and become a werewolf's apprentice? My own life had taken such a weird path. It had never occurred to me that you would also be capable of revenge. But don't you think it's an amazing coincidence that we have both got involved with the same group of people, even though on opposite sides?"

"It's no coincidence. These people rescued me from the psychiatric hospital. They trained me and gave me purpose. And they chose me because of what you had become."

"So they gave you the formula to beat Thorn and me."

"Yes, they needed to stop you. The only thing capable of beating a Dragan or a vampire is a werewolf. They knew from talking to me in the hospital that I wanted to find you to take my revenge at your betrayal. So we came to a deal. As you can see, I'm stronger than before, and they have trained me to fight vampires. You are no match for me."

"So your formula is transforming you into a werewolf, as mine is transforming me into a Dragan."

"No. It has made me stronger. It has made me faster. It has improved my senses. The transformation does this to anyone when they transform into a werewolf and back again. But it will never give me the permanent powers of a werewolf. Only the bite of another werewolf can do that. Although stronger than most, I will always remain human, whereas your formula has stopped you from being human. I will be doing the world a favour when I destroy you. Vampires and Dragans have no remnant human left in them. Whereas werewolves are human most of the time."

"So you're in league with the Turned and the Hunters, trying to find the formula, trying to understand how it's changed me so they can have the power. Don't you understand that there are too many Turned vampires in the world and they are bloodthirsty? We can never let them have this power. Otherwise, all humanity will be at risk."

"Whereas you want to keep the power for the Dragans and make those who they enslave suffer. I will help them destroy the Dragans, and I will be there to ensure the formula is used properly, so the Turned are controlled and their suffering eased."

"You're wrong. They are using you to get to me. Once you have completed your mission, you will be discarded and killed. They don't want anyone watching over them in their New World order."

Norris walked over and stood behind Giles. "Stop the chit chat. You've had a chance for a proper reunion. Do as Bramel ordered and kill him."

Giles gritted his teeth together, clenched his fists and growled at me, the sideburns on his face bristling up and hair standing on end. He was summing up his werewolf strength in his human body.

But I was part Dragan. I was a hybrid. I was sure he couldn't be strong enough to beat me, but there were two of them. "Giles, don't listen to him. I am your friend. Remember all the good times, playing video games, and watching films together? I don't want to hurt you. I am half Dragan already. Please, just walk away."

"I never walk away, not like you do, not like you did at those school gates."

He raised his fists and front kicked. He caught me by surprise, and I stepped back enough to avoid its full force. But I tripped over a gravestone and stumbled back a few paces.

A roundhouse kick flew in from the left. I swung my shin up to block it and then raised my hands to deflect a right hook. I lashed a fist out to gain some space, and Giles darted out of the way. He swung in another punch from the left and caught me on the chin. It whipped my head back, and I spun backwards and scrambled away.

He bore down on me, but this time I was ready. I took the attack to him, doing a leaping, spinning kick. He blocked it, but the power behind it was enough to send him sprawling to the floor. He rolled over and stood back up with fists clenched in the guard position.

I placed my fists up by my chin as well and shuffled forwards, remaining light on my toes. We exchanged kicks and punches, blocking and counter-attacking. They had trained him well, and he was definitely stronger and faster than the average human. Better than the Hunters that I had fought. But in his human form, he still wasn't as fast as a Turned or as strong as a werewolf like Max.

I gauged his strength and speed, looking for an opening, a way in which I could stop him without hurting him too much. Plus, Norris was on guard, ready to join the fray if I did too well. I had to stop Giles and get past Norris. I blocked a few more punches and managed a few body shots around his kidneys, which slowed him down. Giles winced and backed away from me. "Norris, give me the injection."

"No, it's too public. You will have to fight man to man. Now find some courage and fight him like I taught you. Remember how he betrayed you? Let your rage fuel you."

Giles tensed his muscles up and charged in swinging wild punches. I defended and took the blows, waiting for him to run out of steam. I knew the tactic. It was the same way Thorn had taught me to fight, using my anger to attack in a blur of fury.

He panted, and I launched my attack, pushing his guard out of the way, cracking an elbow into his jaw. Blood poured from his mouth after he crashed to the floor. He wiped it with his hand and looked at the blood, then launched himself up again.

I danced around him, waiting for the perfect moment. The other mourners were leaving the graveside and heading back to the car park. A few of them looked over at our fight, and one of them had pulled out their phone to film it while another was dialling. I assumed he was calling the police.

I couldn't get caught by the police, and I knew the Hunters could control the police, so Giles and Norris wouldn't need to worry.

I manoeuvred Giles around, so Norris was directly behind him. Most of the mourners were close to their cars. I stepped in and took a couple of blows around my arms, guarding my face. I flung my hands around his neck and pulled him down and kneed him. "I am not your enemy. Remember our friendship," I shouted in his ear as the knees cracked into his ribs. His body dropped in my hands, and I released my grip and front kicked him in the chest, sprawling him into Norris.

Norris caught hold of Giles, and they both crashed into a headstone, dislodging it from the ground.

"Another time," I said and sprinted off to the car park, weaving through the gravestones.

The mourners stopped and stood back, waiting to see where I was going. Once I got to the car park, I looked back to see Giles still on the floor with Norris stood over him. Norris's face reddened as he shouted at Giles, then kicked him twice in the ribs and walked back to the car park.

The police would arrive soon if the mourners had called them. I couldn't hang about, though I wanted to see if Giles was okay and try to convince him we could still be friends. However, I reckoned I would see him again.

I jogged over to my black Audi, jumped in and drove out of the car park before Norris could catch up. Fighting Norris would be a different matter.

I had again left my friend in the hands of a bully, but there was nothing I could do. Nothing was keeping me in Leeds. It was too dangerous to revisit Kieran O'Keefe in case Giles and Norris were waiting for me. I couldn't stop Giles from having his revenge on the O'Keefes. I certainly wasn't staying to protect them. Giles and Norris were more interested in me. They went after the O'Keefes suspecting I may also be watching. The best thing I could do was to return to Thorn to get them to follow.

Chapter Five

I got back to my purple and white hotel room. The sheets had been changed and new towels were laid out. I stripped off and took a shower, and the soapy water stung my wounds. I dried off and then examined all the bruises and cuts from my fight with Giles.

I couldn't help replaying the image of him being beaten by Norris for his failure at the end. I felt guilty, just like I had done when I left him in the hands of the bullies at school. Then, I hadn't gone to rescue him and hadn't saved him now, either. Both times, I justified it to myself that I would have been badly hurt. At school, I would probably just got a beating. This time, Norris could have captured or even killed me. As a full werewolf, even in human form, Norris could have beaten me one-on-one. I was only a hybrid, but I would have stood a better chance in my proper Dragan form.

I had to forget about Giles and concentrate on my current situation. I had a first aid kit in my travel pack, so I attended to my wounds. Then I cracked open two mini whiskey bottles from the fridge and down them in one instead of taking painkillers.

I sat on the bed and phoned Thorn on a secure line. I needed to tell her what happened and find out how we could meet up. I wanted to be back with her again, where I knew I would be safe. The phone rang for a while and I was about to give up.

"Hello V, is that you?"

"Yes, it's me. Is it safe to talk?"

"Yes, we are fine to talk. It's the middle of the day. You just woke me up."

"Sorry, I completely forgot. I really wanted to talk to you and tell you what happened."

"Did it go well? I was suspecting to hear from you tonight. Did you really get your revenge so quickly?"

"None of it went as planned. I followed Kieran from the prison where his mother and sister met him outside. They drove to the cemetery to meet the rest of his family and pay his respects to his brother and father."

"So you gave him a beating at the graves of his brother and father and in front of his family. How poetic."

"No. Once I saw them grieving, I couldn't do it. They have suffered enough. But that's not all that happened. While I was watching them and deciding what to do, Giles arrived with the other werewolf, a man called Norris. It appears Giles had tracked Kieran down and wanted to take his own revenge. But unfortunately, Norris detected my scent and called me out. There was nowhere to run, so I confronted them."

"Well, that was unexpected. But I suppose it wasn't a complete surprise, as we knew Giles had become a werewolf apprentice. But by the fact that you're calling me, I assume Norris didn't get to you."

"Giles wanted revenge on the O'Keefes but also on me. In the end, I think he was more interested in taking his revenge on me. The O'Keefes escaped as I kept Giles busy."

"So, are you taking your revenge on the O'Keefes tonight, then?"

"No. I told you I can't hurt them anymore. They are already in enough pain with the death of their brother and father. They may be bad people and have hurt people, but we shouldn't have killed them. I won't be taking any more revenge on the O'Keefes. I think they have learnt their lesson. And if not, I will find a better way to bring them to justice next time."

"Oh V, sometimes you are still the innocent little boy. There is only one type of justice these sorts of people understand. But it is your choice, it is your revenge to take or not take. Tell me instead what happened between you and Giles."

"Don't worry, if the O'Keefes step out of line, I will resolve the issue. I may not kill them, but it won't be pleasant either. Anyway, Giles clearly blames me for getting bullied. He said I betrayed him when I walked away at the gates and when I ignored him at school, and for the fact, I never helped his mother in her court case. I can't say I blame him. I am at fault. I betrayed him. He wasn't interested when I tried to apologize and remind him we were kids. Norris was clearly encouraging him as well."

"So, what happened?"

"I asked Giles how he came to work with the Hunters. That surely it wasn't a coincidence he was now working with a werewolf and me with a vampire."

"We are not vampires. How many times do I have to tell you?"

"Yes, yes. I know, but it's easier to explain than Dragans. Anyway, they recruited him because he was my friend. And they wanted someone to hunt me down. It was clear from what happened to him that he had the motivation to come after me. They took him from the psychiatric hospital, and they have trained him and brainwashed him to believe that we are the enemy. He has physically changed as well. He is taller and stronger than before, but he told me that the werewolf formula does not permanently change the person into a werewolf. However, changing into a werewolf has some side effects of leaving them stronger than before, but not to the extent of making them a hybrid like I am."

"I'm guessing that eventually you fought and you won, else you wouldn't be talking to me."

"Yes, we fought and I won. In his human form against my hybrid form, he didn't stand a chance. But they will not stop. He may take the werewolf formula, and I doubt I would have enough power to stop him. I can't take the vampire formula for another four days."

"You're right. You can't risk taking the vampire formula until those four days pass. Else we might not have enough formula left to complete your full transformation. There needs to be the rest period in between for it to take one hundred percent effect. I would recommend you get out of England and find your way back to me. But there is a problem."

"You still don't want me around. Stop making excuses and tell me the truth."

"No, that's not the problem. I have received some news from our private investigators looking for Scarlet. I'm sorry to say that they have found her."

My heart jumped. I tried to control my obvious excitement and took a moment to control my breathing before I said another word.

"Is she okay? Where is she?"

"V, it's bad news, I am afraid. They only found her through a story in a newspaper. The body of a young redheaded girl found in the woods. Her body ripped to shreds by an animal. Bite marks on her neck and claw marks down her back. It looks like the Turned or the werewolves found her before we did. They have killed her. The funeral is tomorrow in London."

My breath caught in my throat, and I gripped the phone hard, the screen bending to my supernatural strength.

"V, are you there? You don't need to say anything to me. I will message over the details in case you want to say goodbye. But I would imagine the Hunters will be watching, so be careful and don't get too close. You don't have to pretend that you are okay. When you are ready, give me another call, and I will tell you where we are and will arrange a meeting."

I was glad she hadn't asked me to pretend. All I wanted to do was slam the phone against a wall and burst into tears and cry until there was nothing left. "Okay," I said, as it was all I could manage.

"Sorry to be the bearer of bad news. It brings me no pleasure to have told you that. I know you may think otherwise, but you promised yourself to me, and I considered the matter between you and her closed. I will say goodbye now and leave you to your grief. Call me when you are ready. Take care, V, I love you and will see you soon."

The phone went dead, and I dropped it onto the floor and slumped back onto the bed, staring up at the blank white ceiling. My tears burst out, but I did nothing to stop them. I lay on my bed and curled up into a ball. The tears flooded out on to the purple bed sheets, creating a damp spot. I wiped my hands across my eyes to clear the tears away.

I lay in the soulless hotel room just as I had done before, with Scarlett in the room next door. On that occasion, I had purposely stayed away from her to avoid temptation. I wish I had knocked on her door that night. Just the one night when we could have been together and happy. No matter that I had made a promise to Thorn, I would definitely never be with Scarlett now. Maybe I had always held out a fantasy that if things changed, then Scarlett would be there for me. It was an arrogant, stupid fantasy to think she would wait, which could never happen now. Maybe I still hadn't fully committed to Thorn, or I was more in love with Scarlett than I realised.

I cried for hours, cocooned in my hotel room, with no fear of being seen or heard. Images of Scarlett flashed through my mind. Her beautiful red hair and smile as we talked at college. Then I couldn't help but picture her face down in the mud, body cut to pieces, her stunning red hair matted in leaves and dirt. It was my fault she was dead. They obviously caught up with her in the end, and I can only assume they killed her as a form of petty revenge.

I would go to her funeral in London to say my goodbyes and bury the past for good. I would not involve any members of my family or any friends ever again. This human pain was no longer something I wanted. With Giles trying to kill me, and Scarlett dead, my last fingerhold on my mortal life had slipped away. Maybe that was a good thing.

Once I was clear to retake the vampire formula, I would. And then, I vowed to take the formula as regularly as possible to complete my transformation. I wanted to be a Dragan, above the emotions of human pain, to be immortal and to be with Thorn, where no one could hurt me anymore. Then I could take vengeance on the Hunters and the Turned, who were destroying my life and killing my loved ones.

Chapter Six

The next day, I rose early and set off to London. I had booked a hotel room which I would go to after the funeral. I just had enough time to drive back to London and catch the ceremony. Scarlett wasn't being buried; she was being cremated.

I drove down the motorway, trying to block out images of Scarlett being torn to shreds. Along the way, I had a few pit stops and cups of coffee to keep myself awake. I hadn't slept much the night before, too many tears and too much guilt.

I knew without a doubt that Scarlett would still be alive if I hadn't had revisited her in London after coming back from America. I only asked her to go to Leeds with me to visit my dad because I was lonely. I hadn't thought about her safety at all. I had acted selfishly, and I needed to consider others in the future. I was a dangerous person to be around. The death of Scarlett and my father had proved that. Also, Amber had suffered because of our relationship. I could not put the life of any more humans at risk. I would keep to my own kind.

`An hour before the funeral,` I arrived at the crematorium. I turned through the gates that were chained back into a large wooded area. I drove down the road, followed the signs to the chapel car park and parked in a space in the back corner. Other tree-lined roads led off to a visitor's area and facilities.

I watched the other visitors and scanned the area to check if anyone was waiting. It would be the obvious place to find me if the Turned were looking, especially if it was the Turned that had killed Scarlett. I couldn't see anyone suspicious, but I left and circle the crematorium a couple of times. I checked no one was following me and no suspicious vehicles nearby.

Being a hybrid, I still had some small psychic abilities and an enhanced sense of smell and sight. I used these to good effect as I drove around trying to tune into any unusual thoughts or emotions. I had the window rolled down, letting the air flood in, trying to detect any out of place smells. I was trying to sniff out the rotting stink of the Turned, as I couldn't hear their thoughts or emotions. However, I would hear the thoughts and emotions of any Hunters nearby. I couldn't detect anything out of the ordinary, so I drove back into the crematorium car park to wait for the funeral procession to begin.

The crematorium was eerily quiet. The surrounding trees absorbed all the sound from the road outside. Everything had been done to limit the noise to keep the area peaceful. The only noise was that of the birds in the trees and wind rustling the branches. I spotted a squirrel scurrying along a branch and diving into a hole in the tree. A rabbit hopped around the tree trunks, over the wildflowers and onto logs. It sat up and looked at me and then bounded off deeper into the woods. Above the trees, smoke billowed out from the crematorium chimney into the greying sky. The area had been created as a sombre space to grieve, but nature had turned it into a thriving sanctuary for wildlife.

While waiting, I texted Miss Jones, the homeless shelter manager, and told her I was back in town. I would visit her tomorrow and see if she needed any assistance.

The people from the previous funeral said their goodbyes. The empty hearse drove out, and the family walked towards a limousine. As the previous mourners dispersed, new cars arrived. Out of the first car were Scarlett's ex-boyfriend and his parents. This was the boy I had hit when I came back from Vegas to find Scarlett. He had blotchy red marks under his eyes. I felt some guilt about my assault on him, as it was apparent his feelings for Scarlett were real. Maybe she could have made a life with him if I hadn't interfered. His dad helped him walk to the front of the chapel to wait for the main funeral group to arrive.

I wondered what other people from college would come to pay their respects. I wondered if Scarlett's best friend, Mary, would attend. A few of the class turned up, including our teacher, Mrs Goodwin.

The large group of sombrely dressed mourners waited outside the chapel. The dark clouds whisked overhead, cutting off the sun and plunging the area into greying light. They pulled their coats closed and zipped them up.

A hearse drove along the entrance road, the black car flashing through the tree enclosed route. It drove into the chapel area with two limousines trailing it. The hearse, bearing the coffin, pulled around to the front of the chapel, and the limos stopped behind it.

To the sides of the coffins were flowers in her name and a set of lilies on top. Men in black suits climbed out of the vehicles and opened the limo doors. Scarlett's mum climbed out of the first car with a helping hand from her boyfriend. In the car behind, a man came out with another woman;

Scarlett's father and his girlfriend, the one he had an affair with.

The funeral attendants opened up the back of the hearse, removed the lilies and then pulled out a stained oak coffin and hoisted it upon their shoulders.

With the mourners lined up behind the coffin, they proceeded through the open chapel doors. At the front, Scarlet's mum being held up by her boyfriend. Next, her dad and his girlfriend. Finally, the rest of the black-clothed mourners followed in, including her ex-boyfriend. Once the main funeral procession had entered, a funeral attendant shut the doors. As the chapel closed, the black clouds unloaded their contents and rain lashed across my windscreen.

Tears rolled down my cheeks, and I rubbed them away with the back of my hand. I couldn't go inside the chapel and say goodbye. Even if I could, I doubted I would be welcome. I had to be content with hiding behind the tinted windows of my car.

I wanted to talk to Scarlett's mum and apologise for taking her daughter away and putting her life at risk, which ultimately led to her death. But how could I ever explain that vampires hunted me? She would have thought me crazy and believed I killed her daughter. I was sure the police had already named me as the prime suspect, considering my record.

I wiped the tears away, having resolved to stay until the funeral was over and the mourners had left. I thought about ways of taking revenge. I knew Bramel and the Hunters had ordered her death, so my best bet for vengeance was winning the vampire war and destroying the Turned for good.

A knock against my window snapped me away from my thoughts. I must've been too caught up in my emotions to have sensed the person approaching. I already had a gun loaded on the seat next to me. I grabbed it in my left hand and pressed the window button with my right. The window rolled down, revealing a crouching figure. I held the gun up, ready to take a shot.

The person was a woman with black hair, a few silver earrings, and a silver Bluetooth earpiece. She held an umbrella over her head as the rain battered against it. I had expected to see her at some point but had been surprised she wasn't one of the mourners. The woman was Mary, mine and Scarlett's college friend. I breathed a huge sigh of relief and removed the gun.

Mary gave me a weak smile and pushed her wet black hair out of her eyes. "It's good to see you again. May I join you and get out of the rain?"

I nodded and buzzed back my window, and she walked around the front of the car. She opened the passenger door, sat inside and closed her umbrella before pulling the door to.

"Terrible weather for this time of year," she said as she ran her hand through her black hair and then brushed the raindrops off her jacket.

"Why aren't you inside with everybody else?" I asked her.

"I wanted to talk to you," she said.

"You want to know what happened, I guess. Well, I can't tell you, I don't want to risk anyone else's life. All I can say is I am sorry for what happened. I guess you know she ran off with me."

"No, Jon. That isn't what I wanted to talk to you about. I know why she ran off with you already. I wanted to talk to you about what happens next."

I raised my eyebrows and gave a derisory laugh. "Mary, you might think you know why she ran off with me, but believe me, you could never possibly imagine what has really been happening. I don't want to risk anyone else's life, so it's probably best you go. They might be watching me. The same people that killed Scarlett."

"Jon, stop being such an arrogant little twit. You need to listen to me. I know exactly what happened that night in the park when you killed the gang and the events it put into motion."

I leaned across her and opened the door, letting the rain in. "I'm sure you think you know. You think I just attacked them and have been on the run since? Then I came back to see Scarlett and took her to Leeds to visit my dad where I just got into more trouble, or you think I attacked and killed her? Best you go now, for everybody's sake. Don't delay, you're letting the rain in."

Mary gave me a cold, hard stare, barely holding back her evident annoyance. She looked different from how I remembered her. Her hair wasn't jet black any more but just a normal dark colour. The piercings in her ears had gone down to a couple, and they were relatively normal. She wasn't wearing any of her usual trademark black Gothic make-up, which was a surprise considering she was at a funeral. She leaned towards the door, grabbed the handle and slammed it shut.

"V, I really do know everything."

I literally jumped out of my seat towards the door and banged into it. Her calling me V meant she really did know everything.

"What the..."

"Yes, V is your vampire, or should I say Dragan name. You are currently going by the alias of Christopher Lee. Typical of Thorn to use a name with meaning, flaunting your true identity to the entire world. When I say I know everything, as you can tell, I know everything. I know of the vampire formula. I know of your rescue of Thorn. I know of the killing of Barry and the monster he changed into. I know of your trip to Vegas and then your road trip to Seattle. Then your return to England and taking Scarlett up north. Your capture by the Hunters, your torture, and finally your escape. Oh, and of course, your recent confrontation with your boyhood best friend now turned werewolf apprentice, Giles. Anything I have missed out?"

My mouth was wide open as I was trying to think of something to say, trying to figure out how the hell she could know all of this. I held up my finger with the Union Dragon ring. "I got married."

"To Thorn I assume."

"Yes."

"You mean a Union, not a marriage."

"Yes. But how do you know all of this?"

"Let me tell you a story. My real name isn't Mary. I know you always believed someone was watching you at college. You believed for a while that Scarlett was keeping an eye on you, working for the Hunters. Someone was watching you and it was me. But I don't work for the Hunters. I work for MI5," she said.

I reached down to the gun, and she quickly grabbed my wrist. "Jon, I'm not afraid of you. There are several snipers with their cross-hairs aimed at you right now. I only have to give the order, and they will put a bullet through your heart," she said and tapped her finger against her Bluetooth earpiece. She pointed at the misted windscreen, which had several red dots swirling around on the raindrops. I looked down at my chest as the blurred red dots danced above my heart.

I relaxed my hand and put it back on my lap. "Well, I guess you better tell me everything, then." I felt a fool. All this time, Mary knew precisely who I was and what was going on. I kind of expected to tell her my strange story and her to be surprised. But now the shoe was on the other foot. She could have me killed in an instant, and I had no idea who she really was.

"MI5, as you know, is concerned with national security. We keep an eye on all national security elements, which includes the Hunters and Vampires and any other such organisation. The Hunters report to a different department within MI5. However, MI5 has always kept tabs on them. It was clear the Hunters' organisation had gone rogue. We had a few spies inside that would feedback information. We discovered a deal had been done with the Turned in order to destroy the Dragans and find out their secrets. The genetic research your father carried out on the werewolves had caused a stir. They wanted the same results with a Dragan. Then, somehow, they were able to catch Thorn, the prime genetic example on which to base their research.

So we know the Hunters arranged the bullying and attack on your friend Giles. Although we suspect it was supposed to be you. However, it had the same effect and convinced your dad to leave Leeds and move to London to work on a new research project. The safety of his son was obviously paramount to him. I was assigned to attend college and become your friend. The idea being I could keep an eye on you. Maybe get to know you better and therefore, find out what your dad was up to. We had people watching your father as well."

"So, if you were there to keep an eye on me, why didn't you stop everything that happened?"

"I'm sorry, Jon, we hadn't realised the attack on you outside the college was a ploy for you to take the formula. We thought it was just an unfortunate event."

"Why didn't you stop the gang on that day? You could have fought them off."

Mary smiled. "I may be a spy, but I'm not some sort of superhero martial arts expert. Yes, I can handle myself a bit, but I'm not sure if I could have fought off those three teenage thugs. And even if I could have beaten them, it would have completely blown my cover. My mission was to watch and observe to become your friend. Someone you could trust and would tell your secrets to. That is why I arranged to be one of your buddies when you first arrived. That is why I dressed in Gothic clothing. I was trying to be someone who you could connect with."

"What do you mean, exactly? Do you mean you were trying to be my girlfriend?"

Mary scratched her chin and took a deep breath. "Well, this is a little bit awkward. I was supposed to become your friend, and if that meant I had to become your girlfriend as well, I was supposed to allow that to happen. It would have ensured our friendship, and it would have ensured access to your father's secrets. But I didn't need to become your girlfriend. It was obvious from the beginning you and Scarlett had hit it off. I realised all I needed to do was become Scarlett's friend and encourage the relationship between you. It's not that I don't like you, Jon, but I am a few years older than I actually look. And it would have been morally incorrect of me to encourage such an intimate friendship."

I shook my head and sighed. "I wouldn't have worried about the age gap if I were you. As you know, my current girlfriend has many more years on me."

"A few hundred more years on you, so I understand."

"I really don't know what to think of all of this. I did find you attractive, and I always felt we had so much in common as well. I had often wondered if Scarlett hadn't been there, if we would have been closer. But I feel weird about the fact that this was all an act on your behalf. You were just a honey trap."

"I know it is weird. And I'm glad I never had to go to that stage of pretending to be your girlfriend. It is not something I wanted to do either. I was so relieved when your friendship with Scarlett took off. And all I had to do was encourage it, which took quite a bit of work. And without me, you probably would have never have got together."

"And if we hadn't had got together, Scarlett would still be alive today. Maybe you are as much to blame as me for her death," I said and stared at her.

"Don't blame me for her death or yourself. It's quite clear the Turned hunted her down and killed her. I suspect this was an act of revenge for the death of Carmella and the other Hunters. But this is why I'm here to talk to you today. Now we have our true identities revealed, we can talk about how to exact revenge and stop them."

"You want to work with Thorn and me to defeat the Turned and the Hunters?"

"It's much more than just me, John. I'm here representing MI5 and, therefore, the whole of Her Majesty's government. The Hunters and Turned working together pose a clear and present danger to national and international security. We need to stop them. Therefore, I have been given permission to engage with the Dragan community to see if we can form an alliance."

"You want to work with Thorn and me to stop the Turned?"

"Not just you and Thorn, but all the Dragans and the werewolves that want to stop the Turned. We have the same goals."

"And how can we trust you? Do you think Thorn will want to work with MI5?"

"It wouldn't be the first time she has worked for us. She acted as an assassin and spy in the Second World War. I'm sure she must have told you about this."

I remembered her stories of roaming France and Germany during the Second World War. Her knowledge of languages, her ability to read people's thoughts, and of course, her supernatural strength was an enormous asset in fighting the war. "She has told me that she worked for the British government during the Second World War and on other occasions. I'm sure she'd be willing to listen."

Mary reached into a jacket pocket and pulled out a USB stick and handed it to me. I took it from her. "What's this?"

"This," Mary said, looking at the USB stick, "is a gesture of goodwill. It contains some information Thorn can use. It also has details on how I can be contacted via secure channels. But in the meantime, my old mobile number still works if you need to contact me in an emergency. Do you still have my number?"

"Yes, I still have it saved." I put the USB stick into my jeans pocket. "So what's next?"

"Speak to Thorn; put forward our proposal to her. With our intelligence and military resources, and with her supernatural powers, we can stop the Turned for good and bring the Hunter organisation back into line."

"And take revenge for Scarlett."

"Yes, and take revenge for Scarlett. Also, long term, it would be useful for this alliance to continue."

"If we win this war, then you want the Dragan's to work for you full time?"

"Why not?"

"I don't think it's Thorn's style to work for anyone. Those few times she has worked for the government, it has been exceptional circumstances."

"The world is changing. Thorn probably knows this already. She needs to adapt if the Dragans are to survive beyond this fight."

"Yes, genetic research has brought everything to a head."

Mary shook her head. "Not just advances in technology and sciences, although this does make a big difference. We humans have the weapons and tools to hunt down the Dragan and Turned. We also have the numbers. But reality itself is changing."

I stared at her, hoping the answer would spring to mind. "What are you saying?"

"Reality is changing. The magic that made the Dragans, which has been considered gone, is returning to the world."

"Magic is coming back. But how?"

"Something has broken the balance that was created when the Mages fused themselves with Dragons and created Dragans. That act drained the world of most of its magic and poured itself into those beings. There was a remnant amount left over, but not enough for normal people to detect or use. But something has upset the balance."

"How? What happened?"

"Several theories are doing the rounds, which include you at the centre of them."

"Me. I haven't done anything."

"You became a Dragan. Not through birth but through genetic manipulation. The experts believe a sudden additional Dragan in the world has punched open a gateway for the transformations to occur. This has let magic back into the world from the original source. The gateway is open and every transformation draws in more magic. Especially considering your change to a dragon in the warehouse battle. It must have secured the gateway."

"I have to die on every transformation, and I always see a bright light and faces and voices of the dead."

"So it does open a gateway to another dimension."

"It's my fault then?"

"It doesn't really matter whose fault it is, but unusual things have happened. And we don't have the Hunters to help us control them. This gives the Turned or Dragans possible other allies or enemies. It is in our interest to bring these potential friends or foes into our department. I will need the Dragans to help us control this new world."

"I see. I will speak to Thorn and see what she says."

"Like I said, I am sure Thorn has already detected this change in the world."

I shook my head. "She hasn't mentioned anything to me."

"And does she tell you everything?"

I looked away and gritted my teeth.

"I guessed as much," she said. "Just ask her about it and we can discuss you joining my department."

"So, what is this department called?"

"The official title is MI5-S, the S standing for supernatural. But we have a few nicknames that the rest of the security services refer to us by. Spooky crew, Scooby gang, and Ghostbusters."

"Imaginative, aren't they?"

"It's just been shortened to department S by most people."

"What are the things that have happened? Is there anyone that could help us?"

Mary took a moment and placed her finger on the earpiece and flicked her eyebrows at it. "Nothing I can discuss. These other people with supernatural powers are rogue at the moment, or we are unsure of their suitability. We have our hands full containing them. Only time will tell if they can be of use or need to be eliminated. One way or another, Department S will need to expand."

"Oh. I understand." It was clear from her gestures that she couldn't talk about it, as other people were listening. Maybe she would tell me another time.

"I'm going now, Jon. Speak to Thorn as soon as possible. Don't leave this opportunity too long. If we don't hear from you within a few days, then we assume you are also our enemy. There is no sitting on the sidelines or being neutral. You're either with Department S and Her Majesty's government, or you're an equal threat as the Hunters and Turned, and any other hostile powers."

Mary grabbed hold of the door handle, pushed it open, got out and slammed it shut. She walked out into the car park, and a car zoomed from the other side, stopped by her and she opened up the back passenger door and got inside. The car then screeched away out of the car park and back onto the main road.

I couldn't believe I had just had that conversation with Mary. All this time, she was watching me, and I thought she was just a bystander.

I would wait until the funeral was over, and then I would head back to the hotel and contact Thorn. I would put forward Mary's proposals. But it seemed the most logical choice, especially as Thorn had worked with them before. We could benefit from a strong alliance. Everything was coming together. My path to vengeance was now clear.

Chapter Seven

Scarlett's family and friends had left, and I gave it another half an hour to pull myself together and think of a plan of action. I would go back to the hotel at nightfall and call Thorn to discuss the proposal from MI5. Afterwards, I would get some sleep, and then I would visit Miss Jones in the morning.

The final stragglers finished talking and drove off as the next set of mourners arrived for another funeral. I decided now was my time to leave amidst the incoming traffic. I started the car up, drove through the tree-lined roads and out of the crematorium.

As I left the crematorium, the sun was ducking behind a wooded area across the muddy ploughed fields next to the country road. I followed my satnav, thinking about what Mary had said, thinking about my revenge and doing everything, not to think about Scarlett.

The car jolted forward, and I slammed into the steering wheel. I pushed myself upright and yanked the steering wheel, skidding the car off the edge of the road to remain on track. In the rearview mirror, a blue pickup truck surged into view. I hit the accelerator to gain some space, but the truck rammed into the back of my car again; its front bars tangled into my rear bumper.

I tried to accelerate away and steer off the front of it, but the truck had too much power. It pushed me further forward, driving me off the road. The pickup truck slammed on its brakes. My car's back bumper ripped off, as stuck to the pickup truck's front fender. My car smashed through a wooden fence and bounced into the wet, muddy field. A wheel hit a tree stump, and the car flipped around in the air. I closed my eyes and braced for impact. My body strapped in and spinning around within the metal cage.

The car crashed down on the roof and skidded along. The windshield smashed to pieces, spraying glass into my face, and the airbags burst open at the front and sides, encasing me in a pillow of safety. As the car ground to a halt, wet mud poured in and covered my face.

The airbags had protected me but trapped my arms inside. I reached down and unclipped the seatbelt and slumped onto the ceiling of the car. I punched and clawed my way through the airbags until they deflated.

Free to move, I wiped the mud off my eyes and crawled through the broken window, its glass sticking into my hands and knees. I crawled out onto the muddy field with the headlights of the pickup truck casting beams of light. Out of the truck, two figures climbed out and clambered down the embankment into the field.

It was the same truck from the cemetery in Leeds, and I guessed it was Norris and Giles. I took a big sniff of the air, but the smell of the countryside and the petrol pouring from the car was overpowering anything else. I wasn't going to wait around. Even if it wasn't Giles and Norris, they certainly didn't want to be friends.

I stood up, but my knees buckled, and I fell face first back into the mud. My legs were bruised, and my body screamed in pain. I felt inside my jacket for the case containing the vampire formula needles. It was still intact.

If I took it, then it would heal my wounds and allow me to escape. However, I should only use it if necessary because once I had injected it, I would have to wait another week before retaking it. That meant I would have to rely on my natural skills and strengths to survive.

I gritted my teeth and pushed myself back upright, screaming through the pain. After I wiped the mud from my face, the woods were visible across the far side of the field. I hobbled away, hoping I could walk off my bruises and run towards the trees. The wet mud sucked at my feet, pulling on my bruised and aching muscles. I squelched a step at a time.

As I walked, the blood pumped through and the adrenaline kicked in. I could hear the feet of men behind squelching through the wet mud, and I forced my feet onwards. I searched ahead for a dry spot and picked my way through the worst of the field to hit solid ground. The movement and fear dulled the pain, and I got into a half-decent run as I picked my way through the muddy field.

I stumbled into the thick woods as Giles and Norris ran across the field. The last glimpse of the Sun gave enough light to confirm my suspicions before it dipped below the horizon and darkness took over.

"No point in running, Jon. I can smell your disgusting vampire stink. There's nowhere to run to, no one to protect you. You have to face me, once and for all, you betrayer."

I grabbed my phone from my pocket. The screen had shattered upon the car crash. The touch screen just about worked but cut my finger ends. I pressed the button on Mary's contact.

The phone rang. "Hello Jon, so soon?"

"Mary, I need your help. Giles and Norris are hunting me. They ran my car off the road."

"I will send a squad to rescue you. If you press the GPS button on your phone and leave the call running, it will help us pinpoint your location."

"I will but you just need to distract them. I'm not coming with you. You need to give me some time to escape.

"Jon, the team is coming. They will help. No one is taking you captive, not even us. Get running." I opened up the settings, hit the GPS location button and stuffed the phone into my jacket pocket.

I scrambled into the woods, weaving through the trees, when a howling sound pierced through the air. I skidded to a halt and looked around. The moon shone from the other side of the woods, providing a faint light. The shape of a giant creature bounded through the tree trunks, with steam evaporating off its fur. I would have to face him. I couldn't outrun a werewolf.

I pulled out the needle case and opened it up. I grabbed the vampire formula and stabbed it into my neck, slamming down the plunger, forcing the formula into my bloodstream. The vampire fuel mixed with my blood and set it ablaze.

My knees buckled and stomach twisted in knots. I keeled over into a ball on the floor, and my heartbeat pounded in my ears. The gap between each pump elongated out until it ground to a fatal halt. I clutched my chest as my heart stopped, and my blood ceased its circulation. The world went black and cold as my consciousness drifted away to a distance bright light, and the voice and shapes of my parents reached out.

My heart exploded and blood surged through its veins. My spirit crashed back into my body. I opened my eyes to multi-coloured lights of energy in the woods. A burst of yellow light exploded out of my body and absorbed into the surroundings. I had seen it on other transformations but not taken any notice, as it was fleeting. Maybe this was the new magic I had brought back through the gateway.

Ahead, the werewolves emitted red energy as they stalked through the trees. Their musky smell flooded my nostrils, and their red rage assaulted my psychic senses. As they approached, birds scattered from the treetops, leaving a trail of heat and fear.

My muscles strengthened, forcing me onto my knees. I stood back up and let forth my own growl as I released an overload of supernatural energy. The wolf bounded through the last of the trees and smashed into me. We tumbled through the undergrowth of branches and leaves and into the trunk of an oak tree.

I laid on the ground and the wolf crouched over with its huge canine teeth snarling back, steam evaporating off its wet fur. Its eyes were black, ears flattened, and jaws snapped at my face.

I got a hand up to slam its jaws away, avoiding its snapping canines. The wolf pushed itself back up onto its hind legs and then swiped down with huge front claws. I shielded behind my arms. The wolf's claws slammed into my flesh and raked across my forearms, ripping open my jacket.

I screamed as its claws lacerated my skin and tore into my muscles. It dropped and snapped its enormous jaws at my face again. I rolled out of the way so it bit into the dirt. I twisted back and lashed a fist across its jaw. He staggered for a moment. I smacked a knee up into its belly and then rolled my legs up to my chest. I kicked upwards and outwards, sending the wolf hurtling backwards. He twisted round in the air and landed on his paws. He turned and snarled, flattening his tail down, fur rising across its back.

I jumped back onto my feet, the pain in my arms still coursing through me, blood dripping onto the floor. From behind, I heard footsteps running through the leaves. I spun around as Norris approached. He stopped and held out his hands. "This fight is between you and Giles. I'm just here to make sure you don't escape again," he said, and then began the transformation into a werewolf.

I had no choice but to fight Giles head-on, and then if I won, I would have to tackle Norris.

Giles prowled around me in a circle, snarling and growling all the time. Once Norris had changed into a werewolf, both of them howled up into the air, and then Giles went back to stalking me. The pain in my arms remained as the blood poured out at a rapid rate. I thought I could just take the attack and the wounds would heal as they had done before. But I guessed there was something special about werewolves' claws because my body showed no sign of recovery.

Giles coiled back and then sprang forward, flying, claws out and jaws wide. I jumped to the side and pirouetted out of the way. He landed, skidded and bounded back, smashing into my stomach, catapulting me into a tree. My head and body jolted on impact. The wolf thumped its giant claws into my body and cut them across my stomach. I lashed out another fist, but the wolf had already moved.

I rolled over and crawled away. He landed on my back, knocking me face first into the dirt. I twisted around. He jumped onto my chest, pinning me to the muddy ground, his jaws snarling and snapping at the air above my face, taunting me with his supremacy.

I had fought monsters before, but something about the sight of the werewolf had invoked a primitive fear. I guessed it was my human side. All I wanted to do was run and hide. I couldn't think of what to do and how to fight. The other wolf, Norris, walked around the side, sat down and howled at the moon. Giles sat on my chest and howled up into the air, a cry of victory.

When I won the battle against the turned, I had summoned my dragon. I had to spark my rage and do it again. I remembered the electric shocks and smashing of my feet from Patrick's tortures. The gun shot killing my father in the car park ambush. The pain of Scarlett's death also weaving into my emotions. I let it build up, ready to release it and ignite the dragon within.

Giles's face transformed back so his features were recognisable and he could talk. "This is the end for you, Jon. I will have my revenge, and then I will finish the O'Keefe family."

Seeing Giles's face killed off my rage. I had abandoned him and his family in their time of need. However, I realised his transformation back meant he had to reduce his powers. I pulled my hands together over my head into a double fist and hammered them into his face. His nose burst open and blood streamed down. His weight released off my chest, and I tipped my body over, pushing him off to the side. I scrambled away and hauled myself up against a tree.

I hobbled away when Norris barrelled me into the dirt. His jaws snapped at my face, and then he stood back and barked over at Giles.

Giles had transformed back into a full werewolf again, blood running from his snout. He replied to Norris with a series of barks and padded across to me. I guessed he wouldn't make the same mistake again. He walked over and stood over me. Giles pushed himself back up onto his hind legs, claws high in the air, ready to swipe down to finish me off for good.

Gunshots fired out in the dark and wood from the trees splintered off. More gunshots fired and more of the trees splintered and broke under the hail of bullets. Two shots hit Giles, and he fell to the ground, twisted around and whimpered. Norris barked at Giles and then turned and growled at the approaching footsteps. He turned and barked at me, then dashed off through the trees and Giles sprinted after him.

I didn't want to be taken in by MI5. I didn't fully trust Mary and their proposed alliance, so I had to escape. I scrambled to my feet and ran through the trees, jumping rocks and logs, trying to shake them off my trail. They chased after me, and I realised they were still tracking the GPS on my phone. I took it out of my pocket, threw it away and headed off in the other direction.

As a Dragan, I would be faster, but I would also leave a strong heat signature. I had to put some distance between us and cool myself off.

As I ran through the woods, I heard the sounds of a river and headed towards it. I reached the edge of the riverbank, and I looked back as dark shapes weaved through the trees, kicking up leaves and breaking twigs under foot. The dark flowing river, which had swollen in the rainstorm, curved around and swirled off. I stumbled down the slope and waded in. The icy water forced my retreat, but the shapes grew closer. I gritted my teeth and pushed onwards.

The current tugged at my legs, but I staggered out until it whipped my feet from under me. The river gathered me up and washed me downstream, swirling and curving off into the darkness. I also hoped the cold would stop the swelling of my wounds and slow up the bleeding.

The river swept me away from the soldiers. I could just make out their shapes looking out from the riverbank. In the distance, a buzzing of a helicopter approached, converging to their position. They were searching for my heat signal, and I hoped they would not spot me in the freezing cold water under the trees.

I focused ahead to keep myself away from jutting rocks or large debris. In front, a large log was jammed against a couple of rocks downstream. I swam to the side to position myself directly upstream. I let the river guide me in, and I grabbed hold of the log, pulled it off the rocks and used it to give myself some buoyancy.

I washed along the river, gripping onto my log. The water twisted around to the left and then swept back across a reed bank, brushing over my legs. I jammed to a stop; the river pushing me forwards but my legs stuck, entangled in the reeds. The river flow forced my head underwater, and I had to let go of the log to push myself above the waterline. With my legs tangled in the reeds, I had to fight against the water to take a breath.

A log hit the back of my head and the water seeped into my mouth. I snapped my head back and spat it out. I couldn't last forever stuck in the reeds and struggling for breath; the fight with Giles had already weakened me. I pushed up for one big breath and dived, slashing my claws at the reeds and kicking my leg loose.

The river hauled me away with the tether of the reeds gone. I swam to the surface as the icy river eddied into a bank, swung around and down through a series of rapids. The water cascaded over my head and forced me underwater. I held out my arms and legs to ricochet through the rocks as the river flowed through the danger.

I plunged deep underwater as it swept me through the rapids and out into the slower running river. The water gushed in as I ran out of breath. I kicked out to the surface and coughed out the swallowed water.

The water was calmer as the river opened up. On the river banks, a few houses ran down to the water's edge. I cheered to see civilisation again, as it meant I could get out of the freezing water and find a way to safety. I thought about swimming to the riverbank and going through a garden or breaking into a house, but I decided it would be a bad idea. Instead, I waited for an easier access out of the water.

The number of houses along the river bank increased, and traffic noise and people echoed down the river. The lights of a town centre blurred in the distance. Small piers and boats tied up to them lined the edge of the river.

My teeth were chattering and hands had gone numb. I couldn't survive in the freezing cold water for much longer, even if it was stemming the flow of blood. If there were boats nearby, there would be people and cars. I could climb out of the river and borrow a vehicle to get to safety.

I would try to get back to the hotel, though I wasn't sure of its location having not yet booked in. I was relying on the car's satnav to guide me back, but that was now wrecked in a muddy field. But I knew where the homeless shelter was on Winchester Street. All I needed to do was acquire a vehicle, work out my location and drive. I had a reasonably good knowledge of the roads around London.

I swam to the side of the river, ready to get out and merge into the population. I caught hold of the edge of a rowing boat tied up to a wooden pier. My legs felt like a dead weight as I hauled myself up. I slumped into the boat and hugged myself to warm up. The air froze above me as I lay on my back, and I stared into the starry night sky.

As the boat rocked back and forth, I gathered my strength, but I would not get better if I lay still. I had to get moving. Twisting around in the boat, I pushed myself on to my knees and grabbed the rung of the pier ladder. I gritted my teeth and screamed inside as I hauled myself up the ladder until my leaden legs and feet moved onto the bottom rung. Gripping on tight to each rung, I pushed myself up until I collapsed onto the top of the wooden pier.

A few hundred yards away, there was a car park with vehicles scattered around. In the far corner of the car park, a group of people hung around, admiring and showing off their customised vehicles. A busy takeaway van sat in the middle of the car park.

Thorn had taught me how to steal cars. However, I didn't have any tools or the clarity of mind. Pain wracked my body, the cuts on my arms and stomach still bleeding despite the coldness of the river. I needed to get some bandages around them to stop the blood from escaping. I just hoped in my Dragan form I could keep going for longer than usual.

I stumbled along the riverbank to the side of the car park and hid behind a wall of a pub on the bank of the river. A few people had gathered around the takeaway van.

I would have to take a car. Somehow, I would have to steal their keys and try to scare them off. I couldn't break into one and hotwire it in my present state. My hands were still shaking from the cold and I had no tools. I hoped that my fangs, red eyes and growl would be enough to send most people fleeing.

At that moment, the pub's back gate opened and a man staggered out into the car park. He pressed the button on a key fob, and the amber lights flicked on and off on a black Mercedes. I decided I could do everybody a favour and take his car from him.

He weaved across the car park and dropped his keys. He bent down and scooped them up, stumbling and swaying towards his car. His hands rested himself against driver's door.

I stumbled over to the drunken man. He grabbed the car door handle and pulled it open. He staggered backwards to righten his balance. I ran over, shoulder barged him out of the way, knocking him to the floor and snatching the keys out of his hand in one movement. I jumped in the car, slammed in the keys and shut the door.

The drunken man found his feet and lurched towards me. His face was red, and he swung his fist back. I glared at him. My red eyes fiercely burnt and I flashed my fangs. He stopped for a moment and rubbed his eyes as if to clear the image away. In the meantime, I twisted the key in the ignition and accelerated out of the car park. In the rearview mirror, I saw the takeaway van's customers run over to him and one of them pulled out a phone.

They had to be calling the police. I had to get going quickly. The cops would hunt me, and with the police came the Hunters and Turned Vampires.

I turned onto the road and just followed it, unsure of my location. I was lucky enough that the car had a built-in satnav. Within a couple of minutes, it showed my current location. I knew there was a main dual lane road not far away, and if I could find it, I could program in the rest of the location without slowing down.

I drove through the town and onto the slip road. I floored it to get onto the dual carriageway and put some distance between myself and the carjacking. When the police broadcast my description, I would have both MI5 and the Hunters looking for me if they believed the description from the drunken man.

I accelerated down the road and was only twenty minutes away from the safety of the shelter. I could make it, but blue lights flashed in my rearview mirror as a police car pulled onto the road behind and gave chase. I swerved through the traffic, trying to keep my speed up. The cars behind moved out of the way of the chasing police car to give them a clear run.

With the traffic out of the way, the police made up the ground. The car I had stolen did not have as much power compared to the police vehicle. Then more blue flashing lights appeared, and another two police cars tore down the carriageway. They were right on my tail lights. I wasn't going to lose them on this long road. I had to get off it and try to lose them in some traffic.

The satnav indicated a slip road approaching. I waited for the last possible moment and swerved off to the side, sending two of the police cars shooting past me, but the one at the back skidded around enough to follow. The blue lights helped clear the traffic in front as I drove straight through the roundabout's red lights. I turned hard right, drifting the car around, kicking up smoke from the squealing tyres. I straightened up and went back down onto the dual carriageway again, in the belief the two police cars I had lost earlier would turn around to chase after me.

I accelerated down the slip road, rejoining the flow of traffic. The chasing police car followed using the long slip road to catch-up. I waited until it wasn't far away and slammed on my brakes, so it drove straight into the back of me. The front of the police car smashed into my bumper. I figured the empty back end of my car would break the police car's engine. The police car rolled back from the impact, and I reversed to smash into it again.

I whacked it back into first gear and wheel spun away. I accelerated down the dual carriageway. The police car didn't move; its wheels seemed to be buckled. I slapped the stick through the gears all the way to the top. I rocketed along and moved over to the near side, ready to exit at the next junction.

In my rearview mirror, faint blue lights flashed. I had a reasonable distance on them, and I could lose them at the next junction.

I fired straight up the next slip road and filtered into the flow of traffic. I went through the roundabout, keeping to the left-hand side and turned into a supermarket car park.

The supermarket was open till late, and the orange lights of the logo shone into the sky. The car park had lights all round to guide the shoppers in. A continuous flow of people moved between the building and cars. I navigated through the customers and cars to the far end behind the main building and parked it in-between a van and 4x4 jeep.

Hedges surrounded the car park, making a barrier between it and a shopping mall next door. The area had CCTV allowing the police to find me, so I had to make my way out of the car park on foot. If I kept to the sides by the hedges and in the shadows, they wouldn't see me. Only if they had heat-sensing cameras would they detect something different about me.

A police car swung into the car park, and I ducked behind a red estate car. I crawled underneath and lay flat on the floor, waiting for the police to give up and drive off. It circled around a few times until they stopped over the far end where I parked.

While they were occupied searching around the area, I crawled out from under the car and made my way out, trying to blend in with the other shoppers. Although I realised my blood-stained clothes would attract unwanted attention, but there was nothing I could do to cover it up. I couldn't hang around for too long before I was spotted. In the distance, a helicopter approached.

I had to find another way of covering my heat signature and getting away from the police. The car's warmth sharpened my senses and stopped my hands from shaking. But the escape on foot had opened up my wounds, and blood poured down my arms and out of my stomach. I took off my black jacket and wrapped it tight around my stomach to stop the bleeding.

I scouted around, looking for an old vehicle that would be easy to steal. An old white minivan didn't look like it had an alarm. I went around the passenger side and used my supernatural strength to crack the door open. I climbed in, clambered across to the driver's seat and cracked open the steering column to hotwire it. The engine hummed into life. Another trick that Thorn had taught me. I sat in the driver's seat and turned up the heater.

My blood dripped onto the steering wheel, and I looked around the van to find something to act as a bandage. In amongst old newspapers and junk food wrappers, a wad of serviettes were jammed between the dashboard top and the windscreen. I pushed them onto the wounds, with the drying blood holding them on.

I pulled out of the car parking space, driving like a good, well-behaved citizen to avoid detection. As I left the car park, more police vehicles and a few black vans drove in. I suspected it could be full of Hunters, Turned or MI5 agents. I pulled onto the main road and drove away, hoping that no one had seen me.

I drove to safety, towards Miss Jones' shelter. But as I drove through the night time traffic, horns beeped and lights flashed. A couple of times, I swerved to avoid a collision. My driving had become erratic. My head was swimming, and there was a constant ringing in my ears. I had lost sensation in my hands and feet despite the warmth of the van. The wad of serviette bandages had fallen off and blood ran down my arms onto my lap.

When I finally pulled onto Winchester Street, I couldn't see straight and my eyes were closing. I lurched the van to a halt and bumped it up the pavement. It was about a ten-minute walk to the shelter, and I didn't want to park too close as it would reveal my destination.

I opened the door of the van and fell out. I dragged my feet out of the van and crawled along the pavement until I reached a house and leaned against it to hold myself steady as I stood up. From there, I shuffled down the street, staggering along, bumping against the walls like a drunken man.

I walked past the discarded police tape when a couple of men approached. "Hello, don't I recognise you?"

I gazed into the blurry face of a man. His teeth were sparse and black.

His breath stank of cigarettes and his hair was greased back. "Yes, I do know you. You're the boy who visited Miss Jones the other day. Looks like you've got yourself into some bother," he said, looking at my blood-drenched arms and stomach.

"I need to get to Miss Jones," I said with a slur to my speech.

"Don't you worry, boy, rotten Tommy will take care of you. Anyone who is a friend of Miss Jones is a friend of mine. I promised someone I would keep an eye out for her friends," he said and put his arm around me. The other man went to my other side and put his arm around my waist.

They escorted me down the road towards the shelter. There must have been something about finally being safe, as I couldn't remember the rest of the journey. Next thing I remember, I was waking up alone in a small white room with no doors or windows.

Chapter Eight

I opened my eyes and stared up at a white ceiling and walls. I lay on a bed tucked into the corner of a small room. A TV hung on the wall and a fridge sat underneath a suspended wooden counter with a microwave on top. Through a white archway, there was a shower, sink, and toilet. I saw no doors, but the ceiling had a hatch with a set of bare wooden stairs leading up to it. The room looked as if it had never been used, and the smell of antiseptic pierced the air.

My body had been cleaned, and I wore a pair of black boxer shorts and a black T-shirt. Where I'd been attacked by the wolf, I had bandages around my arms and across my stomach, and I carried a few cuts and bruises.

I pushed myself up on the bed and then onto my feet. I remembered being carried away by rotten Tommy and his friend towards the shelter. But this place didn't look like anywhere in the shelter. It seemed more like a hospital with its clean white walls and sterile smell. But it felt more like a prison with its bare interior and lack of doors and windows. It reminded me of the hospital prison cell Carmella had kept me in.

"Hello, hello, is there anyone there?"

I waited for a reply, but nothing came.

"Hello, Miss Jones, are you there? Where am I?"

There was still no reply. I walked around the bare white room, tapping all the walls and receiving a solid response. I looked at myself in the shower room mirror. My face was cut to pieces and I had a black eye. I tried my fangs and reddened eyes, and both responded. I was still Dragan, which meant I hadn't been in this room for very long, as the formula would have worn off after two days. However, I hadn't healed properly. I walked back out into the main room, past a grey fabric sofa pushed up against the wall, and climbed the wooden stairs to the hatch. I pushed against it, but it was securely locked. There was a small handle on the inside, but the hatch wouldn't budge.

The room was too nice and my treatment too good for it to have been a prison. Felt more like a hospital room with its bare, white and clean surfaces. I decided the best thing to do was wait and regain my strength. After wandering around the room, I felt a little lightheaded. So, I carefully climbed back down the steps and shuffled across the cold white tiled floor, clambering into the bed and pulled the sheets up to my neck.

I lay waiting for the room to stop spinning and for the sound in my ears to die down. I closed my eyes, breathed in deeply and then exhaled. Just then, the hatch at the top of the room clicked open.

Feet appeared at the top of the steps. A pair of black leather boots with high heels. The feet took another couple of steps down and stopped. The feet twisted as the person's body turned back upwards to grab something. They twisted back and continued walking down. The legs came into sight, a pair of skinny blue jeans hugging her hips and a white T-shirt. She was carrying a tray of food. It looked like some kind of stew and rice, with steam coming off it.

Finally, the woman's chest came into sight and then her face. She had neat dark hair and blue eyes. It took a moment or two, but I recognised the woman. I had met her when Thorn and I had broken into a warehouse of human traffickers. The gang had a group of girls bound and gagged, awaiting shipment. Thorn and I had rescued them, and two of the girls had asked to join us and become vampires. Thorn didn't agree but instead sent them to Miss Jones to be looked after. It had been two years since I last saw Lucinda.

Lucinda smiled as she descended, and I smiled back. I knew by seeing her; I was safe. Behind her, another set of trainers and jeans. Again, the jeans were figure-hugging across the hips. I guessed the next pair of jeans belonged to her friend. Annabel came into view shortly behind Lucinda. Her blonde hair tied back with makeup on her cheeks and around her eyes. Another set of feet in sturdy black hiking boots and jeans followed her down the steps.

"You are awake. That is good. I wasn't looking forward to waking you up," Lucinda said, and stepped off the last stair. I sat upright in bed as Lucinda walked over. She sat on the bed and placed the tray on her own lap. The smell of the beef made my stomach growl and mouth water. Behind, Annabel took the last step off into the room. "You are looking much better than you did yesterday," she said. "How are you feeling now?"

"Err, confused."

The last figure in jeans and hiking boots came into sight and it was Marcy, Miss Jones, who had a first aid rucksack on her back. She turned around and pulled the hatch down. Then she took the last stairs into the room. "You gave us all quite a fright. It was lucky that rotten Tommy found you. He has taken to patrolling the area after one of our helpers was attacked on the way here. I never thought it would amount to anything. Rather just a way of keeping Tommy happy that he was doing something. But thank God he was looking out for any trouble."

My memory flashed back into crashing into rotten Tommy as I stumbled and staggered down Winchester Street to the shelter. "I know. I was surprisingly glad to see him. Will you thank him for me?" I said.

"You can thank him yourself later. Once we get you well enough to leave here."

I looked around the room and at the three women. "Where is here?"

Marcy grinned. "You are in the shelter. This is a hidden room that was built in as Thorn's bolt-hole. It's in my office. Just under the desk is a trapdoor."

"How did Thorn convince them to build a bolt-hole?"

Marcy walked further into the room and stood by my side. Annabel joined Lucinda sitting on the edge of my bed.

"Thorn paid for the whole of the shelter to be built. I told her I wanted to help those in need. Those homeless people who had been like me. Thorn agreed, as she saw some use in having the shelter. She insisted we built in this hidden room, just in case she needed somewhere to hide. She still pays for the upkeep of the shelter, even to this day. There is a trust fund in place. But we do also get money from charities to help fund it, which is more of a smokescreen to stop people from asking how we afford it."

None of this surprised me. Thorn was always one step ahead, thinking about how she could leverage her money to good use if not now but in the future.

I looked at the food on Lucinda's lap. "Is that for me? I am starving. I think I need food to get better."

Lucinda stood up with the tray and put it on the table at the side. "The food is for you, but first you need to drink."

"Okay, but I can't see any water."

Lucinda giggled, and Annabel looked furtively away.

Marcy stepped in. "Let me explain. I think Lucinda and Annabel are a little bit too embarrassed and scared to tell you themselves. I guess you are still feeling a bit weak to work it out. Although we have cleaned out the werewolf particles from your wounds, which stopped them from healing completely, you have still lost a lot of blood. If you transform back to human before this blood is replaced, it could make you critically ill. However, Dragans have a way of healing themselves faster than normal."

"So it is as I thought. The werewolf's bite and claws have an effect on a Dragan. I noticed my wounds didn't heal."

"Yes, the bite or cut of a werewolf is a supernatural attack on your body, as such, even your own supernatural abilities cannot heal and react as it normally would. The answer is to wash the wounds out, clear away any sign of the creature that bit or cut you. You should know that it is the same if you bite or cut the werewolf when in your Dragan form. The werewolf would struggle to heal. However, your dive into the river helped clear out most of the werewolf, but it also introduced some other harmful bacteria directly into your wounds. And in the meantime, you lost a lot of blood while drifting along."

"You know I went into the river?"

"Yes, you garbled something about swimming in the river to mask your heat signature and to get away from the MI5 agents. You were also a bit wet still when rotten Tommy found you, so we put two and two together."

"So this drink that I need. Where is it?"

Marcy looked at the two girls. Lucinda smiled and curtsied. Annabel just bit her bottom lip and looked at me from the top of her eyes as she bowed her head.

"Sorry I don't understand."

"You're a Dragan. You need blood."

I hadn't seen them bring anything else down, no packets of blood for me to drink from. And from the reaction of the two girls, I was assuming they meant a more immediate solution.

"Are you suggesting what I think you are suggesting?"

"You need blood. I don't just have bottles of it lying around in my fridge. However, Annabel and Lucinda are willing to help. They believe that they owe you a favour."

I looked at the two young women again. It didn't seem right to be feeding on these two; they were too young and innocent. "Thank you very much, but I'm sure I will be okay."

Lucinda glared back at Marcy. And Annabel seemed to breathe a sigh of relief. Marcy stared at me and shook her head. "No, Jon, I'm not sure you will survive unless you drink. As soon as you turn human again, your body will go into shock. You need to get yourself back to full health before you revert back to normal. As I said, you would become critically ill otherwise."

"So I need to bite them and drink their blood. Wouldn't it hurt them?"

"A pint each from both of them will be enough to restore your health and will not do them any harm. I will be here to time and ensure their safety, but you have little other choices. Surely you have drunk the blood of humans before?"

"I have but it was in the heat of battle, not a direct sacrifice on behalf of the person. I have never done it like that before."

"What about when you and Thorn performed the Union ritual? Thorn consented."

"That was different. Thorn is a Dragan."

"Well, you best get used to it. As you know from Thorn, seducing a person or a willing subject is the easiest way of getting blood."

"Maybe, but I am just a bit uncomfortable about it," I said and looked over at the two girls offering themselves to me.

Lucinda glared again. "You think it is weird that I am willing to sacrifice my blood? To let you bite me. You think I am some silly young girl?"

I didn't answer but just gave a small smile back.

She pursed her lips together."Well, remember this, Jon. I am, in fact, older than you. Just because you now appear older and run around with vampires and werewolves doesn't mean you are more mature and get to look down on me."

I sat up straight in the bed and leaned back from her words. "Sorry. I forgot about that. You just look young. Thank you for offering to help me."

She shook her head. "No, you don't understand. I am not doing this just to help you. I want to do this, as I have a request."

"Okay. I am sure we can help. Is it money or something?"

She sighed. "No. I want you to kiss me first." I must have reacted badly. "Am I that ugly that the idea repulses you?" she said.

"No, you are a beautiful young woman. I am just surprised."

"Surprised. That I would insist on a kiss before you drank my blood. Is it not the way it is normally done?"

"This isn't a film."

"I don't care. I want a long kiss. Then you are to kiss down my neck before you bite me and drink my blood."

"Err. I am not sure. Thorn wouldn't approve."

Marcy waved her hand to push the objection away. "It's not a problem. I have cleared it with Thorn already. As you know, she often kisses her victim before she feeds on them."

"Yes, I know that. But this is someone requesting it, not someone who's been hypnotically seduced into it."

"And you think no one has ever asked for her to kiss them before she feeds on them? No one has ever been with her that knew her true nature before they started. No one ever knew how their encounter may end," Marcy said.

"I suppose so. It never occurred to me that people openly offered themselves to her."

Lucinda shook her head and grabbed my hand and squeezed it. "Jon does none of this ring a bell. None of this seems similar to you in any way?"

I tried to think back to the stories that Thorn told me. I couldn't think of anyone or any time when she said someone had willingly offered themselves to her.

"You really are that blind to the truth?" she asked.

"Okay. You're going to have to tell me. I'm obviously a little bit slow. Maybe it's because of the lack of blood."

Lucinda smiled. "You're going to kick yourself. But the similarity that I am referring to is you, Jon. How did you meet Thorn?"

It hit me. I'd been too self-absorbed to see my own reflection of desire. I had walked into that room with Thorn in the research centre, knowing full well our encounter would end up with her biting me and drinking my blood. I had wanted her to kiss me and to feed on me. Although I had been surprised when she sank in her fangs, I think I would have been more surprised if nothing had happened. Lucinda was just asking for the same deep-seated fantasy that I had. Who was I to say her desires were wrong when mine were just the same?

I squeezed her hand back and patted the other one on top of it. I smiled and let out a small laugh. "You are right. Strange how I couldn't see it myself. Maybe I thought my circumstances were different. But everything you say is true. And as such, I will give you what you want. It would be my pleasure to give you this experience."

"Thank you, Jon, but I want you to mean it when you kiss me. Not just playing a part. If I don't feel it, then no blood."

I understood her. I wanted to completely believe it when Thorn took me into her embrace, kissed me and bit me. I still liked to think she really wanted me that night. It would not be a hard thing for me to make Lucinda believe I really meant it. She was a beautiful young woman. And she and Annabel had helped us out on a few occasions.

"I will mean it, but this is a one-time thing," I said.

"I understand."

I looked past Lucinda to Annabel. "Do you have any requests?"

Annabel looked over at Marcy and then looked back at the floor again.

"Annabel does not have the same request as Lucinda. In fact, she is terrified at the thought of you biting her and drinking her blood. Her only request is you use your hypnotic powers to take away the fear and the pain. She wants to remember it, but she does not want to have nightmares about it."

I nodded my head. "Annabel, don't worry. I will do everything in my powers to make it a pleasurable experience."

Annabel looked up at me with wild eyes. "I don't want to enjoy it. I just don't want to have nightmares about it. Just keep it neutral. I have no romantic notions regarding this. I'm not like Lucinda. I don't want to enjoy it and then want it to happen again."

"Sorry, I misunderstood. I will make sure it doesn't hurt, and it will not emotionally scar you."

"That is all I ask."

"Okay. I'm glad we have that all cleared up. I think you should start with Lucinda, and then you should be able to regain enough of your powers to hypnotise Annabel. I will time the encounter for three minutes, which is about a pint of blood. I will shout stop. And then you must disengage straightaway," Marcy said.

"I understand. Let's get on with this then. How do we start?"

Lucinda stood up, unzipped her boots and kicked them off, and then pulled down her T-shirt on one side. She climbed onto the side of the bed and lay down next to me. I shuffled over to let her on, and I looked back at Marcy, who had a stopwatch. Annabel sat on the grey sofa and looked away into the opposite corner of the room.

Marcy looked from the stopwatch and back at me. "I will start the timer when you bite her."

I looked down at Lucinda, who stared back. Her eyes had gone black, pushing the blue of her iris out to the rim. Her cheeks flushed red, and she displayed a nervous smile at me. She licked her lips and brushed her hair away from her vulnerable neck.

"Are you ready?" I asked.

She nodded vigorously. "I think so. Don't rush the kiss. Take your time. I want to remember this forever."

"I'm sure I will remember this forever as well. You will be my first so to speak."

Lucinda beamed. I gently lowered my lips down and kissed her. She returned the kiss, putting her hands around my back. We kissed, with our lips searching each other's out, taking time to enjoy one another's touch. Our lips tender against each other, not the frantic kissing I encountered when with Thorn.

The act of kissing seemed to bring about a change in me, not the obvious one of excitement and desire. But my fangs tingled as if they knew what was coming. I sped up the kiss and then pulled away, sucking at her bottom lip. Her eyes shone up at me, and she leaned up and dotted one final kiss on my lips like a seal of approval.

Then I followed the rest of the instructions. I kissed her chin and worked my way down her neck, planting each kiss tenderly until I reached her glowing veins bulging on her neck. I leaned forward and planted one big kiss on the mark to let Lucinda know what was about to happen. She took a deep breath, her chest moved under me, and then she breathed out.

My fangs shot out and my eyes burnt. They both transformed ready to feed. I placed my mouth over her neck and squeezed my jaws together. My fangs sliced through her tender flesh, and she let out a little scream as they punctured into her blood vessels. Her hands gripped my shoulders. I sucked the blood in, feeling its coppery taste slide down the back of my throat.

Her body tensed up, and her heart pounded against my chest. Suddenly, images flashed in my mind of a monster eating her flesh; they were her thoughts and emotions. They had swung from a passionate embrace to monstrous devouring. I had to do something before she freaked out. I focused my thoughts on her.

'Stay calm. Everything will be okay. You can trust me. You are safe.'

With those commands, her muscles relaxed and her heart slowed down. The monstrous images faded, and I continued to suck her blood, aided by relaxing psychic messages. I held my left hand on her shoulder and right hand on her waist to hold her steady. As the blood passed into me, I could feel my strength returning.

"Stop. Three minutes is up. Stop, Jon."

It took all my willpower to break off and move my head back to look

Lucinda in the eyes. I wanted more blood; my rejuvenation had not been completed yet. I looked down at Lucinda through my Dragan's eyes, and the blood on my chin soaked into my flesh. She looked up at me; her face recoiling in horror. My body reverted. My eyes changed back to normal and fangs retracted. She smiled as she looked into my human eyes.

Marcy walked over and handed Lucinda a wad of bandages she placed on her neck. Lucinda held them down with one hand and swung off the bed. She stood up and walked over to the side and sat down on the sofa next to Annabel, who had turned around during the event and watched the whole thing.

"Thank you," I said.

"It's a pleasure. Does this now mean we are bonded? As you have drunk my blood," Lucinda asked.

I didn't know the answer. I knew Thorn and I were bonded, but that was because the vampire formula was made from her blood. I didn't know if by merely drinking another person's blood, it created a psychic bond.

"I am not sure. Thorn never told me about this. As you are my first, we will find out soon enough," I replied.

Lucinda seemed to like this answer, and she smiled back as she sunk into the sofa.

I looked over at Annabel, who looked away to Marcy.

Marcy looked over at me. "Jon, Annabel is ready for you."

This time I was going to have to make all the running. I climbed off the bed and crossed over to Annabel. She looked up as I approached, her hands clenched on her lap, her bottom lip tucked under her teeth. I knelt down in front of her and placed my hands on top of her clenched fists. "There is nothing to fear. You can trust me. You can see Lucinda is okay. Will you do me this great favour?"

She nodded back and un-bit her bottom lip, stood up with her hands in mine and looked into my eyes as we rose. I walked backwards to the bed, and she followed and then stopped. "Here will be fine. I don't want to go on the bed. Like I said, I don't have any romantic notions. This is purely transactional."

I nodded. "I understand. We can do it right here, standing up. I will give you a few seconds to prepare. If you want to pull back your clothing and move your hair out of the way."

She looked up into my eyes and nodded, then pulled her T-shirt to one side, and flicked her head back to reveal her bare neck. I could see the

The Enemies of Vengeance

jugular vein pumping away. But I needed to take my time; I didn't want to freak the poor girl out.

"That's good," I said, and I put my hands on her shoulders and stood closer to her, looking down into her eyes. "Look into my eyes. This will not hurt at all. You will feel nothing. You will feel relaxed and calm. When I bite, you will be aware of the sensation, but it will not hurt. As I drink your blood, you may feel it, but again, it will not hurt and it will not worry you at all. You will stay calm the whole time. The more the blood comes out of you, the calmer you will feel. Nod your head when you are ready for me to begin."

She took a deep breath and looked into my eyes again and nodded. Her eyes had gone as black as Lucinda's. I detected excitement. Her heart beating faster, even though her body was relaxed. I leant down to her neck and gently kissed it once, just so she knew I was in position. I then let nature take its course, and my fangs extended and eyes burnt red.

I bit down, cutting into her flesh, and the blood spurted out and shot into my mouth. I sucked the red liquid down my throat and into my body. Immediately, its power surged through me, just as it had done with Lucinda's blood.

All the time, I sent psychic messages to her to remain calm and stay relaxed. In return, I received flashes of images from her. The pictures I received back were surprising from someone who said they had no romantic inclination. The images were of our entwined naked bodies in her bed. And the more I sucked down her blood, the more excited and intense these emotions and images became.

Whereas Lucinda had said this is what she wanted, but she freaked out in the reality of me biting her. Annabel was the complete opposite. She had acted scared and worried, but once started, her genuine desires surfaced. Maybe she was afraid of how she really felt, whereas Lucinda felt like she should enjoy it.

It felt strange sensing and participating in her fantasy. I wanted to stop feeding on her, as I felt like I was actually making love to her. But I needed to feed, and I had no right to deny her some enjoyment from her sacrifice. Thorn had always said leave them something to remember you by, give them something in return for their blood.

"Stop, Jon, stop feeding on her now. Three minutes is up," Marcy said, and tapped me on the shoulder.

I stepped away, wiping my hand across my mouth, closing my eyes to let them go back to normal without Annabel seeing. I retracted my fangs and sucked down the last of the blood before opening my eyes again. Marcy had put an arm under Annabel to hold her steady and applied a bandage to her bite marks. Annabel grinned at me; her eyes sparkling and she licked her lips. "Did you enjoy that?" she asked.

"It was great. Thank you very much. I am feeling much better now," I said, as formally as possible.

She winked at me, and Marcy walked her across to the sofa to sit next to Lucinda. I received other flashes in her mind and thoughts. It was laughter inside her head. I realised she put on the show on purpose, pretending to be shy and innocent and then purposefully filling her mind full of sexy images to fluster me. I smiled over at her. "Was that really necessary?" I said.

Lucinda looked between Annabel and I. "Was what really necessary? What am I missing?" she asked.

Annabel put a hand on Lucinda's knee. "I will tell you later. Let us both get our strength back first."

Marcy pulled out two cans of cola and handed them over. "You girls are always up to no good, always winding each other up. I can't wait to hear what this one was about," Marcy said.

I shook my head and sat down on the bed. The blood had given me strength. Now I had an appetite for solid food as well, so I took the tray and started digging into the beef stew and rice.

Marcy came over and sat on the edge of the bed as I was eating. "We will wait for these girls to regain enough strength to leave. Then I will come back tonight with a phone, so you can call Thorn and make your plans."

I nodded and guessed from her comments it was still daytime, the day after the fight with Giles.

I finished my food, and the girls downed their sugary drinks. Marcy took the tray, and the girls said goodbye and waved. Annabel winked at me, and Lucinda giggled. They both went upstairs to exchange stories and experiences. Marcy went up last and closed the hatch behind her, locking me in the room.

After feeding, I needed to take a rest to fully recover before speaking with Thorn that night. I lay down with a full stomach and renewed energy, and I closed my eyes.

Chapter Nine

I had been asleep for a while when I heard the hatch click open again. My senses were still Dragan, and I sat bolt upright. Marcy came down the stairs, closed the hatch and walked over with a cordless phone in her hand. She handed it to me and passed me a piece of paper with a phone number on it.

"This is Thorn's temporary number. Call her and work out what to do next. I will sit on the sofa and wait for instructions."

She sat down on the sofa and crossed her legs. I dialled the number and looked across at Marcy as it rang.

"Hello, V, is that you?" Thorn said.

"Yes, it's me. Are you okay?"

"Of course I am okay. I'm supposed to be asking if you're okay. How you healing? Did the girls feed you?"

"Don't worry. Feeling much better, and yes, the girls were very generous and let me feed on them."

"I hope you were nice to them?"

"Of course. They are none the worse for the experience. I can't say the same for me. That story is for another time. Anyway, we need to talk about what happened, not just the attack by Giles, but my meeting with MI5."

"So it's true. You really did meet MI5. Marcy heard you ramble something about MI5, helicopters, water, stealing a car, etcetera, but we weren't sure how much of it was true and how much of it was the illness from the werewolf's bite."

"Let me tell you the truth. At Scarlett's funeral, I met Mary I used to go to college with. It turns out that Mary is an MI5 agent and was sent to college to keep an eye on me. MI5 knew the Hunters had gone rogue and had heard of the unsanctioned experiments. They were keeping an eye on me to get closer to my father. They had no idea I would be dragged into it and become a key part."

"I wouldn't believe everything they tell you. MI5 and any of those national security types are always far more involved than you realise. So what did they want?"

"They want an alliance with the Dragans to stop the Turned and the Hunters. If successful, they want a long term alliance to combat new people with powers. As a gesture of goodwill, Mary gave me a USB stick with some useful information. I'm not sure if I still have it, as it was in my coat."

"Yes, we still have it," Marcy said. "It is just drying out upstairs. I haven't looked at it."

"Did you hear that, Thorn? Marcy says we still have the USB stick. I will look at it later and find out what is on it."

"Yes, but be careful, as there may be a tracking virus on it. Make sure your computer isn't logged into the Internet or anywhere close to getting Wi-Fi. It may open up a hidden program that will connect to the Internet without you knowing and send back your location as soon as it knows."

"I will take all the necessary precautions. I will call you back once I know more."

"What did they mean by combat people with new powers?" Thorn asked.

"Mary said you might know already. The world is changing. Magic is seeping back into the world."

"Yes. I have heard things from my contacts," Thorn said.

"Like what and who?"

Marcy coughed like she was clearing her throat. "You shouldn't stay on the call for too long. It's best to keep to the matter in hand."

"Miss Jones is right, it doesn't matter right now. Enough is going on with the Turned and Hunters. These powered individuals can't help us anyway. They have gone rogue. So your fight with the werewolf, how did it go?"

"As you can probably guess from my condition, not very well. I just didn't know what to do against the werewolf. Its sheer size and rage just sent me into a panic. It wasn't like fighting you or fighting the Turned. Something about the wolf itself seemed to disturb me."

"You are just not used to it. Humans have a built-in fear of wolves. Something we Dragans do not have. When you are back with me, I will ask Max to fly over so you can spar and be more prepared for the next time you fight Giles. I'm sure Giles and the other werewolf will keep tracking you until one of you dies."

"Well, that's a very cheery thought. I will have to kill my best friend if I want to survive."

"Sorry to be the one to tell you, but this will not end well."

I knew what she said was true. Giles wanted me dead, and I couldn't avoid him forever. He wasn't interested in talking. He just wanted revenge. It reminded me of my own recent actions, being hell-bent on bloody vengeance.

"What about you, Thorn? What have you been up to? Have you found Cyrus yet?"

"We have a solid lead. We are heading there tonight. Hopefully, next time we speak, I will have some news for you. Talking of which, we must make use of the dark, and you have a USB stick to read. Call me again tomorrow night at the same time. And V, take care of yourself. Remember that I love you."

I glanced up at Marcy, turned my head to one side with the phone. "I love you too," I said quickly, hoping Marcy couldn't overhear us.

Marcy stood up. "I will get a laptop and the USB stick. Anything else you need?"

"Yeah, make sure it's a new laptop, or an old one that you don't want any more. Once I am finished looking at this USB stick, I will destroy the computer to make sure there are no viruses that could track my location."

"No worries, I can get a new one and bring it down."

Marcy disappeared up the stairs and locked the hatch. I lay back down to get some more rest. Marcy returned within the hour with a brand-new laptop computer and the USB stick. She dropped it off through the hatch and then went back to running the shelter.

I set up the computer and inserted the USB stick. I did some basic checks for viruses but found none. But if implanted by MI5, I probably wouldn't have found them. I found nothing suspicious, but the stick could be its own GPS system. Anyway, in the basement, it wouldn't get a clear signal. I opened up the files and looked at the information Mary had supplied.

There were only a few files on the USB. The first one was entitled 'Dragan locations', then a file called 'contact methods'. Finally, a file called 'first generation Turned locations'.

I clicked on Dragan locations hoping I could help locate Cyrus and confirm to Thorn and Cassius they were on the right track. The file gave the addresses of recent sightings, and it sounded like Thorn was in the right area in Rome. The file also contained the location of three other Dragans - Rip and the Twins.

Next, I opened up the contact methods, a set of instructions on how to contact Mary in MI5. I already had her phone number, but I guess that wasn't a very secure way of speaking to her. The document outlined other methods of communication, like sending files and setting up secure lines. The last file was the locations where the first generation Turned had been seen.

All the information would be extremely useful in our continued war with the Turned and Hunters. But I needed to verify it was correct, and the most obvious way was to speak to Thorn and see if she could use it to locate Cyrus. It occurred to me the information could be a trap. Sending us to places where MI5 or the Hunters could be waiting. I only had Mary's word that she was part of MI5, and I wouldn't put it past the Hunters to pretend to be somebody else.

As Thorn had worked with them before, I hope she had a way of validating the authenticity of this contact. Maybe she still had means of communication with MI5.

I had agreed to speak to Thorn again tomorrow night, so everything would have to wait until then. I didn't want to call in case she was in the middle of a stakeout. In the meantime, I got some rest.

Marcy visited later on, and I asked her to purchase another computer laptop. I intended to type the information from one computer to another. It was the most secure means of copying the data by creating a physical air gap. That way, I could ensure no viruses were copied over that could track my location or record my activities online. Marcy reappeared the next morning with the second laptop.

"Is there anything else you need?" Marcy asked.

"I lost my key to the storage locker. I need some cash and a change of clothes. Plus, I could do with changing my passport as well. It appears MI5 knows I go by the alias of Christopher Lee."

"Don't worry, I have a spare key. I will get some cash and clothes, but I can't do anything about the passport in such a short space of time. I could probably get you one in two weeks."

"The cash and clothes will be enough. I will just have to risk the passport. They know my alias and haven't been stopping me so far, so I should be safe to travel. But it will let them know where I am."

"Okay, I will be back with your stuff later. Will you be speaking with Thorn tonight?"

"Yes. We will make some plans. Hopefully, I will leave tomorrow morning."

"And how are you feeling?"

"The blood has worked its trick and restored all my strength before I transformed back to human."

"You're human again?"

"Yes, it must've happened while I was asleep. But it has left me with its usual after-effects. I can feel the extra strength and sharpening of my senses."

"I will return tonight after you have spoken to Thorn. Then I can help you prepare to leave."

"Thank you. Will Annabel and Lucinda be coming to say goodbye?"

Marcy shook her head. "I think they should stay away from you for a while. They obviously enjoyed that brief encounter far too much. I wouldn't want them getting any ideas. Anyway, I must get back to the shelter. See you later," Marcy said, and walked back up the stairs, through the hatch and locked it.

I opened up the other computer and sat it next to me on the bed. Then I started typing across all the information. I knew it would take me a few hours to get the most relevant parts. I would still take the USB stick and the computer with me, just in case I had missed something vital, but I would keep them off the net.

I hammered away on the keyboard for the rest of the day until it was time to call Thorn again.

"Hi, V, feeling better?"

"Yes, thank you, I've also changed back to human again. But the injection has done its trick, as I feel stronger and sharper than before. I'm steadily moving onwards to becoming a full Dragan."

"Good. I was worried about the damage you had received, as it may have slowed the process down."

"Did you find Cyrus?"

"No, however, I believe we were in the right place, as I detected an old scent."

"Well, the file I got from MI5 gives the location of Cyrus. His most recent sighting was in Trastevere, a neighbourhood in Rome. Does that help?"

"Yes, it helps. The place is only a few miles away from here. He must have visited here hence why I can detect the scent of a Dragan. I will go there tomorrow night and see if we can find him. What else was on the file?"

"The location of the Dragans, the location of first-generation Turned and contact methods to speak to MI5."

"Does it say the names of the Dragans?"

"Yes, Rip and the Twins."

"Rip. That is excellent. If you can find him, it would help all of us. As for the Twins, you need to steer clear of them until we are ready."

"How does finding Rip help us?"

"Rip is an excellent fighter. He was the captain of my Royal guard. If anyone can teach you how to fight a werewolf, it would be him. However, he may take some convincing. He has been hiding from me for some years."

"Hiding from you? Why?"

"Rip was in charge of the Royal guard. So it was his responsibility to protect my family and me. He still feels guilty about them breaking in and killing my husband and child. He's been running ever since, too ashamed to face me and probably too fearful that I may take some revenge upon him. However, I think you can convince him otherwise. He would be curious upon detecting you, and that should be enough for you to speak to him. He would run a mile if he sensed me."

"I will look for him. What about the Twins and what about this information? Can we be sure it is from MI5?"

"The Twins are extremely dangerous. But they were in a relationship with Cyrus, and if we get Cyrus onside, he can bring them in. Whatever you do, leave the Twins alone. Steer clear of them on all accounts. Those girls need careful handling. Even I would not tackle them alone. We will do it as a team. As for validating this information, I still have an old contact in MI5 I can speak to. Let's check out if this information is correct, and I will also speak to my contact in the meantime."

"I will head off for Rip in the morning. And I will call you again tomorrow night."

"I will speak to you then. By the way, did you sort out Marcy's gang problem?"

"I haven't heard of any issues, but I will have another word with her before I leave."

"I will make a few calls. They are supposed to know that the shelter is off-limits. It appears they have short memories of what will happen to them."

We said our goodbyes, and I decided to get a full night's sleep to adjust my body clock to daytime living. Tomorrow I would have a long trip to the South of France to find Rip. All I had to do was evade the Hunters and

Turned looking for me, and Giles and Norris trying to kill me. Once there, and if I could find him, I hoped to convince Rip to train me, as I couldn't survive another encounter with a werewolf.

Chapter Ten

I woke up that morning, ready to start a new journey. I showered and put on jeans and laced up a pair of sturdy hiking boots. I pulled on a red t-shirt and a black leather jacket, in which I stuffed my passport into the inside pocket, next to the case for my needles. In the other pocket, I had a new phone. My wallet stuffed with cash in euros and sterling went into my jeans.

I stuffed the remaining new clothes into my rucksack, along with the laptop and USB stick. I walked up the steps to the hatch and tapped against it.

It unlocked and hinged backwards, and I climbed through into Marcy's office, underneath her desk. Soon as I was through, she pushed the hatch down and covered it over with a rug. I had sat in the office only a week ago with no knowledge of the underground sanctuary. I couldn't tell from the office there was an access point. It was the perfect hiding place.

Marcy unlocked the office door. We walked into the corridor, through the busy kitchen with a couple of people stirring a big pot and cutting bread, and then into the main dining area.

Tommy sat in the dining area with his friends and smiled as I entered. I walked straight over to him and held out my hand. He stood up and shook it, and I placed my other hand on top, vigorously shaking it up and down, and then patted him on the shoulder. "Thank you, Tommy. You are an absolute lifesaver. I owe you my life."

Tommy smiled at me. "It's no worry, governor. Just glad I could help. I am only called rotten Tommy because of me teeth."

His friends laughed and insisted on shaking my hand as well, even though I'm sure most of them didn't know what we were talking about. They just wanted to be in Tommy's circle of friends. I turned back to say goodbye to Marcy when a group of four men walked in. A man in a blue puffer jacket and short-cropped hair and flanked by three big men. The man shouted at Marcy. "Where is she?"

I glanced over at Marcy. She let out a small burst of laughter and stepped towards the gang leader; the man wearing the puffer jacket. "You really do pick your moments. She isn't here. But I have someone that will talk to you."

"So bold this time. I thought you didn't like violence," the gang leader said. Behind him, the three other men all flexed their fists and glared around at everyone. One of them was just a massive bulk of fat, but his sheer size was menacing. The other two were muscular and had fresh stitches and bruises on their faces.

Marcy wagged her finger at him. "It's a bit late. We both know you're here to cause trouble if Mary-Anne is here or not. So let's not mess around."

I decided not to bother with smart words or veiled threats. It was clear this was the gang Thorn and Marcy had told me about. They came to hurt people, and it was my job to stop them. I could repay my debt to the people of the shelter. I couldn't be more pleased. A perfect chance to release my pent up anger from my defeat.

I dropped my bag on the floor and walked straight over. The guards stared at me, waiting for some words of warning, but I had none. I slammed a fist into his face, jolting his head backwards. I then skipped into a front kick, lifting him off his feet and into the other two guards.

He crashed to the floor, and the other two stumbled back into the tables and chairs, skidding them backwards and forcing the homeless guests to dive out of the way.

A guard grabbed a chair and threw it. I swiped it out of the way and stomped towards him. He whipped out a knife and sliced the air. I stepped inside the slash and cracked my head into his nose. He dropped to the floor, and the knife slipped out of his hand. An arm wrapped around my throat and swung me around. The gang leader pulled out a gun and aimed it at me. "Keep him still."

I stamped onto my attacker's toes and he released his grip. I ducked down and flipped him onto my shoulder and then threw him into the gang leader. The gun fired into the guard and blood splattered across the floor. I followed up, jumping over his crashing body, performing a flying punch into the face of the gang boss.

He sailed off his feet and smashed into the wall, leaving a blood trail as he slumped into a broken heap. I picked up the gun and stuffed it into the back of my jeans. The residents of the shelter had backed away to the edges of the room. Tommy started clapping and the rest joined in. I smiled and took a bow.

I crouched down in front of the fallen gang boss and put my fingers against his neck. He was still alive, not that I cared. I had adopted Thorn's moral code.

I stood up and looked back at Marcy. "They'll all live. Unless you say otherwise."

"You best be on your way. Don't delay. I will need to call an ambulance again. It will be the second time they've been called here to attend to this gang."

"Hopefully it will be the last. I hope they have learnt their lesson this time," I said, and slung my bag onto my shoulder, waved goodbye and walked out of the shelter to the applause of the residents. I grinned as I walked away. It was nice to be appreciated and payback my debt. Thorn was right, nothing like smashing apart low-level thugs to cheer you up.

At the tube station, I caught a train across to St Pancras International station. I walked up from the tube, out onto the station's main concourse and stood in front of the bank of arrivals and departure boards to find my train. I boarded the euro-tunnel train, which went straight to Paris. The customs official came around, and my passport of Christopher Lee still worked, despite MI5 knowing it. I guessed Mary wasn't blocking my travel, although she would know I was leaving England.

At the Paris Gare du Nord train station, I changed trains to take the last leg of my journey, which would arrive in Bordeaux, the nearest stop to where Rip had been sighted. I spent most of the trip reading through the files Mary had given me, checking the descriptions and locations of Rip and Cyrus.

The train darted through stations, over rivers and roads as it threaded through the French countryside. I glanced up as we sped past green fields, which became browner the further south we went.

Travelling into the last station before Bordeaux, police cars raced along the side of us, the blue lights flashing and the sirens screaming. I thought nothing of it until I saw they had pulled into the train station.

The train pulled in, but the doors didn't unlock. Something wasn't right. I collected my bag from the overhead rack and packed away my phone and tablet. I put on my leather jacket and walked down the aisle to the doors.

The other passengers looked out the windows and asked each other what was happening. A few of them started filming on their phones. The people at the doors pushed on the door buttons, but they remained locked. A man slid the window down and shouted over to the guard, who walked away, pretending he couldn't hear.

In the end, an announcement came on over the train loudspeakers that there was an engineering issue. But about twenty Gendarme, French police, rushed into the station. They were dressed in dark navy jackets, trousers, and black boots and carried pistols on their hips and cuffs at their side. Behind them, two normally dressed men walked in last.

I wondered what was going on. Maybe a terrorist attack or they were hunting a criminal. One of the plainclothes policemen was over six foot and had shaven light brown hair and the other was shorter but stockier with curly brown hair.

The taller man turnaround, but I already knew it was Giles. I had become too relaxed. With only one station left, I thought I was already home and dry. I didn't think they could reach me in France. The police talked to Giles and Norris, who handed them some leaflets with a face on them, my face. They were showing them to people on the platform. And then they headed to the doors, waiting for them to open.

They penned me in. Sooner or later, they would identify me. I fished a baseball cap out of my rucksack and pulled it down over my head and then put on a pair of sunglasses as well. I had to make a run for it.

From inside the train, I glanced around the platform and then through the opposite windows to the other platform across the train tracks. The way ahead was swarming with police, and Giles and Norris were scanning the crowds. I had to find another way. I stood near the train door and hung back a little, so the police would talk to a couple of people first. The doors clunked to unlock and a police officer at every exit stepped inside and started showing my face to the passengers.

I waited until our policeman was showing my picture, and I tried to skirt around the side of him. He noted my reluctance to stop and placed his hand out in front of me. "Excuse me, sir. Could you take off your sunglasses and hat, and then look at this photograph," the policeman said in French.

My French wasn't great, but I didn't need a full translation to know what he wanted. Outside the door was a couple of policemen talking but not really paying attention. My time had run out. I grabbed the policeman's hand, twisted it round to lock his arm into a hold, and then slammed him into the side of the train. I spun around and leapt out the train door, leading with a kick. My foot smacked into the back of the policeman and catapulted him into his colleague. They tangled together and thumped to the floor.

I sprinted down the platform with the startled policemen scrambling back to their feet and chasing. The other police officers on the platform turned and pursued, as well as Giles and Norris. A policeman on the platform bent down to rugby tackle. I ran at them and swerved, forcing them to check their tackle. Another policeman ran in at the side, and I planted my palm on his face, which tipped him away. The third went for their gun. I whipped off my baseball hat and flicked it. The cap spun around with the peak hitting their eyes. Their hands reached up to protect, and I swiped the gun from their holster as I ran past.

I sprinted the train's full length until I had a clear view of the platform across the tracks. In the other direction, a train hurtled down the tracks. It was a freight train, and I guessed it wouldn't be stopping. I leapt off the platform onto the railway and sprinted across the two tracks as the train approached. I jumped up onto the opposite platform as the freight train whizzed by. The gush of wind propelled me forward, and the driver blasted his horn.

A small group of waiting passengers dispersed as I leapt onto the platform. Some ran out of the station into a small adjoining car park, and others took cover behind benches and pillars. A woman held up her phone to film, her hands trembling and eyes wide to take it all in. I had jumped six foot from the train tracks to the platform in a single leap. An impossible feat for any human. Luckily, I was still wearing my sunglasses. Thorn would be upset if she saw the video.

The police could not follow as the freight train blocked their way, nor could they make the impossible leap onto the platform. I didn't have much time before the train was gone or they found another way round to the other platform. An adjoining bridge went over the top of the rail track and down, but that would take a few minutes to run up, over and down again. I had enough time to make an escape.

I ran for the exit, hurdled the barriers and into the train station car park. At the exit, a young man was pulling on his helmet, having already started the engine on his scrambler motorbike. I shoved him over and jumped on the bike. I flicked up the stand, slapped it into first and sped away onto the main road.

I didn't know where I was going, but that didn't matter. I had to get as far a way as quickly as possible. It wouldn't be long before the police cars found a road to crossover, or they contacted someone on the other side of the train tracks. Eventually, they would catch up. The police could put in roadblocks or send in a helicopter. I was a stranger on a stolen bike and it wouldn't be long before they cornered me.

The Enemies of Vengeance

I rode out of the main town and away from the CCTV cameras that would ensure I could never be anonymous. I burnt through the town roads, looking for any sign that would say I was heading towards less congested areas. If I carried on a straight line for long enough, I figured it would lead me out of the town.

The buildings density on either side of the road diminished, and soon brown sunburnt fields took their place. I got a couple of miles out and ditch the bike behind a hedge and under a tree, covering it over with loose branches. I ran across the fields and into a forest area as the police sirens wailed in the background. They were getting closer.

I was right to have ditched the bike, as I would have been entrapped on the roads. They would assume I was somewhere ahead of them still. It would be a long time before they realised I'd gone in another direction. And they may never find the bike that I had hidden.

I sprinted across a sun-baked field into the cover of the trees until I was in a dense enough wooded area that even a helicopter couldn't spot me.

I picked my way through the woods, checking behind and overhead for any sight of the chasing police. The day grew late and the light dimmed as the sunset cut through the trees. I wouldn't make it to my destination before nightfall. I didn't want to break cover either. Nor did I want to blunder around in the dark too much, even with my enhanced eyesight. If I made it through the night, I hoped they would call off the search.

I wasn't sure where I was, or in which direction I should be heading. I fetched out food from my bag to re-fuel and collect my thoughts. After I had eaten, I gathered some branches and built a basic den against a tree trunk. Using my rucksack as a pillow, I lay settled down for the night under my wooden roof.

In the morning, I would try to find another road. I had to work out my bearings and head in the right direction. My phone had GPS and could provide an exact location. But I was reluctant to use my mobile just in case it had been hacked, and then it would lead the police, or Giles and Norris, or MI5, directly to me.

The trees overhead blocked out even the faint light of the moon and stars. The wood descended into pitch black, and the wildlife roamed around. Through the dark, I saw shapes giving me a wide steer. I picked up the scent of the animals and heard the padding of paws through the undergrowth. I could feel their hunger turn to fear when they sensed me. At least none of them would bother me in my sleep.

I put on as many layers of clothes as possible and zipped my coat up tight. I wrapped my arms around myself and tried to sleep. It took a couple of hours to get used to the sounds and smells of the local wildlife. Although they left me alone, their presence would snap me awake each time. I finally fell into a light sleep late into the night. But the cold seeped through the ground into my bones, preventing me from going into a deeper sleep. I curled into a ball and tried to block out the pain. I dare not light a fire in case it gave away my location.

As soon as the sun rose, I packed my gear and set off. I wanted to get moving and get my blood pumping to warm up. In the early morning, I could cover a lot of ground without being spotted. I walked out of the woods into a field to get the morning sunlight on my face. From the rising Sun, I worked out which direction I needed to head in. The village I was going to, Malrevers, was to the east. At the next village, I could work out my location and ask for directions.

I must have been deep into the countryside, as it took a couple of hours before I stumbled across the next road. A single track road with a few passing places for vehicles to get by one another. Eventually, the road led into a village. I went into the local shop and bought myself a packet of cold meat and a loaf of bread and then sat on a bench in the town square, munching on some thrown together sandwiches. I also bought a local map and worked out that I was only a few hours' walk away from Malrevers.

I decided to rest up for a while before making the last walk. I would try to hitchhike the last part to get there quickly. In the village, there were no wanted posters for me, so I assumed it wasn't a national manhunt.

I wandered out of the village, heading south. I walked along the main road for half an hour before sticking out my thumb. I hadn't seen that many cars, and it was another twenty minutes before the fifth car pulled into the side of the road.

I ran to the car and leaned down by the window. The driver, a ginger-haired man with glasses, buzzed the passenger window down. "Where are you going to?" The man asked me in French.

"Malrevers, please, if you are heading that way," I replied in my best French.

"Ah, you are English." The man replied to me in English with a heavy French accent.

"Yes."

"Jump in, my friend. I am driving straight through to the village on the other side. I can drop you off on the way."

I opened the passenger door, jumped in, put my rucksack on my lap and shut the door. "Thank you very much."

The man signalled and pulled back onto the road.

"I lived in England for 20 years. I am married to an English woman. Last year I convinced her to move to France. But my job is still in England, Reading. So I work there during the week and come back every other weekend. It will only be for a few more years until I retire."

I wasn't sure what to say. The man seemed to want to talk. "So she's enjoying France?"

"Yes, I think she's enjoying it. My kids love it. And you, what are you doing in France?"

"I've come to find my long lost uncle. My father recently died, and he left some items of sentimental value to his brother. We don't know his exact address or have any other contact details. We just know the village he lives in. I have to find him and reunite the family," I said, having already prepared my story in case anyone asked.

"Good luck to you. Malrevers is not a very big place. I'm sure someone will be able to help you."

We carried on in silence for a while, and then the man talked about everything under the sun. He started off on the state of the economy in Europe, and then onto bitcoins, and then politics in America, and the state of education in the UK. He seemed happy to talk and I let him ramble on. I gave an occasional agreement and nods to keep the conversation going and keep my driver happy. I didn't feel I could tell him to shut up, and it was good to be in the company of another human being after my long night of isolation in the wild. I guess he hadn't spoken to anyone for a while on his drive to the south of France. However, the topics he discussed I had no idea about. I had lived in a bubble of ignorance for the last couple of years, and the events of the world seemed to have passed me by.

After about half an hour, we drove into the village of Malrevers where the man pulled over to the side of the road.

"Here you go. Best of luck with your hunt for your uncle. Remember what I said, it's too late for bitcoins now, the stock market is shortening the odds, and the bubble will burst."

"Thank you for the lift and for the advice. I will look into the other crypto-currencies instead," I said and shut the car door and glanced around the village. The man waved, smiled and pulled back onto the road and drove out of the village.

I stood next to a white stone water feature at the edge of a small town square. White stone buildings formed the edges of the square, with a church at the far end with a bell tower and clock facing into the square. A row of benches on a grey brick pathway cut through the middle of the square. On either side of the benches were a few parked dusty cars.

The largest building in the square had double wooden doors with a hotel sign above. The hotel went up three stories with stained brown window frames and half-height rusty metal barriers at each window.

I should have arrived last night, and I had booked in for two nights. I would see if they would still allow me to stop, and I would promise to pay my previous night's fee.

I walked across the square with the little boules area on the side next to the church. There were two men outside tossing the silver balls towards the Jack. They both looked at me and exchanged quick words. I guessed it was in French slang, as I couldn't understand it.

I pulled open the wooden doors into a bar area and the customers turned around at my entrance, holding glasses of red wine and lager. I weaved through them seated at tables in the centre of the room, surrounded by high-backed wooden benches set against white-washed walls.

A blond-haired man with a ponytail stood behind the bar counter, which had beer taps on the top. Behind him, glass shelves with bottles of spirits and a big wine rack half full. The man glanced up as the door shut and stared at me as I crossed the floor.

"Can I help you?" he asked.

"I have a room booked. It was from last night in the name of Mr Christopher Lee," I replied.

"Ah, yes. You did not come last night. You didn't think to call us and tell us you would not be arriving."

"I am sorry. Unforeseen circumstances meant I could not use my phone. But I will pay for last night and tonight immediately."

"You are English?"

"Is my accent that bad? Yes, I am English."

The barman raised his eyebrows and nodded at me. "Okay, I will give you the bill now, and once your payment has gone through, you can have the key to your room. What brings you to our little French village anyway?"

"Looking for my long lost uncle. My father died and my uncle is due some inheritance. I am also due some inheritance, but I need to find my uncle as part of the conditions."

The barman looked intrigued. "And what is the name of your uncle? Maybe I know him and I could help."

"His name is Raymond. But we believe he is using a false name, Rip, as he doesn't want to be found. But I could give you a description." The barman nodded in agreement and I continued. "My uncle is about 6 foot tall and has blue eyes. He has a scar above his left eye. His hair is dark brown. And the last time we saw him, he had it shaven. But it could be any length now. He is quite a muscular man and is very strong. He is a bit of a night owl. Probably you would only see him in the evenings, maybe coming into this bar. People would describe him as a loner."

The barman rubbed his chin and glanced around the bar. "It could describe a few people I know. How do I know you are telling the truth? How do I know you aren't the police or something else?"

"I suppose you don't." I opened my wallet and took out a hundred euros. "But maybe this would make things easier."

"Young man, if money were my main concern, I would not be living in the back of beyond. I'm here for peace and quiet. And I don't want anyone disturbing my way of life, whether it is for legal or illegal reasons. People fitting your description come here for a drink, so if you are inclined to find them, come in here tonight for a drink and talk to the locals and you shall probably find your man. But I don't want to get mixed up in anything that could cause me harm."

"I understand. If I just pay my bill then, I will go to my room, shower and change, then come back for some food and drink and see who arrives tonight. Thank you for letting me know."

I went to put the money back in my wallet, but the barman placed his hand over it. "Thank you, I shall consider that a tip for your stay."

The barman went to the till and grabbed a key. He then flipped open the screen of a laptop and typed in some details. The printer burst into life and churned out a piece of paper. He passed over the invoice for the two night's room rental. I counted out the cash and handed it over, and he gave me the key.

"Go through the door on the side and up two flights of stairs. Your room is number six and overlooks the market square. Enjoy your stay," he said and went back to playing on his phone.

I went through the door and up to my room. The room had a dark oak bed pushed up against white flowery wallpaper. The windows had white Venetian shutters closed across them. Through the back of the room was a small shower area with a sink and toilet.

After my night sleeping rough, I wanted to clean up, so I locked the door, dumped my bag, stripped off, and showered. I still had a few hours before the evening and potential suspects to view. I decided to get a couple of hours of sleep, as I may be up into the small hours of the night.

I slept solidly for a couple of hours, and I was glad I had remembered to set my alarm to wake up. I went down into the hotel bar to see most of the same people still drinking. I ordered a glass of lager and some food, and took a seat in the corner with a stool and a small round table where I had a clear view of everyone entering.

To my side was a high backed bench with a group of two men on either side of the rectangular table. They chatted away and gave me suspicious glances. The rest of the main bar had a few round tables and stools. At the edges of the bar were bigger tables with proper chairs where a few people were tucking into meals.

As the evening approached, a few people left. I guessed they were going home for dinner. There was a small lull in the number of customers, but some of the same people returned and new customers joined in as the light darkened through the windows. I assumed they came in after work for a drink.

The barman seemed to know everyone and chatted to them as he poured drinks. Most of the new customers glanced over at me. I guessed it was unusual to have visitors at the hotel. Some of them spoke to the barman about me, and the barman just said I was looking for a long lost uncle. They eyed me with suspicion and then went to sit with their friends.

I allowed my senses to open up, to glimpse their thoughts and feelings, hoping to find something out of the ordinary, something that would give one of them away as a Dragan. They would also detect something strange about me if they were a Dragan. I hoped their reaction to me would be enough to reveal their true identity.

Many men came in by themselves. Most of them found people to speak to, and they talked over a glass of wine or lager. The hotel was the only drinking spot in the small village. And as the barman had said, the type of person I described would come in there for a drink, as there was nowhere else to go.

Every person who came in looked over and asked the other customers about me. He replayed the story over again, but I could tell most of them didn't believe it. A few of them believed I was up to no good, hunting someone down. I sensed their distrust, and I felt as lonely in the crowded bar as I had sleeping rough in the woods the night before.

About 10 o'clock at night, a man walked in that fitted the rough description. He was 6 foot tall, looked muscular and wore a tie-dyed t-shirt, surfer shorts and sandals. He had long brown hair hanging down in front of his face that he kept brushing back with his hands. I noticed his hair and stubbly beard had flecks of grey in it. He looked like an old hippy that hadn't grown up.

But most importantly, he had the scar above his left eye as described in the MI5 notes. I thought it unusual that a Dragan would have a scar. Surely, with their powers, they would heal completely. Something I would have to ask him about.

I focused my senses on the man to see if I could psychically pick up anything or speak to him. But the man followed the same pattern as everyone else that had come into the bar. He'd gone to the counter and ordered a bottle of red wine and a glass. He exchanged a few words with the barman, who nodded over towards me. The man looked at me for a moment and then turned back to the barman and shrugged. He took his bottle and glass over to another table where two men were already sitting. He exchanged words with them and poured himself a glass of wine and each clinked their glasses together.

I sipped my drink and scanned the bar but kept coming back to the man who matched the description. But I sensed nothing from him. I took a more direct approach and psychically sent him a message. *'Thorn says hello. Everything is forgiven.'*

He did not flinch away from his conversation or even look at me for a second. *'My name is V. It stands for vengeance. I am a friend. I come here in peace.'* I said psychically, but the man did not break stride in his conversation about the recent French presidential elections.

I sniffed at the air to see if I could detect any difference in his smell. But with the overcrowded bar and the smell of alcohol wafting around, I couldn't identify anything unusual.

I went to the bar and ordered another glass of beer, which allowed me to stand a bit closer to my suspect. I focused my mind on him again to see if I could catch glimpses of his thoughts. But his brain was fully engaged in his conversation with the two other men. There was no hint of anything unusual in his thought patterns. He wasn't reacting to the obvious presence of another Dragan in the room. Even if I was only seventy percent Dragan, I was sure another Dragan or Turned or Werewolf or anything supernatural would cause a reaction.

My last option was to talk to him directly. I considered that this may have been a trap in the first place. Something set up by MI5 to lure me to this place alone. I decided to wait and see if this was merely a coincidence or another man may enter with the same description.

I kept drinking my lager and looking at my phone. I kept trying to engage the man, but he did not respond to any of my attempts. The night grew late and he was one of the last few customers in the bar. He finished his second bottle of wine, said goodbye to the barman and then staggered through the tables and chairs. I followed him out into the open air. Without the noise and confusion of the other people, I could focus on him and trigger a reaction.

I followed him out into the cooling night air and down the street. Once outside, the man stopped and lit up a cigarette. He looked up at the sky and blew out a long cloud of smoke and then stumbled on. I focused my senses on him.

His movements were erratic and impaired, and so were his thoughts. They were a random mess and blur after his couple of bottles of red wine. This didn't seem like a man who could be a Dragan. Alcohol couldn't affect a Dragan, as their superior healing would burn off the alcohol instantly. He did not seem like a man who was a captain of the Royal Guard, the best warrior of the Dragans.

The man stumbled into an alley where he undid his shorts, peed against the wall and sucked on his cigarette. I gave up. He clearly wasn't Rip. I turned around and went back to the hotel.

I looked up at the stars as I walked and considered what I would do next. A force smacked into my back and sent me sprawling onto the flagstone floor. I spun around to face up. A dark figure flew up into the air and landed with his knees on my chest. His hand shoved my head down, and his snarling fangs shot into view. His red eyes pierced down and hot alcoholic breath streamed over me.

"Who the hell are you?" The man with the scar shouted.

"I'm V, and I guess you are Rip. Thorn says hello."

Chapter Eleven

"Thorn," he screamed, and pulled his hands back, unleashed his claws and swiped down.

I bucked my body upwards and sent him sprawling. I flipped onto my feet and took a few steps back. "Please listen to me for a moment. Thorn wishes to give you a message. If you aren't interested, I will leave immediately." I held out my hand and whipped out my mobile phone.

The man was back on his feet, claws and fangs out, and his eyes blood red. His face contorted to a sickening grey, and his hair spiked on end as the muscles tensed. He marched forwards, fury burning in his eyes. I pressed play on the video clip and pointed it at him.

I had watched the video clip, and I hoped it would have the desired effect. There was no way I could stop this Dragan if he wished to kill me.

The video played of Thorn stood in front of a plain concrete wall. She wore jeans and a white vest top, and her tousled black hair hung down onto her shoulders. "Hi Rip, long time no see. Please listen to what I have to say before you run away or kill the messenger. And I would prefer it if you didn't kill the messenger as I am in a Union with him."

She smiled at the camera and then continued. "I know a lot has happened between us, and I know you feel bad about what happened to my family. It was hundreds of years ago now. I haven't seen you since that night, but I know you've been running from me ever since. And maybe, in the beginning, I wanted revenge on you. I am not going to deny it. You are too smart. But we need to put our differences aside and bring all the Dragans back together. The curse of the Turned has spiralled out of control. They have formed an alliance with the Hunters. We need to put right what we did wrong. And that means burying the hatchet and forgetting all the old feuds. And to prove to you, I mean it, there is someone here I want to introduce you to."

The camera moved around to reveal a man standing beside Thorn. He had blond hair swept back with a parting down the middle. He was about 6 foot 2, had icy blue eyes and chiselled features. With his sharp features came an elegant but obviously muscular body showing through his tight black T-shirt and jeans. The man smiled at the camera and then at Thorn. "Hi Rip, just in case you have forgotten who I am or forgotten what I look like. I'm Cyrus. If Thorn can forgive me and discuss an alliance between us, then you should have no problem."

Rip's features reverted to normal, his fangs and claws retracted. His eyes cleared to normal as he wore an expression of surprise. The camera moved back to Thorn again. "The person with the message is called V. And I know you can tell there's something different about him. I will let V tell you his story. But I am hoping you will train him and then accompany him to meet up with us. I think you will find his story fascinating and hopefully, it will be enough for you to trust me again, as I will trust you. We all hope to see you soon."

The video then stopped, and the screen froze on the image of Thorn standing next to Cyrus.

The man just pointed at the phone. "How could she? That man is evil. If it weren't for him, we wouldn't have the Turned or had the civil the war. We wouldn't have lost our kingdom and been scattered to the four corners of the Earth."

I put the phone back into my pocket and stared at the man, waiting for a response. He put his head in his hands and shook it around, scratching at his hair. He looked up at me again and shook his head. Then spun around and walked off.

"Hello, excuse me. What is your response?" I shouted after him.

He waved behind his head. "I need more drink, so I am going home. If you want to know more, then you can follow."

I ran after him, caught up and walked by his side. He stopped and offered me a cigarette. "No, thank you," I replied.

"Take one. It can't do you any harm. I don't know what you are, but I'm guessing a cigarette will not damage you. And I hate to smoke and drink alone. So, if you want to talk to me, then you must keep me company."

He shook the cigarette packet at me, and I took one out. I put it to my mouth, and he pulled out a lighter and lit the end. I had never smoked before, so I was unsure of what to do. I breathed in, pulling in the smoke and then started coughing. He chuckled to himself and then lit his own cigarette and carried on walking.

We walked out of the town and down a country lane with dark fields to either side. We jumped over a wooden fence and walked across a field to a small cottage with a garage next to it and a gravel pathway leading onto the road. He opened the cottage door and flicked on the lights.

We entered through the back door into a rustic kitchen and the smell of stale cigarettes and red wine. I walked onto the terracotta tiled floor and stood next to a big wooden table with red wine glass marks. On the centre of the table was a big ashtray with a mountain of ash and stubs of cigarettes.

Rip swiped a bottle of red wine from a collection on the wooden kitchen worktop. He opened the cupboards above and pulled out two wine glasses. Cigarette packs were piled on the shelf next to it.

He poured out the red wine, pulled back a chair and offered me a seat opposite him. I sat down and continued to puff on the cigarette. He had guessed I wasn't entirely human but not entirely Dragan either, by the fact he said the cigarette would not harm me. I knew every puff of the cigarette smoke was damaging my lungs, but I also knew my enhanced Dragan powers were healing my body.

Rip raised a glass of red wine, and I picked up mine and we tapped them together.

"So, you have a story to tell me. I have a bottle of red wine here, so make sure you have finished it by the time we get to the end. And if I find it interesting, we open another bottle and I will tell you my story."

"I am not used to drinking. I'm not sure I can handle all this and smoking."

"Well, you better get used to it, as it will be an important part of your training. Anyway, I suspect you can handle your drink. You have abilities. These abilities should make you Dragan, but I smell far too much human on you and sense too much human emotion. So we start off with you explaining to me who you are and what you are?"

"You're right. I'm about seventy percent Dragan and thirty percent Human. And one day I hope to be one hundred percent Dragan. But I guess your question is how that could be even possible. I best start at the very beginning. One day I was leaving school to find my best friend at the school gates," I said.

I then told him everything. I told him the story of Giles' kidnapping by the local gang, his mum trying to rescue him and accidentally paralysing one of the O'Keefe gang. I told him that I found out that the kidnapping was meant for me to encourage my dad to leave Leeds and move to London. This twist in fate had extra meaning, as without the accident and the subsequent bullying of Giles, he would have never been recruited by the Hunters and turned into a werewolf.

My story carried on with my move to London and how I ended up meeting Thorn in the research centre. I explained my transformation through the vampire formula, Thorn's escape and our life on the run. I told him the full story of Vegas and the road trip, my meeting with Cassius and learning that we weren't vampires. And then onto my fleeing of Thorn and my return to England.

He listened intently to the entire story, his ears pricking up as I mentioned names and places he had heard of, like Cassius and Cyrus. I told him of my capture by the Hunters and torture at their hands, and the rescue by Thorn, Max and Cassius, and my transformation into the Dragon form during the warehouse battle. This particular point sparked his interest, and he spluttered on his red wine, but he signalled me to carry on.

I brought him right up to speed with my Union to Thorn, my return to England again to encounter Giles as a werewolf. All of which led me to meet Mary again, discovering she was actually an MI5 agent, which was how I tracked him down to France.

He downed his last gulp of red wine, which meant we had finished the bottle. I wasn't feeling as drunk as I expected after drinking half a bottle of red wine. Rip looked drunker than I did, which I couldn't understand. He grabbed another bottle, opened it and poured us another glass each.

"That is an amazing journey. You have great potential. To turn into the Dragon form is a feat that few have managed. Thorn knew I would be interested in training such a person. It has been such a long time since I could instruct anyone. Studying martial arts and training others was my great passion. It has been so long since anyone wanted to listen to me. It's been so long since I was willing to train anyone. Teaching humans isn't the same."

"But will you train me? Will you teach me how to fight a werewolf?"

"It doesn't look like I have anything better to do. And if this means I can win back the favour of Thorn and return to the company of Dragans, then I will take the risk. I cannot live another seven hundred years hiding from everybody."

I grinned, slugged back more of my red wine and topped up my glass. "So, when does the first lesson begin?"

Rip grinned and blew out a puff of smoke, sank down his red wine, and slipped off the chair and landed on the floor. He lay on the floor, laughing his head off, holding his red wine high in the air. "I have not spilt a drop. How about that for agility and speed?" He laughed more and hauled himself back up.

After finishing the rest of the glass, he grabbed another bottle of wine.

He pulled out the cork, poured himself a drink and sat back down. He stubbed out his bent cigarette into the ashtray and lit another one. "Drink up, boy. Drink up."

I stared at him in utter disbelief. Surely this was not the man who would train me to beat werewolves, the man who was supposedly unrivalled in the Dragan martial arts. I took another drink and then slammed the glass on the table.

"What is wrong with you? How can you be so drunk? I'm only seventy percent Dragan, and my body is healing and burning the alcohol off. But you are utterly wasted."

He smiled and took another drag of his cigarette. He winked at me and sipped back more red wine. "This is your first lesson. You're right, how can I possibly be drunk? Am I pretending?"

I opened up my senses to hear his thoughts and feel his emotions. But I only got swirling random thoughts. I had sensed the thoughts of drunken people before, and his were exactly the same. "No, you are definitely drunk."

"And how, possibly, could I be drunk?" He slurred at me.

"I have no idea. It shouldn't be possible. Thorn could only get drunk if she took the alcohol in somebody else's blood. And even then, it would not last long due to her fast metabolism. Maybe you are damaged in some way."

"Did I seem damaged when I attacked you earlier on? Were my movements that of a drunk man?"

"No, you were fast and strong. The moments before, when I was following, you were as drunk as you are now."

"So how am I getting drunk, and how was I able to sober up so quickly?"

"I am unsure."

"Let me ask you another question. Where does a Dragan's power come from?"

I sipped my wine and mulled over the question. "From the fact that the vampire formula has changed me physically, I suspect it is a genetic enhancement. We are stronger and faster than humans. Our brains more powerful to send psychic messages."

"This is very true. But it is not the whole reason behind the Dragan power. Tell me everything you know about Dragans."

"They were created from a merging of a mage and dragon. Silver hurts them because of the silver swords that were used to kill dragons. But Dragans can only live at night due to the dark magic used to create them. They need to drink blood to survive, another part of the dark magic."

"Dark magic helped create the Dragans. We drink blood, not just because of the dark magic and the blood sacrifice it represents, but it is the easiest food source to replace the iron we need. The Dragan body needs more iron than a human and burns through it. Silver hurts us due to it hurting dragons. A Dragan is made from a mage and dragon. So we were literally created by magic from magical and human creatures. And you believe our power is purely down to genetics?" he said and shrugged and sighed.

I nodded in acknowledgement and took a puff of my cigarette and coughed again. "So magic is important as well. Hence how Dragans can make the Turned. I understand Dragan blood still teems with magic."

"Dragans still teem with magic. The blood merely carries it around, but every part of a Dragan's body holds magic. Considering this then, why is Thorn the strongest of all Dragans?"

"Because she is closest born to the first Dragans."

"This is true. But genetically, she is not as big and strong as Cassius or me."

"But her genetics are stronger, more dragon in them?"

"Maybe slightly, but not enough. Her true power lies elsewhere, as we have discussed."

"She has more magic in her."

"Good. You are on the right track, and I think this is what everyone believes. But through my studies, I have come to a different conclusion. I believe our Dragan bodies can hold only so much magic. We are limited in our physical capacity. And we can only use this magic within our bodies because of the constraints of the original spell."

"She can hold more magic? But it is not a physically bound capacity due to size. Maybe because she is closest born," I said.

"Maybe it is a physical and genetic limitation. Maybe a body can only hold so much at any time. Some Dragans can hold more because of size and genetics."

"Then what are you saying? What makes Thorn special?"

"What makes you and Thorn special don't you mean to say?" he said, pointing his cigarette and ash dropping off the end.

"Both of us?"

"You are made from her blood. You became a Dragon. You are special."

I gulped and took another sip of wine. "I don't know."

"It is not that you hold more magic, or you are significantly genetically stronger. But I believe you can channel the magic from outside and into your bodies, giving you a greater source. I think all Dragans can channel magic, else we would have dried up long ago if we can only hold so much magic. There must be a way it is replaced. But some are better than others at channelling magic, driving their abilities to greater levels."

"But I thought all magic had gone from the world as used up to make the Dragans."

"That has been the general understanding, but I believe the access to magic by everyone other than Dragans was stopped."

"But why do you think that?"

He puffed on his cigarette and poured more red wine. "I have seen things in this world that can only be explained by magic. While Thorn was gathering great wealth and power, I sought knowledge and experiences. I studied with great masters and learnt ancient teachings. Some humans have abilities that are beyond normal. I detected powers in them. Only a few in all these centuries, but somehow they could tap into the ancient power. I suspect they may have been descendants of the mages."

"They could still perform magic?"

"Not perform magic. No fireballs shooting from their hands. But they could channel something to give themselves skills. I believe these few could find the magic still in the world that surrounds us. So it is not just within us, but we have the power to tap into it. Plus, recently, I have heard of things that indicate this power among humans is on the rise. The source of magic may well be returning to humans. They may have channeled it, or more magic exists."

"Yes. Mary said the same thing to me. The world is changing. Reality is distorting. Humans with powers have been detected," I said but left out the part it could be my fault. "So can a Dragan perform magic? Could I perform magic?"

"I have tried and others have tried as well. But it seems it has to be channelled through our bodies. Hence, why we have to feed it to other creatures for them to take on our powers."

"Okay. So the Dragan's power comes from magic that is channelled from the outside and its genetic abilities. But how does this explain why you are drunk?"

"I think the drink is affecting you more than you realise. Is the answer not obvious?"

"No. Your fast metabolism should burn off the alcohol in seconds. Whether it is your enhanced genetics or your magical power, you shouldn't be able to get drunk."

Rip shook his head and sunk back more red wine. "Genetic abilities are hard to control as they are hard wired. However, as you know, magic can be manipulated and directed."

I stared at him, the realisation of what he meant hitting home. "So you are choosing to be drunk? You are using your magic to stop yourself from healing."

Rip sipped down the last of his drink, put the glass on the table and slowly clapped his hands together. He stubbed the cigarette out into the ashtray and then leaned back in his chair. His eyes glazed over red with the black slits in the middle, and he breathed upwards, flames shooting out of his mouth and a haze emanating around his body. He tilted his head back and sat up straight. The red glow of his face from the alcohol had gone, and his skin was a normal pale colour again. I opened up my senses and could feel sharp and concise thoughts, which were quickly blocked.

"Finally, you have learned your first lesson. I chose to be drunk and I can choose to be sober. The magic can be used to control my abilities. I can blend in and enjoy a lovely bottle of red wine," he said and poured me another glass. "Now it is your turn to get drunk. This is your first training exercise."

"Get drunk. Are you kidding?"

"No, you drink. You will learn to control your powers. Stop yourself from healing, and the more you drink, the harder it will become. As you drink, you can answer some questions."

"As I get drunk, you hope to interrogate me?"

"Yes, you will loosen up and speak the truth."

"I will play the game. But you must answer a few questions as well."

"A question for a question, but only if you get drunk."

"Deal," I replied, and we shook hands across the table.

I raised my glass in the air and gulped down the first glass. I focused my thoughts on not healing, but it was an alien thought and the alcohol burned off. Rip grabbed another couple of bottles of red wine.

"Try again," he said. "But drink a little slower. We have all night. You should learn to enjoy your wine as well."

I took another glass full and swallowed down a few more mouth fulls. This time I tried to enjoy the wine a little more. I was getting used to the taste. Again, I focused my thoughts on the alcohol, but it burnt off all too quickly, leaving my head clear.

Rip grabbed my arm and pushed up my sleeve. He flicked open a claw and slashed open my flesh, leaving a thick line of blood swelling to the surface. I gritted my teeth at the pain.

"Focus your energy. Stop it from healing."

The blood was drying up, the Dragan genetics fighting to protect itself. I tried to focus on the blood but to no avail.

"How?" I snapped back.

"I hoped it would be instinctive. You turned into a dragon. How? What did you feel at the time?"

"I was in a rage. I had just found out they had killed my father. Thorn had shot me and I thought she was trying to kill me. I had just spent the last few weeks being mercilessly tortured. I was in a fury of anger and hate. I had never felt so explosive before. As the formula healed me and transformed me, then the rage within triggered the change, lighting up the Dragon genetics hidden within."

"Your anger and rage fuelled you?"

"As Thorn had taught me. She told me to use my emotions to drive my actions. To use it to focus my powers. Usually, I had to remember events and relive memories to drive my powers, but on that occasion it was immediate."

Rip nodded his head. "It seems Thorn understands this power better than I expected. She knows how to use it to accelerate her Dragan powers."

"So I need to get angry."

"No. You need to fuel it. Anger is but one emotion, and in certain circumstances, it is a quick and available source. But we can't always rely on being angry."

"Other emotions, like love?" I said and laughed. It sounded ridiculous considering everything I had been through.

Rip drunk some wine and then contemplated the glass in his hand. "Why not?"

"But we are dark creatures powered by dark magic. How can love be something that focuses our energy?"

"Just because we are created by dark magic doesn't mean that we have to become it. All emotions have power. Love is one of the most dangerous emotions in existence. How many people have died because of love? The need to protect your loved ones. The justification of an act because of love. The jealousy of seeing the one you love with someone else. Crimes of passion resulting in murder. Love is dangerous and even more powerful than hate or fear. People commit atrocious crimes without regret and all in the name of love. The desire for love can cause terrible acts. Due to the lack of love, some people turn to darker thoughts. Love has a dark side beyond compare."

I couldn't help but agree. We all seek love and peace, and when we don't get them, it can cause hate and anger. Even trying to get love or to protect it, people commit evil acts and justify them. "So I need to feel love to fuel my magic and prevent my genetics from healing."

"You use whatever is at hand. If you feel nothing, then you are at peace and you are contented. It is but another emotion. What is it you feel now?"

"Confused by this situation. But also pain from the cut, and background of fear and guilt from my encounter with Giles."

"Then let's focus on the present. Don't invent your emotions or relive memories as it takes time. We feel something every moment of our lives. Focus on those emotions, don't block them off, let them run wild."

I did as he said and relaxed, letting all my worries take hold. With them came my love for Thorn and sadness at not being with her.

"Now, imagine your magic as a light within you. Your emotions channels into a ball of light, making it burn brighter, sucking in magic from the outside. Do you see it?" I nodded. "Good. Now think of the outcome. Picture the wound on your arm staying as it is, your magic surrounding it and blocking the body's natural reaction."

I imagined a big ball of purple light, with fiery lines of different colours of my emotions sparking around and enlarging the fuel lines of purple magic streaming in from outside. The ball grew more violent, shaking around, sparks buzzing off it, as more magic channelled in from outside as my emotions of love and sadness opened the gateway. I then pictured my arm and the outcome of the wound staying open and the purple light surrounding it flowing from the ball of magic.

I opened my eyes and looked at my arm, the blood welling back up to the surface and the stinging pain returning.

"Well done. Now hold it."

I kept my focus and kept the wound open. Once I had started, it felt easy to maintain it. In my mind's eye, I imagined the purple sphere being fuelled from the outside and then streaming off to my arm. My emotions were just the key to unlocking the fuel lines of magic.

Rip poured me another drink. "Now I want you to drink and use your newfound power to stop your body from burning off the alcohol. I want you to let it seep into your bloodstream and race around your body and mind. I want you to get drunk."

I picked up the glass and tipped it into my mouth. At the same time, I watched the wound on my arm and kept the ball of light focusing around the cut, preventing my body's natural reaction to heal it. I let that same feeling spread around the rest of my body, blocking off my body's natural response to burning off the alcohol through its fast metabolism.

I knew it would take some time or take a lot of alcohol to discover one way or the other if it was working. I sped up the process by finishing the glass, pouring myself another and downing it again.

"Hold on, young man. That is a vintage bottle. I will get you some spirits if you are intent on getting drunk quickly," Rip said and grabbed a bottle of Vodka from the side. He cracked open the sealed and poured it into my drained red wine glass, tinting it pink. I grabbed it and sunk it back in one, swearing as it burnt the back of my mouth. My concentration slipped temporarily and the wound on my arm healed, the blood sinking back in. I focused again, keeping the magic around the wound and holding back my metabolism.

"Let's talk for a bit. There are things I want to know," Rip said.

"Yes, let's talk. A question for a question. I have plenty of things to ask you as well."

"That seems fair. But I get to go first. So the first question is, who do you love more, Thorn or Scarlett or Carmella or Amber?"

"That's not fair. Are you trying to get me into trouble?"

"I just want to understand your emotions. I want to understand the journey you went on so I can help you become a well-rounded warrior. It's important to understand a person's motivations to drive them to excellence."

"I love Thorn the most. Surely that is obvious."

"Not obvious. People love each other in different ways. I'm sure you felt something for all of them, and it felt different for every single one of them, but were they all love or were some of them infatuation?"

"Yes, I definitely love Thorn, and I definitely loved Scarlett. Amber, I liked a lot and under different circumstances, it could have been something more. Carmella just used and tricked me."

"You didn't love Carmella or feel something for her."

"Carmella seduced me, she brainwashed me into wanting her. She played Miss Nice to Patrick's Mr Nasty. Whatever I felt for her, real or not, was purely induced through torture. I felt a connection as her story seemed so similar to mine. When Thorn killed her, I felt some level of guilt, but that was just my heart talking. In my head, I knew she was twisted and evil. She allowed them to hurt me until I was broken to her will."

Rip nodded along and sipped his drink. "Yes. But did you love her?"

"I just told you she used me and tricked me."

"But did you love her?"

I pictured Carmella, her brown curly hair and enormous almond eyes. My heart beat a little faster and the wound on my arm healed. I refocused and blocked off the healing again.

"Not sure love is the right word. There was something even though I knew it was all a trick, but she didn't feel the same way about me."

"Are you sure she didn't love you?"

"I am sure. She wouldn't let them treat me that way if she loved me."

Rip paused and stubbed out a cigarette. "Are you sure? She saved you. Maybe it was the best she could do under the circumstances. She needed you to give the Hunters some information to rescue you."

"No. It was all a game to her. I thought she liked me because of my Dragan powers to seduce and our common history. But I am convinced it was a trick. The way she treated me at the end made it clear. I was just an asset to be bargained with. She loved Bramel."

"And if Thorn had never come for you, would you be with Carmella still? Maybe you would have been completely in love with her and her with you. What may have started off as a relationship of convenience could have turned into something real. Two people both snatched from their normal lives and turned into monsters."

"We are not monsters?"

"So you don't see the Turned as monsters?"

"I never said that. But they never asked to be turned. The Dragans did that to them."

"We did. They did, should I say. I have never turned anyone. So you won't fight them?"

"Yes. I will fight them and kill them. Their thirst for blood drives them to evil acts. But inherently, they are not evil."

"So how are Dragans different then? We must feed. We spill blood. We created the Turned. Are Dragans evil?" Rip asked.

I stared at him and then into the bottom of my Vodka glass and took another mouthful.

"Survival. The instinct and desire to survive at any cost. This is why the original Mages and Dragons infused themselves with dark magic. It is why some of the Dragans created the Turned to win a civil war," I said.

"Yes. And let me point out that Humans have committed worst atrocities to each other. It was humans that tortured you. From my point of view, it was humans that drove us to become Dragans in the first place. The Turned are a by-product of that event. So there are no blameless parties in this scenario. Humans have no right to act innocent in these events."

"But it wasn't all humans, it was some humans."

"Yes. It was also some Dragans, but not all that created the Turned. But you haven't answered my question. Would you still be with Carmella and be happily in love?"

"I doubt it. It was clearly just a game to her. My powers of seduction had no effect on her. She only had eyes for Bramel. And Bramel only had eyes for Thorn."

"But even if she didn't love you, do you think you may have fallen in love with her?"

I shuffled in my seat and took another sip of vodka. "I don't know for sure. I felt something. But I had been brainwashed. I had started to see through it."

"How does Carmella's seduction, brainwashing and her relationship with you appear any different from the one you have with Thorn?"

I glared at him. "The situations were completely different."

"Are you sure? Thorn seduced you through the use of her powers. Carmella did the same but in a slightly different way. Your relationship with Thorn was one of convenience but became more. It could have been the same as Carmella. Can you explain to me what is the difference between the two of them?"

I've never thought of their actions or the circumstances of our relationships as being similar. It was true what he said; both of them had seduced me, neither of them wanted me at the beginning. I will never know if my relationship with Carmella would have turned into something real. But I knew there was a difference. "Thorn never tortured me. I went there of my own free will."

"Are you sure? She used hypnotic powers on you. She made suggestions about wanting her. How was that any different to what Carmella offered? At least Carmella told you what she wanted. She was more honest and open about it, but Thorn was deceitful."

"I understand it may seem that way. The difference is that I knew Thorn was trying to seduce me. When I went to rescue Thorn, I knew I was doing as she asked, but I didn't care. I wanted her to seduce me. I wanted to be enslaved by her. I never wanted to be seduced by Carmella, but she brainwashed me through pain and pleasure until I had no other choice but to give in out of pure survival."

"You wanted Thorn to seduce you? You understood what she was trying to do and went anyway?"

"Yes. I wasn't aware straightaway. But once I had time away from her, it became clear. When I returned to release her, I was in Dragan form and her powers had no effect on me. It was my choice to let her out of that cell. I knew what I was letting myself in for. I suspected she would either kill me or turn me into a vampire. Either way, I was happy to be enslaved by her dark power."

"That is a big thing to admit. That you wanted to be controlled by her."

"Lucinda made me see the truth of my dark desire. I had always thought of it in a romantic light of how Thorn and I came together. But the truth is different."

"And Scarlett?"

"Scarlett was my first love. If I hadn't been attacked and met Thorn, I would still be with her. But things happened. I had to change, and I shouldn't have involved Scarlett in my new life. She has paid the ultimate price of knowing me. She's dead."

"So was Scarlett also older than you. Just as were Carmella and Thorn."

"Don't start on the psychoanalytical rubbish. I got that from the Hunters, the inference I was seeking a mother figure. It is just coincidence they are all older than me."

"You put your trust in older women. With Thorn, you wished to be seduced by her dark power and maturity. With Scarlett, I understand again she was older than you, more experienced and mature. And with Carmella, it was the same again. You can deny it or accept it. You have missed the mother figure all your life. It would be no surprise that you would seek, on an unconscious level, someone to fill that gap. This doesn't mean that this is how your relationship now works. It just means it could have been part of the attraction to have a more mature woman in your life. That doesn't mean they mother you."

"I don't go in for all that Freudian nonsense. Maybe I was seduced by Thorn's maturity and experience and power. Our relationship is nothing like that now. Maybe I enjoyed her taking care of me and looking after me in the beginning. I would hate that now. I'm growing stronger every day and one day I will be one hundred percent Dragan. My powers will match that of Thorn's permanently. I have proved through my transformation into a dragon that I could be more powerful than her one day."

"Interesting. You hope to replace her?"

"Not replace her. I want to be her equal one day. But most of all I want her respect, which I will only get if I am her match or I am more than her match."

"Do you think she doesn't respect you now? Do you think it is important that you are as strong as or stronger than her? Remember, Thorn has met very few people as powerful as her."

"Then maybe it is exactly what she wants. For someone else to stand up to her."

"You think she craves to be put in her place?"

"No. That isn't what I meant. I suppose just someone to be her physical equal."

"All relationships have physical inequalities and inequalities in money, intelligence and attractiveness. One person is always stronger than the other in areas. This is a fact of life. A Union is a partnership of common interests and brings qualities to the relationship the other may lack. Maybe you should just accept this part of the relationship. The imbalance in physical strength."

"I already accept the differences between us, else we wouldn't have lasted together. Doesn't mean I wouldn't like to even things up a little. Anyway, enough of you twisting my words and analysing me. It's time for my questions."

"Your questions will have to wait until tomorrow. For now, I want you to take that magic you have been using to hold back your metabolism and healing power of your body. Then let it surge into you, burning off the alcohol and healing your wound as quickly as possible. Focus on that ball of energy and see how quickly you can heal."

I looked down at the line of blood on the top of the wound. I could just take the magic away and let my body do all the work. But the goal was to drive my magic into my body, to accelerate its powers. I pictured sucking all the purple light back into the ball, and I could feel my body following its natural reactions. Then I drove the magic into the feeling of my body healing, driving it through and accelerating it.

The blood on my arm sucked back into the wound. The flesh began knitting back together from underneath and closing it up. I breathed out a huge gasp of surprise and the alcohol-hazed out of my mouth and seeped through my skin. My head became less fuzzy and sobriety took hold once more. My arm healed up completely, and my body was free of alcohol and smoke.

"Wow. That healed almost as quick as if I was already a Dragan," I said.

"You did well. But it should be no surprise you can power yourself to that level. You are seventy percent Dragan, after all. The correct use of magic will be enough to push you to that final thirty percent if you ever need it."

"So I don't need to become a full Dragan to get my full powers?"

"You can use your magic to give yourself a boost. The further you become a Dragan, the more access you will have to the magic, and the better you will control it, and the better your genetics can accelerate to their full extent. Even with the focusing of your magic, you would still not be able to beat Thorn at your current level of transformation. You will need to be a hundred percent Dragan before you could manage that feat. Remember, Thorn was one of the first born and is the most powerful of all Dragans."

I nodded in agreement and played with my glass, swirling the vodka around in it. "So, what is next?"

Rip looked out the window and then at his watch. "It will be light in a couple of hours. I wish to take a stroll in the moonlight. Go back to your hotel and sleep. Come back here tomorrow night once dark. Bring all your things with you and check out of the hotel. Tell them we have reached an agreement."

"And then tomorrow I get to ask my question. And what else happens next in my training?"

"Tomorrow night, we drink some more. That is your training."

Chapter Twelve

Rip wandered off into the countryside as I walked back to the hotel. I went up to my room and crashed out onto the bed. The excessive drinking had given me a headache even though I burned it off, yet it still left a mark. I drank a glass of water and got some sleep as I knew tomorrow night I would have to do it all over again.

It wasn't exactly what I expected from the great Dragan warrior. I thought we would be sparring and him teaching me secret holds and moves, not trying to get drunk. Although, I understood the reason behind his training methods. He was stating that the Dragan's greatest power was through the control of their magic. We did not need to fight to understand and learn it. I suppose getting drunk was just as good as any other way of learning how to control your power. As the lack of focus that came with getting drunk meant it had to become automatic in your mind after a while.

However, I hoped we would put that magic to use in the form of fighting. I needed to prepare for when I met Giles again, as I couldn't just challenge him to a drinking competition.

After my drinking bout, I slept well. I woke in the late afternoon and went downstairs and ordered some food from the bar. I told the barman I would be checking out of the hotel as I had met my uncle and we had exchanged contact details. The barman looked surprised that my story had appeared to be true. I knew he would tell all the other customers tonight. It would give Rip the perfect cover story when he needed to leave with me. The barman grunted at me and brought me over my invoice as I ate my lunch.

I settled my hotel bill and finished my food. I wanted to head over to Rip's cottage and begin my training, but it was still daylight and he would be asleep. Instead, I tried a bit of training on my own and ordered a bottle of red wine.

Once the wine arrived, I pulled out my tablet from my bag and fired up my Kindle app to read for a while to kill time. I poured myself a glass of red wine, took a sip and focused my senses. I imagined a ball of purple light to simulate my magic inside. Then I needed to feed it with my emotions to channel the magic to prevent the alcohol from being burnt away. I took another sip of red wine and enjoyed the taste. I wondered what I was feeling at the moment, what emotions I could use to control my magic.

I had a background of different emotions. I still felt guilty about Scarlett and anger at my father's death, but hopeful for the future, optimistic that Rip would teach me new powers to help end the war and bring order.

I allowed those mixtures of emotions to fire into my magic and then focused it around my bloodstream, preventing the alcohol from dissipating. I got the feeling locked in my mind with the magic flowing into my body and alcohol rushing through my blood.

I whiled away the next few hours with a couple of bottles of wine and reading until I felt quite drunk. Other customers visited the bar and the barman told them I had found my uncle. Their suspicions went, and some of them even smiled and nodded at me. I had been accepted into the town through association. I hoped that meant if anyone came looking for us, the locals would treat them with suspicion instead.

The day moved on and I noticed the light fading through the windows. I would go to Rip's cottage and show him I had continued to master the skills he taught me. I left the hotel bar and staggered down the street. The road ahead was swaying around as my feet misplaced each step. I stopped for a moment and leaned against a building to re-gather my balance.

A few locals saw my drunken state and watched. I needed to sober up a little bit, so I pulled the magic back and felt the alcohol burn away and clarity return. I then used the magic to block my body from taking its natural course of burning away all the alcohol. It seemed to do the trick. I had sobered up enough to walk down the street without falling over and drawing too much attention to myself.

During my walk and stop to sober up, it had become dark, and I knew Rip would be waking. I'd remembered the path from the night before and approached the field with his cottage at the end. I slowly climbed over the fence and then stumbled along the brown field to his cottage. I went to knock on the door.

"Ah, I see you have been practising," Rip said.

I spun around and saw him standing a few paces away. In fact, I saw a couple of him as my vision had doubled. He wore jeans, army boots and a black t-shirt, and he had tied his hair back and shaved. It was a stark contrast to the surf-dude look of last night.

"Yes, I enjoyed a couple bottles of red wine," I slurred while holding onto the door of the cottage to keep my balance.

"Well, I was going to suggest a little drink and a little chat before we started your training tonight. You have beaten me to the drinking, I see. Let's go inside and sober you up. And I will partake in a little glass of red wine to relax."

I opened the door and staggered in, grabbing hold of the table as I walked through. I shuffled around the table, pulled out the chair and slumped myself in it. Rip took a bottle of wine and two glasses off the side, sat down, and poured us a drink.

I focused on my magic and let it retreat inside my ball of light, allowing my body to heal. I pushed the magic into the healing, and I leaned back in the chair as the alcohol fumes burned through my body and breathed out of my mouth. My body forced the alcohol out, and my T-shirt was drenched through in a wine smelling sweat.

"So, do you feel better now?" Rip asked.

I took a deep breath and sighed. "Glad to be sober. But I wanted to show you I could do it, and I had a bit of time to kill."

"Good. I know you probably think it's a mad thing to do. A strange way to train one's magic. But it is an important thing to control your body, and this is doubly so for you. As you are a hybrid, neither Dragan nor Human, you could pass as either. The control of your magic can make you appear Human. And it could also make you appear Dragan. It would be useful for you to act as one when you are the other and vice versa."

"You're right. I can go places and do things that other Dragans won't be able to do. If I can also pass myself off as a human by preventing my Dragan genetics from giving me away, then I have even more opportunities."

"Good. You understand the true power of your magic and your unique circumstances. Now I believe you have a question for me."

"I have several questions. What happened with you and the Twins and Thorn? Why is your hair greying and why do you have a scar if you have this amazing healing power? What have you been doing the last few hundred years? Are you, in fact, an alcoholic?"

"Well, I see you have been thinking about it. I will only answer one question now, remember our deal, a question for a question. And as you have asked me so many, I will choose which one to answer. Regarding my greying hair and scar, I use my magic to allow myself to age a little to fit in. I've been living here for fifteen years, so I decided it would be unusual for me not to age during that time. I had once drunk a little too much at the local bar and fell and cut my head open. I realised that I had to prevent it from healing to keep my cover. So I had to keep the scar on my head."

"So every day you need to focus on looking this way and preventing your body from healing."

"I've been doing it so long now, it's almost become part of my image in my head. It has become almost fixed within my system. I would actually have to concentrate now to remove the scar and the greying hair."

"So you can control the way you look? You can alter your physical features."

"I suppose so. If I focus my magic in one area in particular, then maybe I could alter it from the way I usually appear. In this case, I've only allowed my body to take its normal course without the enhanced Dragan genetics interference. But I have never tried to radically alter my appearance."

Rip poured himself another glass of red wine and drank it down.

"Now it's time for me to ask you another question to prepare ourselves for your werewolf training."

I acknowledged him with a nod of the head.

"I need you to tell me what happened in your fight with the werewolf. What did you feel? How did you fight? Why do you think you lost?"

"Only one question at a time, remember? Which one shall I answer first?" I said and tapped my finger against my chin.

"Well done, but this is for your own good. I will answer the rest of your questions later on."

I smiled back, still feeling relaxed from the drinking session.

"I lost. The werewolf attacked, and I felt frozen to the spot. It sent an icy fear through me, like an innate instinct to run and hide. I knew I couldn't run, hence why I was stuck. Luckily, my Dragan senses kicked in, and I was able to fight him off. But I took a lot of bites and cuts."

"It is scary the sight and sound of a werewolf charging in for its kill. I would guess your human psyche is to blame for the sudden paralysis. Humans keep clear of wolves, and werewolves are even more of a threat. Did Thorn ever teach you how to fight a werewolf?"

"She never taught me to fight a werewolf. I have fought one before, but he was in his human form at the time, and so was I."

"Did you win that battle?"

"No, I lost that one as well."

"So why do you think you lost both these battles?"

The memories of those battles flashed back. Giles's werewolf crashing through the trees and bowling me over. The sheer size and strength of the beast were too much, even in my Dragan form. Again, Max was too big and powerful when we fought in his diner. The sheer ferocity and power of his attacks had me on the back foot. He tackled me to the floor and hit me over and over.

"They were stronger and more aggressive. I couldn't prevent the momentum and power of their attacks."

"So they were bigger than you and stronger. In which ways were you able to defend yourself or fight back?"

"I could move quicker and be more agile. Against Max, I jumped out of the way of his initial attacks. With Giles, I was able to get under him and push him off."

Rip nodded and lit a cigarette. "Yes, the wolf is strong, maybe a little stronger than us. It is certainly more aggressive, and it attacks more direct and ferocious. But we are faster, more agile, and clearer in thought in a fight. The wolf's instinct is to go for the kill, a direct onslaught. So how would you defeat it? How does the smaller, faster and more intelligent animal win?"

He had practically given me the answer, and it seemed so obvious as he talked it through.

"I use my speed and agility to avoid his attacks. Hit him fast and get out. Let him wear himself out."

"Good. But it is unlikely the wolf will run out of energy. He may get clumsy and angrier, leading to uncoordinated attacks. You can use that to lure him into more mistakes to present you with greater opportunities. But what other advantage does the Dragan have over the wolf?" he asked and raised his glass of red wine and presented it to me. I picked up mine and we clinked glasses together. We drank together and I let the alcohol take its course, holding back my healing powers. I put my glass back down and smiled at Rip.

"Magic. I assume the wolf doesn't have the same ability."

"I believe not. Even if they did, I doubt in their wolf form their thoughts would be clear enough to control it. So how would you use your magic to win?"

"I would increase my speed and strength. I could heal quicker."

"Yes. And which of our weapons hurt a wolf?"

"Our claws and fangs, the supernatural powers prevent it from healing, as theirs does to us."

"So what is it in our claws and bites? What gets into the flesh that causes so much damage?"

"With the bite, I guess it's the saliva, and with the claws, it's the bacteria. Part of our body gets embedded in theirs."

"Yes, so we get stuck inside them. Parts of the claws stick inside and the saliva from the bite mixes in with the werewolf's blood and gets in the bloodstream, which affects the whole body."

"So I should bite it if possible. Use my magic to increase my saliva and bite the werewolf."

"Correct. Your claws and fangs should poison it, but don't drink its blood else you will poison yourself. Use your speed and agility to avoid its attacks and counter-attack with your own. Use your magic to accelerate your powers and maximise your poison. However, I should warn you that I have never tried out this strategy against a werewolf. And it is hard to remain clear of thought in the heat of battle. Don't fight on its terms and get involved in a battle of pure strength and size. It will win, especially if it is a full moon."

"What if I have to fight Giles on a full moon?"

"I would use the same tactics. Its main threats are its size and strength. At the full moon, these are just exaggerated. Your strength is your magic and ability to use the magic to enhance your existing powers. You are more agile. You will move faster than a werewolf. You are strong but don't have the aggression that the werewolf has when it has transformed. We have rage and anger, but we have to incite it and feel its emotion. For a werewolf, it is immediate. It is a red rage from the pain of being transformed."

"Okay. So I use my speed and my brainpower to win. How can I train in the meantime?"

"Drink up. Let's go outside and see what we can do."

Rip poured back his drink and stubbed out his cigarette in the ashtray. I downed my drink to keep up with him as he was heading out of the door. I followed him into the night, and he walked into the field that surrounded the cottage. He looked down at his wristwatch and then back at me.

He pointed across the field to the fence line. "I want you to run as fast as possible and back, but without using your magic, just relying on your pure genetic strength. And then we will do the same again with your magic. Let's see how much of a difference it can make."

I agreed and put myself into a starting position. Rip looked at his watch, and I waited for the signal. "Go," he shouted and swiped his hand down.

I bolted forward, pounding my legs up and down, pumping my arms, pushing with every stride to get maximum pace while breathing in and out. I skidded towards the fence line, tapped it with one hand and turned around and sprinted back to him. As I ran past, he pressed the button on his watch. "Excellent, thirty-five seconds. Now take a moment to get your breath back, build your magic up inside and then we will try again using your full potential."

I placed my hands on my knees as my lungs sucked in the air. My eyes closed and I pictured my purple sphere of light. I was exhilarated from the run and excited about what I was learning. Those emotions of happiness and excitement fuelled my magic, expanding out my purple light. I imagined channelling that magic into my body, letting it flow into my limbs, pumping my heart faster to drive my legs.

"Tell me when you're ready," Rip said. I gave him the thumbs up and stood back up into a starting position. A few seconds went past as Rip prepared his watch. "Go," Rip shouted and swiped his hand down.

I bolted back across the field as I let the visualisation take hold, and the magic flowed into my limbs, pumping my heart faster. The ground beneath blurred and the fence zoomed into sight. I skidded again, but my momentum was much stronger than before and I barged straight into the fence, knocking part of the wood out. My feet got a grip on the ground, and I sprinted back, letting the magic accelerate me to new speeds.

I sprinted past and he clicked his watch. Again I skidded onto the path just outside his cottage, kicking up a load of dust and gravel, pinging it into the front door.

"Fantastic. Twenty-five seconds," Rip shouted and flung both his hands in the air as if I'd won the gold medal at the Olympics.

"Is that good enough?" I asked.

"Is that good enough! Of course, it's good enough, it's nearly a third quicker. Imagine your Dragan powers are thirty percent more powerful than before. If you can channel your magic directly into your strength, speed and psychic powers, you will be a force to be reckoned with. Now defend yourself," Rip screamed and charged.

I still had my hands on my knees, panting. I looked up as Rip leapt at me, and I put both my hands up to parry his oncoming attack. He barged into my chest and we both tumbled to the floor. He punched down at my face. I blocked with my forearms and tried to dislodge him by bucking my body. He didn't move and followed up with more punches onto my forearms. He stopped and stood up over me.

"Where is your magic? At thirty percent better in your hybrid state, you should almost be as good as a normal Dragan. You should be able to defend yourself and fight me without the formula. So what happened to your magic?"

He was right. As soon as he attacked, I forgot all about my magic. I couldn't do that in a normal fight. I always had to be prepared to push my magic into my body. So I decided on the best way to answer him. I let my feelings of humiliation and anger burn into my magic and let it spark across my body.

I rolled backwards and sprung up, forcing Rip backwards, and I landed on my feet. I lunged forward with a front kick. Rip leapt back and avoided the blow. I followed on with a flying left punch. Rip spun around and blocked it with his arms. With Rip going backwards, I powered the magic into my fists and let them blur towards his face, knowing I couldn't do him any actual damage. After several blocks, I smashed through his guard and hit him clean on the nose. He staggered back and tripped over onto the gravel floor with his hands over his nose.

Blood poured onto his hands and soaked back into his fixed nose. "Better. It took me by surprise, just as I did to you. An important lesson if you're fighting another Dragan. It takes time to get the magic to flow, whether subconsciously or consciously, in our case. Most Dragans can use this magic on an unconscious level. You and I, my friend, are fully aware of its true power and can accelerate it and enhance it to levels that they cannot reach."

I smiled and held out my hand. He reached out, grabbed my hand and dragged me down, pulling himself up. He then thrust himself backwards, coiled a foot into my chest and flipped me over into the air, spinning me into the field behind. I let my magic flow and righted myself in the air to land on both feet. Rip continued with the momentum and rolled onto his feet, ready to attack, when he saw me waiting for him.

He stopped and grinned. "Wow. You really are getting the hang of this. I suggest tonight we call it a draw and have a drink. Tomorrow, we train some more and I will look forward to it. It is the first time I have fought against another Dragan for many years. And the first time I've really used my knowledge of the magic to accelerate my own powers. You will be training me as much as I am training you."

He held his hand out for me. I was expecting another trick, but I walked forward and shook it. He grabbed it and shook my hand with both of his hands, and then slapped me on the back and walked me back into the cottage, where he poured us another glass of wine and lit another cigarette.

I went around the other side of the table. He raised his glass and I picked up mine. "To new friends," he said.

"To new friends," I replied.

Chapter Thirteen

We carried on drinking the rest of the night until Rip checked his watched and looked out the window.

"Daylight approaches my young apprentice. I need some quiet time to plan your training program. I wasn't expecting to work out your next stage of training just yet. But you have advanced quicker than I expected."

"Are you sending me to bed?"

"Yes. Get some sleep."

I sunk back the last of my wine and said goodnight. Rip got a pad of paper and started writing. I had gone to bed at 4 o'clock in the morning, which meant I slept most of the next day. But at least I was awake at night, ready to train with Rip.

As darkness came, I made my way down into the kitchen, searching for food. The noise must have woken up Rip, and he appeared and grabbed his cigarettes from the worktop and went out into the field for a smoke. I wandered after him while munching on a baguette. He offered me a cigarette, and I shook my head.

"You are fine to smoke. It can't do you any harm with your powers," he said.

"I know, but I just don't like smoking," I replied.

"Nor do I really. It's become a habit, a way of feeling something after being alive for hundreds of years. Feeling it burn down my throat and into my lungs. And then letting my body fix itself and expel the toxins. You're right, I should just give up. I have plenty to feel and live for now you are here. We are gonna have great fun," he replied and flicked his cigarette out into the field. Then he walked back into the cottage and threw the rest of the cigarettes in the bin. He poured himself a glass of water from the tap and drank it down.

"So I have a training plan for you. I'm going to attack you to mimic the moves of a werewolf. I will use my magic to make myself stronger and more aggressive. You must use your magic to move faster and more agile. And then tomorrow night we will swap roles. Then maybe you will experience what a werewolf sees when they fight a Dragan. But before we train, I am hungry and need to feed. So we will drive a couple of hours to another town, where we will try to find something. Plus, we need to get you some food as well."

I totally forgot about the need to feed on blood. "I understand. Do you need me to come with you?"

"Yes, it is part of your training. You've already realised you need blood on occasions. After the werewolf attack, you needed blood to heal quickly. The more time you spend as a Dragan, the more blood you will need eventually. You need to learn how to feed and how to find your food."

"Thorn has taken me on her feeding trips before. Do you do it the same as her?"

"Well, that depends on how she does it?"

"She likes to seduce men and then take them somewhere quiet to feed, or she looks for trouble and takes her fill of their blood, usually killing them."

Rip nodded. "Back in the old days, I worked for Thorn. We would fetch her something to feed upon. Rarely did she venture out on her own to find food. She was royalty, after all. But it seems like we get food in very similar ways, which is not a surprise. The ability to seduce is something you are aware of. But also our psychic powers allow us to pick vulnerable people or people that probably deserve to be fed upon. Tonight we need a quick feed, so we head to the rough part of a town and attack one of the local drug dealers. They are easy to spot on the street corners. We attack one of them and get their guards to chase us into a dead end."

"You want me to feed as well? I'm not in my full Dragan state and don't need to."

"Maybe you should try it. See if you can use that magic to produce claws and fangs. Seventy percent of you is Dragan. Test how drinking blood affects it. You can practice your new fighting ability against the dealers even if you don't feed. Come on, let's go. If I get a good feed tonight, then I don't have to go again for a few nights. Then we will have plenty of time to get on with your training."

Rip headed out of the cottage, swooping his hand into the bin for his cigarettes. I followed him out, and he locked the cottage door and then walked over to the small garage. He flipped open the big, long metal door and shuffled down the side of the garage and climbed inside a beaten-up old white Citroen. He started it up and drove out. I shut the garage door and got in the car. He drove out along a gravel path that was overgrown with patches of grass and then turned right and headed out of town.

It would take a couple of hours to get to our destination, so I decided it was my chance to ask him some questions.

"So, what is the deal between you and Thorn?"

"She hasn't told you about me?"

"She told me that you were in charge of the Royal guard. It was your job to protect her and her family during the Dragan wars. And that you probably feel guilty about the fact they broke in and killed her husband and child, and her mother and father. And that you've been running from her, too ashamed to face her, or feeling guilty because of what happened."

Rip stared ahead at the road for a while and wiped his eyes with the back of his hand. "It is true. But did she tell you how it happened, how they got past me?"

"No. She only told me that you were in charge of the guard and would have felt guilty about not protecting her."

"It was my fault that they broke in and attacked Thorn and her family. The Twins, who worked for Cyrus, had distracted and seduced me. They tricked me into letting them in. It was all a ploy to gain access to the castle for Cyrus's Turned army."

"Thorn was with Cyrus in that video. Are you telling me that Cyrus was the one who ordered the raid that killed her family?"

"Yes, it was Cyrus who was at war with her. Hence, if she can forgive Cyrus for what happened, I believe she can forgive me as well. And therefore, I suppose she can forgive the Twins for their part in her family's death. But I'm not sure I can ever forgive them for what they did to me."

"So why was Cyrus at war with Thorn?"

"It's a very long complicated story. How much has Thorn actually told you?"

"Only the Dragans were at war with one another. Through this war, they discovered their magic could turn the recently dead into vampires, hence the name of the Turned. She said the war started through jealousy as such small numbers of Dragans in existence."

"Yes, it was Cyrus who discovered the Turned. It was he who raised an army and attacked Thorn and her family. It was due to jealousy; Cyrus believed he should be the King of the Dragans. And to be King of the Dragans, he needed to be in a Union with Thorn."

"But Thorn married someone else and had a child and made them the King of the Dragans," I said.

"In a way, yes. Thorn had actually been married or in a Union twice before and once to Cyrus. However, Cyrus was unable to father any children with her. The need to reproduce the race was too important, so their Union was disbanded. But Cyrus left in a furious state, vowing revenge for his loss of title. Thorn found another who could give her a child, and she formed a Union with him."

"So Cyrus and Thorn were in love once?"

"I never said they were in love. But it was deemed to be a good match because of their heritage. Thorn was the first child of the original mages and dragons. Cyrus's parents were also original Dragans, and they controlled the other major Dragan House. The Union between Thorn and Cyrus was meant to unite the Dragan Empire. It made sense for them to be together and their offspring would be strong, but it didn't work out. And as Thorn's parents were considered to be the strongest of the Dragans, the others deferred to them and looked to them for guidance. They had become the leaders of the Dragans and were given the title of King and Queen, which meant Thorn was direct in line to be the next ruler. And therefore, her partner would be King of the Dragans."

"So Cyrus wanted to kill Thorn, and her parents and her husband and child, so he could claim the title for his own, as his House was the next strongest? He started the entire war?"

"Yes. This whole mess we are in is because of the argument between Cyrus and Thorn. So you can see why I was so surprised to see them together. And why I now think I must be forgiven if she will forgive him. But if we win this war and defeat the Turned, I suspect the old rivalries will rear again. Unfortunately for you, it means Cyrus will look to take your place and claim the title he believes belongs to him. One that he was once due to inherit but lost as Thorn disbanded their Union."

I put my head in my hands and rubbed my temples, just what I needed: a crazy jealous Dragan as an enemy. "Great. I will keep an eye on him and add him to the list of people who want to kill me."

"Don't worry, my friend. I have a duty to protect you as the new King. I need to fulfil the duty, as I should have done all those years ago. Thorn knew full well I would feel this obligation when she sent you to me. However, it has been no hardship on my behalf," Rip said and smiled at me.

He carried on driving, and I had more questions for him, but I decided that was enough revelations for one night. I would get more of Thorn's mysterious past out of him as my training continued. He promised a question for a question, and I was owed a few.

The car rattled along the single-track country lanes until we joined a normal road. All the time, Rip smoked as he drove. I opened the window and kept my face near it to get some fresh air and to allow the smoke to escape. He offered me a cigarette, but I turned it down. I decided that regardless of my body's healing ability, I just didn't enjoy smoking.

We joined a major route with dual lanes and sped along until we finally reached the town, Saint-Étienne. We drove in from the countryside with houses building up in density and headed through the city centre and out the other side. The atmosphere changed as we drove into the suburbs. The roads had potholes, and we cruised along unnoticed, as Rip's car was old enough to fit in with the other scratched and dented vehicles.

He parked along the street by a shutdown cinema. The doors and windows boarded up, and the car park blocked up with metal wire fences. The cinema had a sign for a film from three years ago, and the car park tarmac was losing the battle with the weeds erupting through it.

We walked another couple miles into the rundown area, past boarded-up houses and broken-down cars with the wheels and mirrors already salvaged by the locals.

Other cars drove past and the passengers eyed us. The people walking the streets kept their eyes fixed ahead and expressions grim. The population carried the same disrepair as the buildings and streets upon which they lived.

Rip dragged us into an alleyway and whispered into my ear. "Look down the street and you will see a man standing on the corner." I looked over at a man dressed in a tracksuit with hair shaven at the sides and long on top. "He's a drug dealer. You go to him and pay the money and then walk back across the street, and a young lad will run over and give you the drugs. What we are going to do, or should I say you are going to do, is run over to the man and punch him in the face and steal all his money. Then run back to this alleyway where I will be waiting.

Other people will appear out of these buildings or cars and chase after you as well. Lead them down the alley, and then I will jump out. I can get an excellent feed off a couple of these guys. We can both practice our fighting. See if you can work your magic up into a big ball before you start. Don't run too fast when being chased; I don't want you to lose them completely. And you are to only use the magic once they are trapped down here. I want you to push out your fangs and claws and attack as if you were a Dragan. If you feel the need to take a little blood as well, it might give your powers a boost."

The Enemies of Vengeance

I stared across the road at the man looking around for customers. I knew he was a drug dealer preying on the vulnerable to make money. But I'm sure he had his own sad tale to tell. I was basically going to trick him into chasing me to get torn apart by a Dragan, who would drain his blood. I felt better to be taking out drug dealers than just picking on a person at random. But I still wasn't convinced this was the right thing to do.

"Are you going to kill him?" I asked.

"Well, I am not taking him out for a five-course meal and giving him champagne," Rip replied.

"But he is still a person. Probably has no choice but to deal drugs to make money. Not saying I agree with what he does, it is just that we shouldn't judge other people. We have no idea what's led to these decisions and this lifestyle."

"You won't get very far as a bleeding heart liberal if you can't feed. What you have to remember is that everything has a consequence. Other people are poor and need to make a living, but they don't deal drugs. If we take him off the streets, then maybe someone coming for their fix will be forced to go clean. Maybe by taking away the drug dealers, it would prevent young people from joining the gang to become drug dealers. Maybe they will look for other employment. If there are fewer drugs on the street, there will be fewer drug addicts and less crime. You may feel sorry for him, but the world would be better off without drug dealers and criminal gangs that control them. What would you rather, I found some poor innocent young girl walking down the street and ripped the life away from an A+ student, someone who might have become a doctor, someone who might have made a difference?"

"I understand. I just wish there was a better way."

"I've been alive for hundreds of years and have yet to find a better way. If you find one, which means I can feed without hurting anybody, then let me know. But for now, punch that man and then steal his money and lure them back here. Just think of us as crime-fighting superheroes, who also drink people's blood."

I had to forget about being human and remember that I was becoming a Dragan and had to see humans as food at some point if I was to survive.

I brushed down my clothes, pushed back my hair, took a deep breath, and then strolled out of the alleyway and down the road towards the man. He stared at me and took a step back. I guessed he didn't recognise me as a regular. He looked up and down the street for his backup. "How can I help you?"

I coiled my fists and sprung forward, using my magic to accelerate myself, hitting him square on the chin. He flew into the brick wall and then slumped to the floor. I searched through his clothes, grabbed the cash and a mobile phone, and stuffed them in my pockets.

I was supposed to hit him so he could chase after me down the alley. But the dealer was spark out, blood running from the back of his head. I looked up and down the street, waiting for his backup. A front door burst open and two men raced towards me. I had my prey. I jumped up and ran back towards the alley, making sure they kept track, letting them catch me up.

I ran down the alley but couldn't see Rip anywhere. The alleyway finished in a brick wall, a dead end. The men ran down and cornered me. It reminded me of the two Hunters confronting me in Vegas. I walked back towards the guys, who started swearing in French slang, which I didn't understand. I prepared to fight them both, pulling my magic inwards, preparing to let it burst out through my fists when a massive bin on wheels skidded across the alleyway and out stepped Rip.

"Hello, my friends, glad to see you could make it to our little party," Rip said and walked towards them with his arms out to block their way. They looked at each other, and then back and forth between Rip and me. They both pulled out guns, one aimed at me and the other at Rip. I should have known drug dealers would have guns. I didn't have one.

Rip kept advancing. "Guns, excellent. A proper test for us, V."

"Thanks. But you realise I don't heal quite as well as you."

The men looked back and forth between us, guns pointed at us both while they stood side to side but facing in opposite directions to keep us in view.

"Well, try not to get hit then. Use your powers to get to them first," Rip said, and he darted forward. The man facing him fired off two shots, but Rip zigzagged across the space.

The man facing me fired his gun, and I ducked and rolled towards him. He squeezed the trigger again, and I dodged to the side, letting my magic power burst through my legs, and I blurred the final space between us.

Rip had already hit his man, knocking my opponent over as well. As he stumbled forwards, I grabbed him by the throat and then slammed him into the wall, knocking him unconscious.

Rip had already opened up the neck of his victim and was sucking down his blood. He looked up at me with blood soaking across his chin. "Feed. There is enough Dragan in you to need blood. So feed," he shouted and pointed at the unconscious man.

After kneeling down by his side, I pushed his head back to reveal his neck. I wasn't fully transformed into a Dragan, but Rip told me to use my magic to force on the extras required. I pushed all my emotions through my magic and then streamed it into my fangs. My teeth broke through and enlarged. I put my fingers to the tip of my fangs, and they cut through the skin, blood welling up on my fingertips.

With the appearance of my fangs, a sudden thirst came upon me, and I bit into the man's throat. I sucked down the blood. At first, it felt great, and I felt a surge of power, just as I had done with Annabel and Lucinda and the other victims I had fed from, but then suddenly I felt sick. I stopped and stepped back and threw up the blood.

Rip laughed and wiped the blood from his chin. "I guess there is still too much human in you. Start walking back and get yourself a drink on the way. I will finish up here and see you at the car," Rip said and then went back to gulping down his meal.

I wiped the vomit from my mouth and staggered out onto the street. I looked around, and the man I had hit on the street corner was getting to his feet. He saw me and ran over. I didn't want him to disturb Rip, so I ran down the street and got him to chase me.

We ran down a few streets. I could get away from him if I desired, but I didn't want to spend the rest of my journey looking over my shoulder. I decided the best thing to do was to confront him. So I did the one thing he least expected. I stopped and turned around and waited for him. The man caught up the ground and then slowed to a walking pace, scouting around, suspecting something was off.

"Are you bloody stupid? Do you know who we are? Do you know what will happen to you when they find you?" the man asked. I walked towards him, and he stepped backwards.

"Here is your money," I said and pulled the cash out of my pocket. It was at least €900.

He frowned at me and looked about once again. "Is it a joke? You hit me and steal my money, and now you're just going to give it back."

"If I take the money, you will get into trouble with your bosses. Maybe you can say you chased after me and was able to recover it," I said.

"Why do you want to give me the money back? Are you afraid now I have caught up with you?"

"I am not scared," I said and stepped towards him, so we were face-to-face, then I forced out my fangs and burning red eyes, using my magic as Rip had taught me, "but you should be."

The man turned around so fast he tripped over his own feet and stumbled to the floor, then looked up at me as I glared down at him. He scrambled to his feet and sprinted back to where he came from. I laughed as he ran away and put the money back into my pocket. Then I realised I had let someone see a Dragan, but I hadn't removed his memory or killed him. However, I doubted they would believe a drug dealer, as he was probably a user as well. No one would believe his tall tale, but I should be more careful and not show off quite so much.

I continued the journey back to the car, remembering a little bar on the way. I stepped in and ordered a pint of lager and drank it down in one go to clear the taste of vomited blood. I walked back to the car and leaned against it, waiting for Rip to return.

He appeared about twenty minutes later. His clothes had splashes of blood down his chest. He flashed a massive grin and his eyes sparkled. He displayed the typical post-meal glow of renewed energy and satisfied hunger.

"You did well tonight. Consider it your next phase of training. We start with the sparring tomorrow night. Now let's go home and enjoy a nice bottle of red wine."

Chapter Fourteen

Rip drove back to the cottage in good spirits. He showed the typical post feed elation I would often see in Thorn. He chatted a hundred miles an hour and drove the same. He chain-smoked all the way back, and with the speed of the car through the twisting roads and the smell of the smoke, it made me feel sick again. Rip had to pull over so I could empty out the rest of the blood from my stomach.

Once we got back, I raided his cupboards for some food to try to settle my stomach acid. Being a Dragan, he didn't have much food. I only found some stale bread and cheese. I toasted the bread and melted the cheese on top and took part in a couple of glasses of red wine as Rip continued to talk.

He told me about the adventures he'd had in the last few hundred years. He talked about training with kung fu masters in a remote Shaolin Monastery in China. I asked him how they accepted him into their community, considering he was a Dragan and fed on blood. He could hide his true nature using his psychic abilities. He trained with them only at night and explained it by saying he was a hunted man and should not be seen during the day.

He would bring them food and clothing at night as gifts, and in return, they trained him. Through their meditation and training, he discovered the truth about Dragan magic.

He told me about visiting great libraries, studying ancient texts on martial arts, meditation and spiritual understandings.

He had also fought in many wars, just like Thorn had. But he chose not to work for governments or countries. In the Second World War, Rip helped with the French resistance fighters. In the other wars, he usually switched sides to whoever offered the greatest challenge. Wherever he could find the best fight to practice his skills and find a good feed in the surrounding mayhem.

We finished our wine as the Sun rose. With the first streaks of light coming under the doorway, Rip said good morning and headed off to bed. I decided to take in a bit of daylight and went outside to watch the rising Sun. We had already gotten into a similar training pattern, feeding and fighting that I had developed with Thorn. Rip promised me that the next night we would begin sparring.

The Enemies of Vengeance

I stayed outside for an hour, letting the warmth of the sun hit my face while I contemplated the day's events. I needed to see the Sun once in a while and view the world in daylight rather than in the cold of the dark.

I took in the fields surrounding the cottage. The woods at the edge of the fields and the broken fence I had caused on my practice run. As I headed off to bed, I saw the cottage for the first time in the daylight. The white stone walls and terracotta tiles on the rooftop. The cottage had a small extension to the side, and I realised I hadn't looked in any of the other rooms apart from the kitchen, bedroom and bathroom.

I headed inside and snooped around the other rooms. A study room with a desk and computer. The walls lined with shelves crammed to bursting with books. The books were categorised into different topics of military strategy, martial arts, spiritualism and meditation.

The next room had a TV and a long leather sofa. Then a dining room with a small table and chairs. There were a few photos on the wall of sceneries: the great wall of China, Vegas casinos, Eiffel Tower in Paris, and the Houses of Parliament in London.

I went to bed and slept the rest of the day, preparing for our night of combat. I woke late at night, having slept longer than I expected. The previous night's activities had taken a toll on my system. Drinking the blood hadn't agreed with me and vomiting it up left me feeling weak.

I heard Rip walking around in the kitchen and then uncorking a bottle and pouring wine. I jumped out of bed, put on my jeans and t-shirt, and stumbled down the narrow stairs and through the kitchen door.

"I thought you would never join us on such a good clear night," Rip said and held his glass up to me and took a swig.

I sat down and slumped my chin onto my hands, with my elbows on the table. I grabbed an empty glass and held it up to him. He poured the red wine in, and I took a big gulp back. I kept my healing back and let the wine take its effect on my system. It felt good for it to numb the pain a little. Rip puffed smoke into the air and leaned his head back. "Are you ready for the rest of your training?" Rip asked.

I downed the rest of the red wine and put the glass on the table. "Yes, let's get on with it."

"Good. Because this will be your last training before we meet Thorn. While you were sleeping, I had the chance to phone her and discuss what happens next. They are moving out as they had a tipoff from your MI5 friends about the location of some first-generation Turned."

I was surprised to hear that. Thorn hadn't said she was now willing to work with Mary and MI5. She just decided without telling me. Probably reassured by the strength of their information so far, finding Cyrus and Rip.

"So we will meet at a new place?" I asked.

"Yes, Thorn has given me the location they are heading to. We will meet them there."

"And is Max still joining them?"

"Max is your werewolf friend. If so, yes, I believe he is flying over to prepare you to fight against Giles, but I also have some training for you. Tonight, I will play the part of a werewolf, and you will try to defend yourself."

I pushed back the chair and headed out of the door, keen to get on with the training. Rip stubbed out his cigarette, finished his glass of red wine, and then followed me into the moonlight.

I turned around to make sure he didn't get the jump on me and walked backwards to keep an eye on him. He might attack from behind to prove I should always be on my guard. It's just the sort of thing Thorn would do.

"Good. I see you are prepared. Let's go into the field and give ourselves some room."

I walked into the field, keeping a wary eye on Rip all the time. Likewise, Rip kept moving around as we walked, ensuring that I kept my senses alert, looking for a weakness and a lapse in concentration to attack. I stopped in the middle of the field and balled my hands into fists, ready to fight. Rip stopped and likewise, tensed his muscles and flexed his hands into fists. He seemed to be building up his aggression, as I saw his face change, the muscles contort, and the Dragan fangs and eyes appear.

I felt apprehensive and scared. He wouldn't severely hurt me, as we were training. Even so, Rip in full Dragan mode looked frightening, and it reminded me of the monster within. I let my magic build up by using the fear and nervousness to create a spark. I tensed my legs, digging my feet into the ground and coiling the muscles ready to spring out of the way.

Rip's muscles enlarged. His shoulders and fists grew larger, his canines grew bigger. He seemed to use his magic to take on the characteristics of a werewolf. Finally, he allowed his energy to explode, and he bounded forward, dropping his hands to the floor and running like a wolf at me. He leaped into the air, hands out front with claws whistling. I waited for the last moment and spun out of the way, whipping my hands around and hitting him on the back as he sailed past. He rolled on the floor and sprung back up. I knew if that had been real and I was a Dragan, then I would have slashed my claws straight down the wolf's back.

Rip stood up and smiled, and immediately ran back at me, but this time, he didn't leap. He skidded a few feet away and sliced his claws at my face. I ducked underneath, hitting him in the stomach, then spun out of the way and kicked him in the back. He turned around and jumped into the attack. I front kicked him back onto the ground. I went in for the kill and jumped up and landed on top of him. Rip dragged his feet back underneath and kicked into my stomach, ripping the feet back and forth down my gut, and then kicked me up into the air and out of the way.

He stood up and strolled over. "Remember, the wolf's hind legs are powerful weapons. Do not expose your stomach to them as he will gut you open. Remember, you are fighting an animal. Hit it from behind, where its weapons can't reach you. Never let all of its four claws and mouth have free range to hit you."

I nodded back and then stalked around in a circle, trying to think of the best way to attack. Rip brushed himself down and tensed his muscles. He eyed me up as I walked around him and then he bolted forwards. I darted to the side as his fists swung. He swiped backwards, and I blocked with my forearms, kicked him in the back, and he fell to the floor. With his back facing me, his weapons would all be out of range. I jumped onto his back and pretended to claw down at him, across his head and then pretended to bite his neck.

He lashed back with an elbow and caught me in the ribs. I rolled off. He sprung back to his feet and dived at me. I lay on my back, pulled my knees up to my stomach and kicked out, hitting him square in the chest, pushing him off balance. He collapsed in a heap at my side. I sprung back to my feet and jumped back to gain some space. Rip got up onto one knee, grinned and then stood up.

"Well done. Hitting me across the back was perfect. If I were a werewolf, I would not have been able to reach you. A wolf's weapons are at the front. They cannot reach around or over. It has to twist around to get you. Remember not to get involved in a strength contest with it either. They have more aggression and outright natural strength."

"But Thorn told me we were stronger than them, faster than them. Are you saying she was wrong?"

"She's not right or wrong. It depends on where that strength lies. They have outright aggression, which they channel into a direct full-frontal attack. In this respect, they are stronger than us in that type of battle. However, we are stronger overall because we can focus our magic on particular parts of our attacks. They cannot do this. We are faster as well regarding agility and punching and kicking. But in an outright foot race, they would win. After all, they do have four legs compared to our two."

"So, there's no point in trying to outrun a werewolf?"

"That's right. You can run from it. But make sure it isn't in a straight line, twist and turn, make use of your surroundings. Like climbing trees or up the sides of buildings, the werewolf cannot follow you. Try to ambush it, attack it from behind but beware of its incredible sense of smell. It is better than our sight or hearing. If you are to ambush it, then make sure you are downwind, so your scent isn't carried to it."

"Okay, so let me get this straight. I can't outrun it, can't simply overpower it. The werewolf will always know where I am through its superior senses."

"Yep, I know it sounds bad, but think of what Norris has told Giles about how to fight you. He would have told Giles to always keep you in front of it, never let you circle around the back. Make sure you stay downwind of the Dragan, so its scent is carried to you. Try to hit it quickly and powerfully and pin it to the floor. Don't let the Dragan move freely around. Take the battle to the Dragan, try to anger it and get it to engage in an all-out battle of power and strength. It would have said the Dragan is faster and more agile."

"So if I don't play its game, then I need to dictate the terms of battle. I need to decide how and when we fight against each other."

"It will do the same to you. It will try to choose the battleground. So Giles will use his knowledge of your relationship to anger you. He will say stuff to make you attack him head-on and play to his strengths. By remaining calm and passive, it is likely to anger him and make him attack you wildly. You can then use your agility and magic to outmanoeuvre him and hit him from behind. Get those claws and fangs into him quickly and then move away again. Let the poison take its toll, debilitating him and slowing him down. Then you can prepare to make your final move and kill him."

I recoiled back. "I just needed to beat him, not kill him. He was my best friend, after all."

"Well, that is very honourable of you, but they would have trained him to kill you. They would have brainwashed him into believing it was the right thing to do. They have turned him against you. He is no longer your best friend. He is your worst enemy. You are going to have to accept that one of you will have to die."

Chapter Fifteen

Rip and I sparred for most of the night, stopping a few hours before daylight to pack our bags so we could start off as soon as darkness came around again. The activities of the night before must've been tiring, as when Rip woke me and I had not heard him enter the room.

Rip told me to get the car started and load the bags. He packed a few essentials, which meant a few bottles of wine and some cigarettes. He gave me the coordinates of Thorn's location, which was in a cabin in the Spanish mountain forests just over the border. According to the sat nav, it would take six hours to drive. We could easily do it in one night and not have to worry about being caught out in the daylight. Yet, Rip wanted to get started as soon as possible to avoid any potential delays or incidents that may cause him alighting in flames.

I drove the car out of the garage and opened the door for him. The light had faded. Rip put his hand outside to check if there was any reaction. When his skin stayed normal, he jumped out of the cottage and locked it. He then dashed over to the car and climbed into the passenger seat.

He immediately lit up a cigarette, wound the window down and blew out a puff of smoke. "Are you okay to drive?" he asked.

"Yes, I'm fine to drive. I haven't driven much on the right-hand side of the road, but I'm sure I can adapt."

"Excellent. It's just in case the sun hasn't fully gone down. I wouldn't want to swerve the car off the road. If you drive the first two hours, then I will finish the rest of the journey. You can have a sleep in the car and be fully refreshed when we meet Thorn."

"Okay. That sounds like a plan," I said, and hit the start button on the GPS and put the car into first gear but the car didn't move.

"Pump the clutch," Rip said.

I pumped the clutch twice and tried again. The car rolled forward, and we crunched over the gravel, flattening down the weeds.

I flicked the headlights on and followed the green arrow on the satnav, driving us out of the village on single track roads and heading towards the main route south and over the border into Spain, then through the mountains into the forest where Thorn was hiding out.

The driving was easy through the quiet roads, even though I was driving on the opposite side of the road. Rip kept an eye on the GPS timer, chain-smoking cigarettes until he felt happy that we were making the timescales to get there before dawn. I wound down the window to let the smoke out and air in.

After a few hours, Rip asked me to pull in to a lay-by. He flipped open the bonnet and fetched a bottle of water from the boot. He filled up the radiator with water. I stretched my legs a little.

"Is there a problem?" I asked.

Rip poured in the last of the water. "The radiator has a little leak. If I top it up now, it should last until we reach Spain."

"Are you sure? Your car seems to have a few issues."

Rip dropped the bonnet and put the empty water bottle back into the boot. "Of course, it's a classic. Don't worry."

"I'm not worried. But I'm fine if we break down and the sun rises."

"It won't break down. Jump in the back and try to sleep. I will drive the rest of the way. I will awake you when we are about half an hour away so you can help scan ahead for any potential threats," Rip said.

"From the Turned."

"Or from Dragans."

I lay down in the back seat and undid my coat and used it as a pillow. Try as I might, I couldn't get to sleep, as I was jostled about in the rattling old car. After about forty minutes, I asked Rip to pull over so I could get back into the front passenger seat. We talked for the rest of the journey. Rip told me more stories of his time in hiding, and I gave him more details about my time with Thorn.

The GPS timer counted down as we passed through the border into Spain. We hit thirty minutes left until we arrived at the location Thorn had given us.

"I want you to open your mind to listen out for any psychic noises. And open the window as well; you may pick up a scent or a sound."

I lowered the window, tipped my head back, and closed my eyes to listen for any psychic messages or unusual sounds. But the car was old, and the engine was noisy, and the exhaust was smelly.

We continued into the mountain forest, the car winding through the trees and the headlights flashing through the trunks, illuminating wild animals running for cover. Rip flicked the lights off and we carried on. I knew he could see without the headlights, and it would cover our arrival.

We continued on, heading back north as we went into the national park and back up the mountain.

"Up to the right is a log cabin. I can see strong heat signatures coming from it. It's probably our guys, and the GPS seems to agree that we only have a few metres left. Be prepared for anything, just in case Cyrus has betrayed Thorn and is waiting for us."

"Shall I just call Thorn and let her know we are nearly here?"

"Yeah. Good idea. Let's stop for a moment while you call her. They have probably already detected the car and are circling around us."

I looked out of the window and flicked my eyes around, looking for one of the Dragans stalking us. Even with my improved eyesight, I saw nothing. I turned my phone on and speed dialled Thorn.

"Well, hello. I guess that is you making that noise just down from the cabin," Thorn said.

"Yes, it is us, so please don't attack. Is everything okay up there?"

"Of course it is. Bring the car up to the front. We will come out to greet you, so you know there is nothing amiss."

I hung up the phone. "They are waiting for us at the front of the building. Drive around. Thorn has promised me everything is okay."

"I hope you are right. I'm trusting you, V. But apart from that, no matter how fast Thorn is or how much you have learned, I could still rip your throat out quicker than they could attack me. So remember that once we get up there, just in case you have some plan against me. I am not called Rip for nothing."

"I think you've been hiding out too long. You're paranoid."

"Being paranoid saved my life many times. Just because you're paranoid doesn't mean they aren't out to get you," Rip said and drove the car up around the road, twisting around the roads back and forth until we hit the road heading straight towards the log cabin.

Out of the cabin door, four figures walked down to the track where two jeeps were parked. The cabin was on one level, but it was elevated up on a platform to make it flat due to it being built on a slope. The porch and front door were on the slope side, and the stairs led down to the forest floor.

I could tell three of them were Dragans from the smell, and I guessed the final one was Max, the werewolf, as I detected a familiar musky odour.

Rip brought the car to a halt and flicked on the headlights, making them shield their eyes with their arms. Rip jumped out of the car and slammed the door shut.

"Here I am. If it's revenge you want, then let's get it over with. I can't run anymore," Rip shouted and pulled his hands into fists.

The Enemies of Vengeance

Thorn ducked out of the beam of light to the side. "Rip? Is that really you? You're looking older than I expected."

"And you are looking just as wonderful as ever."

Thorn walked towards him, and behind her, the others stepped out of the light to follow. Cassius and Max, and the third Dragan was Cyrus. Cassius and Max both towering over everyone else. Max dressed in his faded jeans and a white t-shirt. His hair tied back and a stubble beard. Cassius in a black tracksuit and white trainers.

Thorn and Rip stood only a few yards apart. "Rip, there is nothing to forgive. There is no need for you to hide anymore. We are and will always be friends and family. She opened her arms up, and he stepped forward, and they hugged each other.

Rip and Thorn stood back from one another. "What's with the scar and grey hair?" Thorn asked.

"We all get old," Rip said, and Thorn frowned at him but said nothing more and stood to the side and gestured back to Cassius.

"I assume you remember Cassius?" she said.

Rip stepped forward and Cassius walked over to greet him. They shook hands, and then Cassius wrapped his big arms around him and gave him a hug, and Rip hugged him back and then tapped him on the back. Cassius released him and stepped away. "Good to see you again, old man."

"Good to see you too, Cassius," Rip said and then looked back to where Cyrus stood.

Cyrus stepped forward with his hands out. He wore designer jeans and a polo shirt, and his blond hair had a neat centre parting. Rip crossed his arms and glared at him. "Are you kidding? After everything you put me through," Rip said.

Cyrus opened his arms. "Not going to give me a hug, either?"

"Give you a punch in the face if you like, but that's the only physical contact you will get from me."

"Rip, the feud is over. You have to get used to having me around. Thorn and I have agreed to share power."

Cassius and Max both slyly glanced at Cyrus and shook their heads. Rip and I looked over at Thorn, who shrugged her shoulders. "We have to learn to share. It's a big planet. I'm sure we can come to some agreement."

Cyrus then walked past Rip towards me. "And you must be the infamous V?" he said and held out his hand.

I had no history with Cyrus, so I shook his hand. "And you must be

Cyrus."

"They have told you about me?"

I looked to Thorn and Cassius and then to Rip, unsure what to say. They had only ever told me they had been a war with him and that it was he who created the first army of the Turned. I decided it was best to avoid the question. "Thorn doesn't tell me much. She thinks I can't handle it."

Cyrus laughed and slapped my arm. "Sounds like Thorn." He turned around and looked at her. "Hey, darling, I see you haven't changed that much."

She smiled back sarcastically, and Cyrus walked over to her, put his hand on her shoulder and stood by her side.

"And nor have you, Cyrus," Thorn said and placed a hand on his and removed it from her shoulder.

"Sorry, V. Thorn and I have history. I'm sure she will tell you all about it. We had some good times together once, and I'm sure we can be good friends again."

Thorn smiled at him again and gently placed a hand on his arm. "We can all be friends again. There is no need for any more wars between us."

I hated the way he touched her and talked to her. I could have accepted that if in isolation. But Thorn seemed to respond in kind. She seemed to be almost encouraging him. I felt my blood rising, and I gripped my hands together to control my temper. I wanted to say something, but I knew Cyrus could easily beat me. And I knew Thorn could look after herself. I'm sure she had it all under control.

"I am willing to let the past be forgotten," Cyrus said. "We have all taken losses. Thorn took her revenge all those years ago. She wiped out my entire house and killed my mother. Only the Twins and I survived from the House of Smoke. Remember, it was Thorn that created Bramel who leads this Turned army."

"But you started it. Without you, there would have been no need for revenge," Rip said and took a step forward towards Cyrus.

"I started it!" Cyrus responded. "As I remember, you and Thorn had an affair while I was still in Union with her. I had every right to be outraged."

I glared back and forth between Thorn and Rip. Neither of them had mentioned it. She hadn't told me of her and Rip, but she had said she had tried to have a baby with every Dragan male, so I should have worked it out.

"It wasn't an affair. I was just trying to help further our race. Something you seemed incapable of doing with Thorn," Rip said and stepped closer. Cyrus jumped forward and pushed out with both hands, knocking Rip backwards.

"So it was the honourable thing to sleep with your Auntie."

Auntie! Someone could have told me.

"It wasn't like that and you know it. We don't use human terms to define our relationships. But that hardly excuses you using the Twins against me to break into the castle and kill everyone."

Cyrus's fangs jutted out and claws ripped through the flesh of his fingers. Thorn jumped in between, with hands out to make peace. "We all know what happened. What is done is done. We have to stand together and defeat the Turned, which we all created. If you can't control yourselves around each other, then keep a distance."

Rip took a few steps back, and Cyrus retracted his weapons.

"I suggest we get some sleep. It will be light in less than an hour," Thorn said, and everyone muttered in approval.

I walked back to the car to get my bag out of the boot. Rip came with me and took his bag out as well.

I looked at Rip. "Auntie?"

He shrugged. "We were made from four Dragans. Of course we are all related. But he is using human terms on our relationships. We don't think like that. We can't afford to think like that."

Max walked through the crowd and held out his hand to me. I went to shake it, but he picked me up instead and squeezed me tight. He put me down again. "Good to see you again, little man."

"I'm hardly little, Max. I am over 6 foot."

"You will always be little to me," Max said and laughed.

Rip stood at my side and looked warily at Max. "Rip, this is Max, he's a werewolf," I said.

"I can tell," Rip said. "I understand you are here to train V, in case he ever has to fight Giles again."

"Yes, I understand you have been training him to fight werewolves already. Tomorrow night, let's find out how good that training is. Maybe we should chat first and devise a training program for our little colleague."

Rip grinned. "Yes, I think that will be a good idea. Maybe we can enjoy a nice glass of red wine together."

"Sure, if you got no beer, then red wine will do. I will show you inside to one of the spare rooms." Max led the way in and Rip followed him in with Cassius at his side. Thorn held out her hand to me. I placed my hand in hers, and we walked inside. Cyrus stood in the way and glared at us both. "What are you doing?"

"We are going to bed. What do you think we are doing?" Thorn answered.

"You're going together? I thought we had an agreement about the sharing of power."

Thorn stopped and squeezed my hand tightly as reassurance. "Sharing of power, Cyrus. That is all we will share. V and I are in a Union."

"You said we would share power again, and you admitted that we once had good times together."

"Our time is long gone, Cyrus. You killed my parents, my husband and my child. If you think we will ever share a bed again, then you are crazy. No amount of time will ever make me forget that. But we now stand together to defeat a common enemy that we created. We undo the damage of the feud and then go our separate ways. I suggest you go to bed and think it through."

Thorn pulled on my arm and dragged me past him into the house. She pushed me in front of her, keeping her body between Cyrus and me. I glanced back and saw Cyrus glaring at me with raging red eyes. Thorn ushered me down the hallway and into a bedroom. I put my stuff down on the floor next to the bed as Thorn shut the door.

"Don't worry about him. I will have a long chat with him tomorrow night and clear the air. I said sharing power and meant we could divide up whatever was left. Even if we defeat the main Turned army, there will be stragglers to clean up. I was going to suggest we assign countries to rule. There are very few of us and many countries in the world. In the past, there were more of us and fewer places to rule."

"I'm not sure he cares about territory. I think it's you he wants and the title of King of the Dragans."

"Well, he can't have me, and he can't have your title. He can call himself whatever he likes in his territory," Thorn said and walked towards me, pulled off her top and flung it to the floor. "Enough of Cyrus. Enough of the Turned. Enough of werewolves. I wasn't sure if I would see you again. I've been so worried about you after you were attacked by the werewolf. We shouldn't talk about anything else. We are together again and there's only one thing we should be doing," Thorn said, putting her hands around my head and pulling me into a kiss.

Chapter Sixteen

Thorn lay next to me with her arm across my chest. I checked my watch. It was midday. I'd had a bit of sleep in the car and now felt wide-awake. I heard a few footsteps outside in the corridor, and I guessed it would be Max wandering around.

It had been great to be back with Thorn and celebrate our reunion. But I couldn't lay in bed for the rest of the day waiting for her to wake. So I decided to get up and talk to Max and then take in my surroundings in the light of day.

I carefully removed Thorn's arm, and she rolled over and wrapped the duvet over the top of herself. I grabbed my clothes from the floor, took my t-shirt off the antlers of a stuffed deer's head on the wall and pulled them on. I shuffled around the side of the double bed crammed into the room, and carefully opened the bedroom door to make sure no sunlight was streaming through. The light in the corridor was dim. They had tightly shut the curtains to ensure no stray beams of light. I stepped through and quietly shut the door behind me.

I walked down the log wall hallway towards the smell of sizzling bacon, which triggered my stomach to growl, and into a small rustic kitchen area.

"Morning, sleepyhead," Max said. "Would you like my special fried breakfast? I have hash browns, sausages, bacon and eggs."

"You must have read my mind. That would be perfect, thank you."

"Right on it. Help yourself to coffee and take a seat. This will just take a few minutes."

On the kitchen side was a big coffee pot three-quarters full. I opened the cupboard above it, grabbed a mug and poured the coffee in. A big wooden table took up the middle of the kitchen. I grabbed a seat facing Max, who was busy at the hob.

I sunk down the coffee to wake myself up. The coffee was a little hot, but it was welcomed and had the desired effect. "So when did you arrive, Max?"

"I have only been here a couple of days. Thorn called me and told me of your problems with the werewolf. She asked me to fly over and give you some one-on-one practice."

"Thank you for coming. I really need your help. I got badly hurt in my last encounter, but Rip has helped train me up."

"Excellent. Rip and I had a bit of a chat last night. Sounds like he was giving you some good advice. But we shall see tonight whether you can put that advice into practice."

"Do we have to wait until tonight?"

"I can only transform at night time. And I have to change tonight anyway, as it's a full moon."

"A full moon! But you will be at your maximum power."

"Yes. It will be excellent practice for you. And it will be doubly difficult, as Thorn has told us that you can't take your injection either."

"What? I wouldn't stand a chance without it."

"Tonight, you will learn to evade and counterattack. If you can do this with me, on the full moon and without your formula, then it'll be easier against Giles next time you face him. But mostly, I think Thorn didn't want you to waste one of your injections on training. You may need to use it properly in the next couple of days. If you use it tonight, then it will prevent you from using it within the next week."

Max presented me with a plate of sausages, eggs, hash browns and bacon. He grabbed a knife and fork from the drawer and placed them next to me. He sat down across the table with a cup of coffee. I thanked him for the food and dug into the sausages first.

"Tonight, we will spar for one fight only as it will be very tiring for you. Then I will go off and try to scout out the first-gen Turned. We believe there is one about thirty miles away. In my heighten werewolf form, I can cover the ground quickly and will sniff them out. If they do sense me, it won't necessarily give away the rest of our presence," Max said.

"Why not?"

"It wouldn't be abnormal for a wolf to be in the woods. The Turned can't always sense werewolves as well as Dragans. I would be able to sense them from much further away. So it's unlikely I would even come into their range."

"So we could be launching an attack in the next few days?"

"Yes. It looks like the war is starting."

I polished off my food and drunk down the last of my coffee. We were about to fight back, and I was excited and scared. I could get my revenge and eliminate the constant threat of the Turned from trying to cut me open. I had no choice but to fight them, and this was the first time we could take the battle to them, even if it was just one first-generation Turned. But with each first-gen gone, their potential to grow their army diminished and we furthered our goal of defeating them.

I changed the conversation. "So, how is everything going back at the diner? How are Eleanor and Amber getting along?"

Max drank his coffee. "Everything is going well. Amber has taken the money that you gave her and invested it into revamping the diner. She convinced me that a fifties style diner was old hat. Nobody was going to drive out there to eat. And passing traffic didn't always stop. We had to make it a go-to place, so we had to make it different, something special."

It sounded interesting, and I shoved my empty plate to one side and got a refill of coffee. "So what is it now?"

"You will not believe this, but Amber wanted to literally revamp it. So it has become a cafe with the Gothic theme. It embraces everything to do with vampires and werewolves. Amber has some steampunk vampire outfits that she wears to serve in. The walls have pictures of famous vampires and Gothic settings. We have fake spider webs around the door and along the counter. The menu is horror themed. We have the first bite burger and bat wings. All served with Mummy fries and werewolf milk. She's been running a social media campaign on Instagram and Twitter. We offer a discount if you re-post."

"Thorn would find this highly amusing. The restaurant is doing well then?"

"Thorn did find it highly amusing. Especially as I have to pretend to be a werewolf. You know how much she loves to mix the fact with fiction, almost rubbing people's noses in the truth. Anyway, the restaurant is doing fantastic. It appears that people want an eating experience now, not just casual dining. It has become the go-to place to be seen in. Amber has done a fantastic job. She's worked in so many places, so she has a wealth of experience, as well as the money you gave her."

"Excellent news. I felt so bad for what happened to her with the bikers. I'm pleased it has all worked out for her in the end. Please say hello to her when you go home."

Max shook his head and scratched his nose. "I don't think she would want to hear that. Your name isn't particularly well thought of by her."

"She blames me for what happened with the bikers because I gave her that money?"

"No. She knows you gave her the money with good intentions. You didn't arrange for the bikers to kidnap her. But she is annoyed with you over the way that you met. She learnt about your powers of seduction, the chemical hormones that you can release as a Dragan or half Dragan. She feels that she was used."

"Ah. I did use my powers on her. It has occurred to me since that I seduced her by using my powers. I wasn't sure how much effect I had on her until I met up with Scarlett again and saw the reaction she had to me. I can only apologise for what happened, but on the night, she seemed just as eager as I was."

"You can't be sure that she was completely willing, as your powers cause overwhelming emotions. I know you didn't force her into that room, but your powers were an unfair advantage and something she wouldn't have been aware of. She would have thought her feelings were real and meant something special. You need to learn to control yourself."

"Yes. You're not the first person to say that to me. Thorn said the same. But then again, it was her idea to practice on Amber in the first place. I'm not sure what to think anymore. Part of me feels guilty for what I have done, and the other part couldn't care less. When I first became V, after Barry's death, I felt no emotions whatsoever. I just felt cold and numb. All I wanted was to become a vampire and take revenge. But after a while, the desire went and my actual emotions returned. Meeting Amber helped me regain some of my humanity. Seeing Scarlett and my dad helped it all return. But seeing him shot, and my kidnapping and torturing has left its toll. As time goes on, I seem to care less about how I have hurt other people. Rip and Thorn don't care about how they hurt people. Cyrus definitely doesn't care about who he hurts."

Max nodded and sat up straight in his seat. "It's not just the things you have been through, you are becoming a Dragan, and therefore, your humanity will drain away. As a Dragan, you will need to feed, and I doubt you will survive for long if you worry about the people you may hurt or trick. You will be driven by instincts and humans won't seem the same to you once you have fully transformed. You may lose your sympathy for them."

"So what can I do? I have to become a Dragan to survive and to be with Thorn. How can I try to keep my humanity intact?" I asked.

Max stared up at the ceiling and took a deep breath. "Maybe you can't. Maybe you have to accept you will become different. After a hundred years of living as a Dragan, you won't care about humans anymore. Seducing them against their will is the least bad thing you could do. It is easier and quicker just to kill them outright."

"But Thorn cares about humans still."

"What makes you think Thorn cares about what happens to humans?"

"She is with me. I am human. In the past, when I wanted to kill Barry's sisters and mother, Thorn stopped me."

"Maybe this is more to do with Sisterhood than humans. But I take your point. Maybe it is possible to keep some of your humanity intact."

"Plus, I've seen that Thorn could have killed people before but chose just to feed on them instead. She even takes away any painful memories and leaves them with something happy to remember."

"That is good to hear. Maybe you can ask her how she does it."

"I will. She has a moral code about who she kills and who she doesn't. I thought it was weird and twisted, but now it's making some sense. She has rules of engagement."

"Maybe, for now, your answer is simply to follow those same rules. Or make your own rules to ensure you have empathy and feelings for other people."

"I will try it."

We sat in silence for a few moments and continued drinking our coffee. I tried to think of something else to chat about, but I didn't want to start unnecessary small talk. Somehow it felt beneath us to discuss the weather.

Max broke the silence after he finished his coffee and took the cup to the sink. He turned back around and leaned against the kitchen side. "How about we get in a little practice before tonight? A bit of man against man. A rematch from our first encounter in the diner. Let me see how much you have learnt."

"Okay. We should go out into the woods and get a bit of space. But let's not go one hundred percent. You will heal tonight when you change, but it may take me a little longer, and I need to be at my best if I am to practice tonight."

"You have a deal."

We headed out of the kitchen through the hallway and passed the other bedrooms with sleeping Dragans and out the front door.

The forest looked different during the day, with the sun streaming through the tall pine trees' branches. I had noticed last night the area was devoid of wildlife. There were no animals in the local vicinity. I guessed they all sensed the Dragans and Werewolf.

The open forest floor outside the lodge was hard-baked in the summer's sun. We walked across the mud baked floor into the wooded area where the ground was covered in pine needles and twigs.

Max crunched the twigs underfoot. He walked further into the forest until we came across a small circular clearing of brown ground. He turned around to face me and took a couple of steps back.

"Is this enough space for you?" he asked.

"This will be fine."

"Let's start. Show me what Rip has taught you."

I nodded to acknowledge, and I observed Max, expecting him to launch into a furious attack. Instead, he paced around me, and I kept my guard up as he stalked about. As I waited for him to attack, I felt nervous. I let that feeling build my magic. I let it store up to make myself stronger. Rip had taught me werewolves attacked head-to-head, so I expected Max would be the same even in his human form, just as he had attacked me at the diner. Therefore, I expected a quick and aggressive full frontal strike at any moment.

But Max took his time circling and watching me. He would turn back in the opposite direction and stop and then spin back again like an agitated wild animal.

I decided to use my speed by letting my magic flood to my legs and arms. As Max walked back and forth, I waited for him to turn on the spot, and then I let the magic explode and darted across the ground.

I flashed a few punches past his slow guard and tapped him on the chin. He lashed out to defend himself as I danced to the side. I kicked him from the side as he turned towards me and caught him in the ribs. He put his arm down to cover and stepped back. I jumped back to gain some space and skipped around the edges of the clearing, making him watch me.

Max nodded and grinned. "He's an excellent teacher. You are much faster than the last time we met. And you took me by surprise. I thought I could wait you out and make you nervous."

"Thank you. Rip taught me to control my Dragan power, even though I am not fully transformed."

"However, it may be a different story tonight when I change into a werewolf."

"Maybe. I hope Rip has taught me how to fight a werewolf as well."

"You know what your biggest advantage over a werewolf is?"

"My agility. My clear thinking. My Dragan power."

"All good strengths. However, you may find a more mature werewolf, like Giles's mentor, will be much clearer of thought. He will know his weaknesses as he knows your strengths. He would be wary and unlikely to give you the chance to use your agility against him. And he would be of clear mind and will have learnt to control his werewolf aggression. As you saw in the warehouse fight, Norris can control his transformation and doesn't have to become a full werewolf. He can fight standing up and control his attacks. Only an experienced werewolf can do this. Giles' hasn't mastered this skill yet and must fight in the full wolf form. But there is one other advantage the Dragans have over werewolves."

I looked at Max for inspiration but couldn't think of anything. I wracked my brain through all the stuff that Rip had taught me. But I had said everything I could remember. "Is there something I'm missing?"

Max simply held his hands up in the air and opened them and closed them. Then he reached down to the floor, picked up a stone and threw it at me.

I dodged out of the way of the stone and stared at him. I couldn't understand what he was trying to tell me. Max leaned down to the floor again, picked up another couple of stones and threw them at me. I dodged out of the way and picked up a rock and threw it back. "Will you stop throwing stones and just tell me the answer?"

Max laughed. "That is the answer. Can werewolves throw stones?"

"Of course they can't. But are you saying I can beat a werewolf by throwing stones at it?"

"No. But the reason why werewolves can't throw stones is that they have no hands. Human hands can manipulate objects. Hands and arms can carry things. They can control things. You can throw stones. Or you could wield a sword or fire a gun. A werewolf cannot hold a sword or fire a gun unless they are in mostly human form. Your hands are your biggest advantage."

"Are you saying I should just shoot Giles in werewolf form? I assume a silver bullet will do the job."

"Why not? I don't think the bullet has to be silver. It would probably help, but enough bullets would kill any creature. Especially if they were in the head. Likewise, a sword would also kill a werewolf if it punctured its heart or severed its head. Why would you not use weapons?"

"Thorn doesn't like guns. I assume it would be dishonourable to use weapons."

"Thorn doesn't need guns. Therefore, a gun would only slow her down. She is quicker and more powerful in the majority of battles without a firearm. But she uses a sword, as you have seen when fighting the Turned. Why limit yourself to just your Dragan's claws and fangs? There is no honour in being dead."

"So I should get a gun in case I have to fight Giles."

"I am saying to use whatever weapons you can find. Whether it be a sword or a gun or a club. The objective is to win and stay alive. No one is scoring you for honourable fighting."

"I get it. It just hadn't occurred to me that I could use a weapon. I spent so much time with Thorn telling me not to use guns once I was a Dragan. I thought I couldn't use weapons at all. But you are right, even Thorn uses swords and once she shot me with that gun."

"Yes. She shot you with the gun containing the formula. If needed, Thorn would use any weapon."

"Thanks, Max," I said.

"No problem. Get yourself a weapon. Now I would like to rest before my transformation tonight. I suggest you get some sleep as well before we embark on your proper training and you have to face me on the full moon."

Chapter Seventeen

After sparring with Max, I went back to my room and lay down beside Thorn, who had cocooned herself in the duvet. I had to wait another four hours until Thorn would awake and we could spend some time together. Afterwards, I would have to face Max as a werewolf. It would only be sparring again, but I was scared. Max would be at the height of his powers, and I was unsure if I could control my fear enough to battle against him.

Thorn loosened off her grip on the sheets, and I slid in beside her. I really wished she was awake so we could talk, but I would have to wait for a few more hours. I turned around to face the opposite direction and then felt her hand glide across my stomach and hug me. Her lips kissed the back of my neck. "Get some sleep," she said. I smiled to myself, put my hand on top of hers and closed my eyes.

I woke again a few hours later with Thorn gazing into my eyes. She smiled and put her hand on my cheek.

"It's night-time and Max will change soon. And I need to work out a strategy to fight the first generation Turned and put up with that insufferable fool, Cyrus. We will both be busy tonight. But we have a bit of time now. So I suggest we use it wisely," she said, and kissed my lips.

I returned the kiss and moved my hands to her waist. She wrapped her arms around my back and pulled me closer as our kissing intensified. She pushed me down onto the mattress and then sat on top of me, flinging the duvet off. The supernatural breeze blew her hair and a mist circled around the room. She grinned, and the redness in her eyes flickered. I reached up, grabbed her and pulled her down towards me. Our lips kissed. We carried on where we had finished off the night before until we were both in ecstasy.

Afterwards, I lay in the bed, catching my breath as Thorn got up and got dressed. She pulled on a pair of black leggings, knee-length boots and a black Lycra top. She tied her hair up into a knot. "Come on, up you get. We have things to do. But hopefully will be back together again before dawn," she said and walked out of the room.

I rolled out of bed and pulled on the clothes I had worn earlier: dark blue jeans, thick army boots, a T-shirt and a thick green fleece with a hood. I strolled out of the room and back down to the kitchen. Sitting around the table and drinking coffee were Cyrus, Cassius and Max. Thorn was pouring herself a drink and handed me one as I walked in.

I grabbed the warm cup in my hands and took a sip. Thorn leaned against the kitchen side, and I stood next to her. Cyrus glared at us, and Cassius raised his eyebrows at Max. Down the hallway, another door opened.

"Good night, everyone," Rip said and made his way to the kitchen side. Thorn put the coffee in front of him, but he uncorked a bottle of red wine he had left on the side and poured a glass.

"It's a bit early for wine, isn't it?" Cassius said.

"It's never too early for wine," Rip replied. "Anyway, it does me no harm."

"So then why drink it if you get nothing from it?" Cassius asked.

"Why do you drink that coffee?"

Cassius shrugged. "It's warm and tastes nice. I get a little kick from it but it wears off."

Rip raised his glass to them and took a big gulp. "Maybe you aren't doing it right?" Rip replied and winked at me.

I knew full well he meant using his Dragan power to let the wine take effect. Cassius could use his ability to allow the coffee to give him a bigger kick. They hadn't worked out the full secrets of the Dragan power. Rip had taught me how to do it, but the time wasn't right to tell the rest of them.

Cassius shook his head. "You have become very strange, Rip. The coffee or wine has no effect on us really. But I like its taste, and I like to drink it hot."

"And I like my red wine at room temperature. I also like a cigarette, so I will go outside," Rip said and fetched a packet of cigarettes out of his pocket and walked out of the room

"He has changed," Thorn said.

"How has he changed?" I asked.

"He used to be extremely serious about his training. It was all he ever thought about. And it's all he ever did were training and studying martial arts."

I laughed and gulped down my coffee. "He hasn't changed as much as you think. I must go outside and get some last minute tips before my practice match tonight."

I drank down the rest of my coffee, put the cup on the side and went outside to join Rip. I found him stood by the car with the wine glass on the bonnet and a cigarette in his hand. He offered me a cigarette, but I waved it away.

"It would be good practice for you," he said.

"Maybe, but I just don't like the taste of it."

"Suit yourself."

"When are you going to tell them about your discovery that the Dragan magic is not just inside of us but something we can channel? That it is almost limitless."

"When the time is right. I don't trust Cyrus. I would not want him to learn this technique, as I fear he would use it against us."

I nodded in agreement. Cyrus's comments last night suggested there was an ulterior motive at hand. He wasn't really interested in defeating the Turned but only interested in gaining back his rightful position.

Max came out of the cabin and walked off into the woods, staring up into the starry night sky and the rising full moon. He did not stop to talk to us; he merely waved his hand for us to follow. Rip dunked his cigarette out into his wine, and we walked after Max. As we walked, Rip placed his hand on my shoulder.

"Remember everything we practised. Tonight, you will see a fully powered werewolf. Max is very experienced and very powerful, so it's unlikely that Giles could match this level of power. Battling against Max will be great training for you."

We followed Max through the tall pine trees, and the moonlight cast a dim light to find our way. Max stomped on ahead, crunching the earth and branches under his feet. We reached the same clearing that we had sparred in earlier in the day. Max stopped and looked up at the full moon shining into our combat circle. Rip took a few steps backwards to the edge of the clearing.

Max's face began to contort and it looked like he was in pain. He was clenching his teeth and balling his hands into fists. His body tensed up, and he wrapped his arms around himself, with the muscles bulging out of his biceps. He pulled off his t-shirt and kicked off his trousers and boots.

The bristles on his beard stood on end, as did his eyebrows and hair. His skin turned red as his muscles tensed under the strain. Eventually, he let it explode out, releasing his arms, spreading them wide and throwing his head up into the air to release a bloodcurdling scream.

Fur erupted all over his body, and his jaw extended out, his teeth growing and sharpening. As his back legs buckled, he threw his body forward onto his hands. His hairy arms expanded and hands transformed into paws, with enormous claws jutting through. His back legs lengthened and pushed out to form the wolf's hind legs.

His ears changed to those of a wolf and pushed up to the top of his head. The spine on his back pushed out a hairy tail. As every bone-crunching change occurred, he screamed out until it became a howl.

He had fully transformed into a werewolf with dark hair and gleaming blood red eyes. He growled at me and stalked around to the side.

I felt frozen to the spot, just as I had done with Giles. The fear coursed through my body, and I relived the moment when Giles bit and clawed into my flesh. My instinct was to run away, but I knew the wolf could catch me in a straight line, and that wasn't the point of the exercise.

Max stalked around, and I mirrored him, keeping the distance between us.

"Remember what I taught you. Use your emotions to fuel your power. Whatever you are feeling now is good enough to unlock the doors to your magic."

I didn't need to worry about trying to find an intense emotion. The fear was intense, even though I knew Max would not hurt me too much. I pictured my sphere of purple magic inside, and I let my intense fear pour into it. My sphere of light expanded at an ever-increasing rate towards the edges of my imagination. I would have to use it as soon as he attacked.

Max stalked me, growling all the time. I scooped down to the floor, picked up a stone and then threw it at Max's head. He ducked out of the way. I followed up with another couple, the final one hitting his head. He coiled back and sprang at me, jaws wide open and claws slashing forwards. I dived to the side and rolled back onto my feet. Max landed on the floor, skidded around and set back after me. I darted off through the trees, zigzagging around them as Max chased. I grabbed hold of a tree trunk to whip around 180 degrees to darted back in the opposite direction. Max skidded to a halt, twisting around to chase after me again.

I ran back into the clearing and turned to face him with a massive tree to my back. Max bounded into the clearing and charged at me. I knelt down and waited for his pounce, letting my magic build up and preparing to redirect it to my legs.

He jumped the final couple yards, and I sprung up into the tree, grabbed the branches and twisted myself up into safety. Max hit the tree head-on, shaking it violently. I held onto the tree as it rocked back and forth. Max whimpered from the pain and staggered sideways, then walked around in a circle, shaking his head until he was facing the tree once more. He stared up at me and then barked and growled.

I guessed it must have hurt hitting the tree. But I was up in its branches and safe. I would just wait in the tree to see what he would do next. He couldn't climb up without turning back to being part human, at least.

Max scraped the floor with his paws as if he was building up to something. He sat back on his haunches and then ran at the tree and jumped, hitting it full on with his paws. The tree shook again, but I held on. But then Max ran around the clearing and jumped back at the tree. This time, I heard a crack and the tree tilted to one side. My extra weight sent it tumbling over as I tried to clamber further up. I leapt to safety at the last second and hit the ground.

Before I could get fully up, Max barged me to the floor, sending me bouncing along the ground into the base of another tree. I shook my head and cleaned the dirt off my face. A giant werewolf's face loomed in front with jaws wide open. I shuddered backwards and put my hands up to my face to protect myself.

Max barked at me several times. I took my hands away from my face. He leapt forward and licked my face, covering it in werewolf's saliva.

I rubbed my face on the sleeve of my shirt, and Max nuzzled my head with his nose. He then turned and ran off through the forest. Rip walked over and held out a hand. I took it and he pulled me up.

"Are we done? Where is he off to?" I asked Rip.

"Your training for tonight is complete. You did well in making him hit the tree. You definitely had him dazed and confused. I think you should have followed up on the attack at that point."

"I wasn't sure how far to take it. I certainly wasn't expecting him to knock the entire tree over."

"Max is strong. Not sure Giles could have done the same thing. At least you know it's always a possibility. You did well; no one was expecting you to win. It was to get used to fighting a werewolf. After practising against Max at a full moon, you know what to expect and can be prepared when you face Giles again."

"Where has Max gone now?" I asked, staring out into the darkness, hoping to see him.

"He is using the advantage of the full moon to scout out a first-generation Turned that lives in this area. His senses will be enhanced, and he can cover a lot of distance. Hopefully, he will find them, and then tomorrow night we can attack. Let's get back to the cabin. Thorn, Cassius and Cyrus should be working out potential battle plans if we locate the first generation Turned."

We walked back through the forest towards the cabin. The lights were on and guided us in. We walked up the stairs through the front porch and heard voices coming from the kitchen and smelt fresh coffee. I stopped off in the bathroom and washed my face to clean off the werewolf spit, and then went and joined the rest of them in the kitchen area.

They stood around the kitchen table with a map on it. Rip was busy pouring himself another glass of red wine while the others stared at each other and then at me as I walked in.

"How did you get on?" Thorn asked.

"I evaded him and then got him to bash into a tree. He was definitely dazed for a while, but I didn't think to follow up. But Max won in the end. I survived but got a face full of werewolf's slobber."

Thorn smiled and uncrossed her arm. "He was bound to win. He's a werewolf and you are not fully transformed yet. There was no real winning or losing tonight. It's just practice."

"Thank you. Rip, can you pour me a glass of wine as well?" I said and headed over to Rip, who offered me the glass he had already poured.

Thorn pointed at the map. "We think they are based here in an old hostel. If it is a first-gen Turned, they will have second and third-gen Turned guarding them. It will be a hard battle in a confined space."

"They will sense us and leave before we can get into position," Cassius replied.

"There aren't enough of us to close in a perimeter line. I suggest one person goes in and forces them out. The others pick them up as they run," Cyrus said.

I went over to look at the map. "Or I could draw them out. If I went near, they might detect me as just a human or come after me. It would draw them out of their hideouts and get them to attack me. If I had the formula, I could transform and keep them busy for the rest of you to swoop in."

"But they would detect us if we were nearby. Nice try, boy, but let's leave this one to the adults," Cyrus said and gave me a disgusted look and returned to pointing at the map.

Thorn glared at him and Cassius raised his eyebrows. Rip walked around to the side of me and took a sip of his red wine. I stared at Cyrus for a moment and drank down my wine in one go and then slammed the empty glass on the table.

"And that is why you don't come with me. We have this stuff called technology. I press a button on my phone or my GPS receiver watch, and it signals you to my exact point. I know these guys can run pretty fast. Can you keep up with them, Cyrus? I should imagine you can. You have been running for long enough."

Cyrus grabbed the table and flung it over. "How dare you speak to me like that, boy? Who on earth do you think you are?"

"My name is V, for vengeance. And I am the King of the Dragans."

Thorn went to put her hands between us, but Cyrus pushed them out of the way. "You're not my King. Thorn promised herself to me as part of the agreement for my help. I am the rightful King. You have just been a sideshow. A means of keeping the biotech away from the Turned. But you should know your place and shut up."

I kicked the table back across the room, but Cyrus stopped it with his foot. "You are not the King and will never be the King. Thorn did not promise herself to you. All of this is your fault. You started the Dragan War. You created the first Turned army. You don't deserve to be King or even good enough to lick our boots," I yelled back.

Thorn pushed me back through the kitchen door and then twisted around to face Cyrus. "I never promised you anything, Cyrus. We had our time together hundreds of years ago and it didn't work. We can share power now for what it's worth, but that does not mean you are my King. I decide who I am with."

"Just like you was with Rip all those years ago while we were supposed to be trying for a child."

"Maybe if you'd spent more time with me instead of the Twins, then something might have happened. You talk of my affairs; you were no innocent. You groomed my girls under my own roof and then took them from me and turned them against me. Why can't you understand that you were only King through our Union? It didn't mean you were in charge of me."

"You mean you prefer this half Dragan to a full blood like me?"

"It means I have decided to be with V. It is my choice. We can share power by each taking a different continent to rule. There is plenty of land up for grabs. And very few of us to oppose one another. Why does this even need to be an argument?"

"Fine. Let's forget I even mentioned it," Cyrus said and pulled the table back up and put the map back on it.

Thorn walked back into the room and went to the bottle of wine for a drink. I stood in the corridor and looked back at Cyrus, who grinned at me, then he flung the table to the side, blocking in Thorn and Rip, and then kicked Cassius in the groin and darted towards me. I spun away to run, but he was too fast and grabbed me around the neck and dragged me down the hallway. He kicked the door off its hinges and flung me down the stairs. He jumped down, grabbed my shirt and pulled me through the dirt. As he dragged me along, he extended a claw and placed it against my neck.

"Stop fighting, little child. We will settle this like men even if you aren't one."

Thorn, Rip and Cassius burst through the lodge doorway and ran after us.

"Leave him alone. I said to drop him now," Thorn shouted.

Cyrus pulled me up straight and pushed his claw against my neck, allowing a bit of blood to trickle out. "We will fight for you and for the rightful position of King. Now I want you to all stand well back. If he fights well, I will let him live at least. He can continue to live as my servant. If he wants to be King of the Dragans, then he needs to fight like the King of the Dragans."

"You harm him, and I will rip you to pieces," Thorn yelled, and her eyes misted blood red and claws appeared at the end of her fingers.

"I said get back, further back, so you can't attack without me killing him first," Cyrus shouted back.

Rip, Cassius and Thorn all stepped away, and Cyrus kept ushering them backwards. He flung me to the floor. "Now get up and fight me, King of the Dragans."

I stood up and clenched my fists, and I saw Thorn and the others were far enough away that they could never get him in time. Maybe I could run towards them. I could probably move faster than Cyrus expected. But he was an experienced Dragan. I couldn't be sure I could get away in time.

"It is a tradition for the King of the Dragans to defend themselves. Or to put down any challengers. The first King, Thorn's father, had to battle many opponents. I am simply invoking the right to challenge for the position of King of the Dragans. Thorn, this is my right as another Dragan."

Thorn shouted back from a distance. "He's not a Dragan at the moment as not completely transformed. You should wait for him to finish his transformations and the war to be finished. We can settle all of this then."

Cyrus laughed and then spat at her. "Why should I wait when it is so easy to beat him now? Anyway, you heard him earlier. He pronounced himself as King of the Dragans, even in his human form. He is willing to use that title in his human form, then he should be prepared to defend his title in his human form."

Cyrus held up his fists and faked a punch to my head. I jolted back with my arms up to protect myself, and he laughed at me again. He circled around and dived in with a couple of fake attacks, making me jump back and flail my arms to protect myself. He laughed again and switched directions. He was trying to humiliate me before beating me, so I would never forget what happened and everyone else would always see me as being weak. I had to put on a good show, at least.

I focused on my fear and anger. The intense emotions opened the pathways to the external magic, and it streamed in and engorged my power. I wish I had the vampire formula to bolster my strength. Thorn was carrying one with her, but Cyrus would never let me take it.

Cyrus jumped in again and faked a punch. This time I didn't move, but he quickly followed up with a real blow to my head, and he spun around with a kick to my side, which sent me crashing to the ground.

He jumped into the air, leading down with a kick to my head. I twisted back to my feet and lashed out with a front kick to his side, knocking him off his flight path and into a heap on the floor. Thorn cheered and Rip clapped. Cyrus jumped back up, his eyes blood red and fangs jutting out, and he mopped the dirt off his face.

"You will pay for that."

"You were already going to make me pay."

Cyrus sneered back at me. "You're right. This is going to hurt quite a lot. I can't understand how Cassius and Rip could consider you as their King. I don't care what Thorn says, she's just a deluded psycho."

"You should hear what they say about you!"

"Very funny. I can guess what they say about me. But I don't care. Just remember, I am only here to regain my power and position. I could care less about the Turned and their motives. They will never be strong enough to completely overthrow the humans."

"You don't understand. They are working with the humans and will try to take over everywhere. Eventually, there will be nowhere left for you to run. If you want to survive, we need to stop them now."

"I understand fully. But we will stop them with me at the head of our little army. I'm not playing second fiddle to some wannabe."

Cyrus lunged at me again and hit me on the chin. I was too busy thinking about what to say next. I tripped over backwards onto the pine needle covered ground. Cyrus walked around me, occasionally kicking the dirt at me as if I was something disgusting to cover up.

He waited until I was back on my feet and had my fists in the guard position, and then he attacked again, pushed my guard out of the way and elbowed me across the nose.

I crashed to the ground once again and put my hand up to my nose. I pulled back my blood covered hands. To stem the flow, I focused my magic on it. While I was checking my nose, he stepped in again and kicked me twice in the ribs. I curled up into a ball, and he kicked me twice on my back and then kicked dirt into my face.

He shouted to Thorn. "This weak little boy does not deserve to be your king."

I spun around on the floor and kicked him through the back of his knees. He upended into the air and landed on his back. The impact of the fall knocked his breath out of him. I rolled on top and punched him in the face, fist after fist. His nose was bloodied and my knuckles stung against his face. He bucked his body up and flung me off, and then staggered to his feet, wiping the blood off his face.

His face contorted and hair stood up as his red eyes darkened and fangs sharpened.

"You little git. This ends now. Say goodbye to Thorn," Cyrus said and then turned to where Thorn was standing. "Say goodbye to your little boy King. He dies now."

Thorn dashed across the forest towards us, and Cyrus charged at me. I just needed to survive another attack so Thorn could be here in time to save me. But I suspected Cyrus was going straight for the killing blow. I focused my power to dart to the side and avoid his attack when a black shape charged through the forest from the other side. It hit Cyrus full on and knocked him into a tree.

The shape barked and growled at Cyrus and stood in between him and me. I could see from Cyrus's face that he would not move. Even he dare not take on a werewolf on a full moon. Max had returned just in time.

Within moments, Thorn, Cassius and Rip had run down to join us. Thorn loomed over Cyrus. "This will not end well for you. If you will not join us properly, then you are against us and I don't have time to fight another enemy."

"Don't be rash, Thorn. You need everyone on your side. But we also need proper leadership," Cyrus said.

As they were talking, Max transformed back into a human. The fur on his body receded, and his face returned to normal, but he didn't revert all the way before speaking, his voice growling at us. "Shut up and listen. They are coming for us. It's a trap. We have to run."

Chapter Eighteen

"Who's coming?" Rip asked.

"Who else. The Turned, the Hunters and two werewolves. They know we're here, and they're coming in large numbers. We can't possibly win."

"Everyone head back to the cabin. We have weapons in the wood store. We have some swords and a couple of guns," Thorn said.

We sprinted back. Cyrus jumped up and followed us. Now didn't seem the time to settle internal disputes. First, we had to survive the attacking Turned and Hunter Army. Max also said there were two werewolves with them. It had to be Giles and Norris.

We reached the cabin and Thorn ran to the firewood storehouse and ripped off the door. Cassius and Rip ran behind and grabbed the swords as she passed them out. Rip hesitated for a moment as Cyrus outstretched his hand. He glared at him for a moment before reluctantly slapping the hilt of the sword into his hand. "We will settle this later. Now the survival of the Dragans is more important," Rip said.

"Whatever," Cyrus said and swung around to prepare for the Turned.

I waited for a sword to be placed into my hands, but Thorn came out, gave me a gun and then handed me a needle box. I wedged the gun in the back of my jeans and put the needle box in my front pocket.

"It's you they are after. You must get far away from us. We will do our best to distract them for as long as possible. If they catch up with you, then use the needle and take the formula. Once you transform into a Dragan, you might as well come back and help us, but only take it if absolutely necessary. I would prefer to save these needles for when we attack them."

"I'm not leaving you. We fight side-by-side," I said.

"No," Thorn screamed back at me and shoved me away. "Without you, we have no chance of winning this war. If they get you, they will perform more experiments looking for the secrets of the DNA transformation. If they find these secrets, then the war is lost and you will be dead. You must go," Thorn shouted and then headed back to where the army was advancing. Max led the way and had transformed back into a full werewolf.

"V, please do as Thorn asks. We will do our best to hold them off. I suspect the two werewolves are hunting you. Be prepared to fight them," Rip said and slapped me on my arm and then chased after Thorn.

"Take care, V. You did well in your fight against Cyrus. I believe in you. Now run as fast as you can," Cassius said, and headed into battle.

In the distance, a wide fan of the Turned army sprinted through the trees. They were carrying swords and guns. At the back of the Turned, I could just make out the figures of two werewolves sniffing the air. I wanted to join the fight. I could take the needle and then run headlong into battle. But Thorn had asked me to run. I would do as I was told for once. I suspected I would end up facing Giles and Norris, which meant at least I was taking them away from Thorn, Rip and Cassius.

I darted through the trees away from the crackling gunfire, clashing of swords against swords, and the cries of the first Turned been slaughtered.

I headed up the hills, hoping the high ground may give me a defensive advantage. Down below, Thorn was slashing away, dispatching two Turned to ash. Max was bounding forward, tearing a Turned in half and then slashing another one to pieces. Rip was moving with precision and controlled speed. He finally got the chance to use his abilities' full power, using the techniques he had learned. Cassius waded in, punching one Turned down, cutting through another at the same time. But there was no Cyrus. I guessed he had already escaped.

My team were fighting well, littering the forest in the ash of vampires, but many more awaited their chance to fight. There was no way they could continue forever. They would have to break and run eventually or be destroyed. Meanwhile, Norris and Giles were moving through the Turned, ready to fight.

I put my head down and ran up the hill, knowing full well the wind was blowing down the mountain, sending my scent down to them. I kept turning back as I climbed, watching to see if they took the bait and left my friends alone.

Eventually, one of the wolf's noses lifted into the air as it caught the scent. It barked at the other wolf and ran up the hill towards me. The plan had worked, but now I would have to fight them both.

I dashed off in the opposite direction along the hill, hoping to get some distance from the main battle. Once they caught my scent, they could follow it no matter where I went. As I ran, I peered around and saw the wolves bounding up the hill, following the invisible trail I left behind.

Rip and Max were right. The werewolves' top speed was much faster than mine, and it didn't take long for them to hunt me down. I had to pick a place to make a stand.

I pulled the gun out of the back of my trousers and hid behind a tree and caught my breath. The wolves raced in as I glanced around the side of the trunk. I jumped out and fired a couple of shots at the biggest wolf, Norris. He quickly dived to the side, the bullets blowing up the leaves as they impacted the earth.

Giles skidded to a halt and then ran around the back of a tree. I had to face him. The gunshots bought me some time. I placed the gun in the back of my jeans, pulled out the needle from the box and stabbed it into my neck. I sunk the plunger in and felt the vampire formula burning into my body.

My veins burned red as the formula hitched a ride within my blood stream. The drug seeped inward, infecting every part of my body. My brains pressed against the side of my skull, and my vision blurred around the edges. My bones twisted into new shapes and sizes. The formula soaked into my muscles and sparked the fibres to strengthen. My forearms and biceps bulged out and chest muscles shuddered. The formula performed a full circuit and collided into my heart, and as per usual, my heartbeat quickened until it could take no more. I crashed to the floor with my hands out in front, and my heart ceased. I toppled over onto my back and seconds of blankness swept over me. Every time I had to die to complete the full transformation; every time the gateway opened to the bright light and familiar voices.

I jolted back to life, my senses on fire, and I heard the paws of the wolf padding around the trees, growling and then sniffing the air. I jumped to my feet and pulled the gun out the back of my jeans and aimed. In wolf form, Giles barked at me and snarled, with saliva dripping from his jaws and the fur on his back rising up.

"Good to see you, old friend," I said and fired the gun.

I had to protect myself, even though he had been my friend. He was already darting out of the way as I fired. He twisted away, and from the other side, Norris bounded up and knocked me over, spilling the gun from my hand. The wolf picked up the firearm in its jaws and ran off with it.

I jumped back onto my feet, and Giles circled around me.

He pushed himself onto his hind legs, and the transformation retreated enough to speak in a deep, growling voice. "No more running. You face me now and answer for your betrayal."

"I told you I was sorry. I should never have walked away that day at the school gates. I went to get help, the caretaker and your mum. It was us that stopped you from being taken by the gang."

"I understand that. You did the right thing. But I'm talking about your betrayal afterwards. You ignored me and allowed the gang to harass me until I couldn't carry on. You threw me onto the fire just to protect yourself."

"My dad told me to do that. He said there was no point in both of us getting into trouble. But you're right, I should have ignored him. It was the wrong thing to do. There is no need for us to fight. You should be on my side, not his," I said and looked over to Norris, who was partly transformed back into a human.

Norris growled at me. "Ignore him, Giles. I'm the one who protected you after what happened. I am the one who gave you this power to fight back. He never came to look for you after what happened. Never came to look for you with his new vampire powers. Too busy enjoying his life with that woman. He cares nothing for you. Kill him."

"You can't hide from me forever, Jon. You can't beat me tonight on a full moon. It is you that is on the wrong side. The Dragans are evil. They created the Turned to fuel their wars. They were born from black magic."

"Did they tell you that they also created werewolves? That means you are born from the same evil. These people only chose you to get at me. They are not your friends."

"Maybe, but they have given me power and a chance to protect myself and my family. All I need to do is kill you. And I will do so with pleasure. Now fight," he shouted and dropped back to all fours. His face changed back to that of a wolf and arms reverted to front legs. The fur on his body grew back, covering him in a thick grey coat. To the side, Norris stayed in his semi-human form, ready to ensure I couldn't run from the fight.

Giles barked to get my attention. He sprinted and dived at me with claws out and jaws snapping at my face. I bolted to the side in time to miss the front claws, but his back legs kicked out and cut across my forearm, ripping through my coat.

He had taken me by surprise and was preparing another full-frontal attack, so I circled around to stop it. I tried to remember my training with Rip and Max. I remembered the purple sphere of magic that I had used to great effect before. My transformation making it easy to connect into, and I felt it glowing within me.

Giles leapt at me again. I released the magic into my limbs and spun out of the way, scooped down and pulled up a handful of loose dirt. Giles launched at me again, and I twisted back to face him. I threw the dirt in his face, but he moved with such speed that he dived through it. His claws ripped my arms again, cutting me, blood pouring out. I could not stop it because of the wolf's DNA embedded within. I focused my magic on healing the wound, preventing the blood loss as much as possible.

I couldn't just play defence against him. I had to hit back with my own weapons if I was going to stop him. He circled around a few more times, and I visualised my own moves on the next attack. He dived for my legs, trying to bite my shins and take me off my feet. I somersaulted over his snapping jaws. The claws on my hands flicked out and scraped down his back. I landed and blood lined his grey fur.

I spun back around, claws at the ready. Giles yelled with pain, twisted around and charged again. He jumped up and dived for my throat. This time I dropped, holding my claws up as Giles leapt over me, and they ripped into his stomach. He hit the forest floor, screaming in pain, the blood dripping onto the leaves.

He rolled around on his back and then licked at his stomach. Then stopped and eyed me, his eyes burning red, snarling through his blood coated jaws. He strained his head up and howled at the moon and then pulled himself back up.

He stalked around with his head low to the ground and his front paws coiled under him, ready to spring. He constantly growled and snarled, eyes burning red and fur stood on end. Blood was dripping onto the ground beneath him, and I knew the longer he bled, the greater my chances of winning, but also the greater the chances of him dying.

He charged back at me and then checked to the side, sending me diving in the wrong direction as he jumped back again and then hit me full on with his head against my chest. We crashed to the dirt and rolled over one another, his paws trying to scratch my face as my hands held him at arm's length. The blood from his stomach dripped onto me, and his jaws snapped at my face. I shook my head from side to side to avoid the sharp canines. He tried to pull in his rear claws to gut me.

I coiled my legs up to block his claws and kneed him in the gut a few times, into the wounds I'd already created. It was enough for him to loosen his attack, and I threw him off to the side. As he rolled in the dirt, I followed him.

I jumped on to his back and latched my arm around his throat, squeezed and tipped myself back. I held him steady in the choke hold, his claws and jaws unable to reach me. My claws on my free hand dug against his throat. His legs were kicking and scraping at the ground, trying to get a grip. His front claws thrashed about, and his head shook from side to side.

I placed my claws against his throat, knowing I only had to dig in, slicing him open to stop him once and for all.

"I'm truly sorry, Giles. But it appears one of us has to die."

"Stop," Norris shouted, and pointed the gun at me.

"Why? You are going to shoot me anyway. I might as well finish him off first."

"If I wanted to kill you, I wouldn't need a gun. Powers greater than me have decided only he can fight you. If he cannot win, then I am to let you go free without stopping you. For whatever reason, you may leave. If the choice were mine, I would transform back into my wolf form and rip your throat out. You may have beaten Giles, but he's an inexperienced pup. But I see you have received some training since our last encounter. Enough to beat a werewolf on a full moon. But you would have no such luck against me."

What he said was true. Having just sparred against Max, I knew how powerful a werewolf could be at the height of its powers. I decided it was worth the risk of trying to walk away. And I was relieved I wouldn't have to kill Giles. Though I was sure Giles would come for me again one day, once fully healed. At least it might buy some time to convince him we could still be friends.

"Okay, just throw that gun away. And I will get up and leave him. I take it you can help him survive."

Norris threw the gun to the floor. "They will find us soon enough, and they have medical supplies to counteract the Dragan poison from your bites and claws."

I lowered Giles to the floor. He was panting heavily, and blood was still trailing out of his stomach. He bled too much to turn around and attack. The wrestling in my arms had only contributed to further blood loss. I was concerned he would bleed to death on the floor and maybe I would do him a greater service to kill him outright. But it wasn't my decision. Norris had his instructions.

I stood up slowly, keeping my eyes on Norris the whole time. I glanced behind me and slowly backed away once I saw the escape route was clear.

"Just keep walking before I change my mind. But one day, you and I will get to find out who's the best."

"I think I have one or two friends who would want to meet you first. By the way, that other werewolf you fought before in the warehouse, his name is Max. I'm pretty sure he'd like a rematch first. Until then, take care of my best friend."

I turned away and sprinted through the woods, occasionally looking around to check that Norris wasn't coming for me.

Through the trees, I saw he had bent over Giles's wolf form. I slowed my pace, nursing my arm and listened out to what Norris was saying.

"You useless, pup. You're supposed to kill him. I'm not allowed to do it. You're such a disappointment."

I looked back at Norris and stepped around the trees to get a better view. Norris raised his fist up and then swung down. Giles whimpered. The fist rose up and then down again a couple more times and each time Giles yelped.

"I'm supposed to save you. Then train you back up again and go after him again. But if you can't even beat him on a full moon, then you will never beat him. You will never break his spirit."

A faint voice replied. "I'm sorry. I will try harder. He was much better than before. I didn't know what to do."

I jumped up a tree and shimmied up its branches to get a better look. Giles had transformed back into human form, with claw marks down his back and front.

Norris stood back up and then stamped down on Giles's stomach. Giles screamed and blood spurted out of his mouth.

"You useless, worthless pup. They will be here any minute to save you. But if you died now, that idiot Jon would be upset. That may be enough to break his spirit. Then I would get to fight him instead. I would rip his body to pieces and present it to his stupid werewolf friend." Norris punched Giles a few more times and stamped on him, and Giles cried out in pain.

I froze to the spot, transported back to the school's front gates, when I walked away and left Giles to the gang of bullies. This time it was different. This time I knew for sure that he would die, but I could also die if I faced Norris. If I hadn't walked away from those gates, we might never have arrived at this point.

In the opposite direction lay Thorn and friends. I could help them battle the Turned and escape. Plus, Giles had tried to kill me. No sane person would expect me to do anything else but walk away and leave him to the wrath of Norris.

Chapter Nineteen

Giles screamed again, and a flash of a fist pummelled into him. I jumped down from the tree and looked towards where Thorn and my friends were fighting and then back to the sounds of Giles being beaten to death. I had to rejoin the fight as soon as possible, but which fight?

Giles screamed again and the clash of swords echoed up the mountain. I twisted the clock face on my GPS watch and pressed the button to set off the tracker. I sucked in the air and visualised the purple magic exploding into my muscles. The extra power ignited within as I dashed through the trees, zigzagging past the trunks and leaping the rocks.

Norris raised his fist again, and I dropped my shoulder for impact. I hit him square on the chest and catapulted him into a tree trunk. The tree cracked and branches rained down on his dazed body.

I stood over Giles and offered my hand. "Never again will I leave you. You are my best friend."

His eyes widened and filled with tears. The years of hate rolled back to our school days. Through shallow, painful breaths, he reached up and placed his hand in mine. I hauled Giles to his feet and put my arm under his shoulder to hold him up. We walked down the mountainside.

"I gave you the chance to leave. I don't care what their orders are. We are going toe to toe right now," Norris shouted behind us.

I propped Giles against a tree, and he slumped down with his back against it, holding his hands over his cut stomach. I turned back and faced Norris, who had dusted himself off the ground. Norris was in a half transformation state, but his eyes were that of a full werewolf, blazing red. His hands were gripped into fists, his whole body shaking through the rage.

"I wasn't leaving my friend again. No matter the circumstances," I said, and I circled around to distract Norris away from Giles.

"Good. I'm glad I won't have to wait to kill you. Fighting me won't be like fighting that useless pup who can only transform into a wolf. I, however, can transform into a proper werewolf. I can control it so I can fight standing up and use my weapons under control. You've seen this before when I fought in the warehouse against Max. You've seen how powerful we are in this form and it is a full moon as well, which means my power is enhanced. I won't be diving at you recklessly, trying to slash you with my claws. I have control, I have power, and I have rage."

I remembered the battle at the warehouse and the fact that both he and Max didn't transform into wolf form like Giles had. They both transformed into a werewolf monster. I guess it took practice and experience to achieve that level of transformation. I also remember my battle at the warehouse.

"You remember the battle of the warehouse, then? You will also remember my transformation that night. I don't think even your werewolf form at a full moon will stop my dragon form. So I will give you this one chance to leave."

Norris laughed, which sounded more of a growl, and then he barked at the moon. "If you have this awesome power, why haven't you used it already? You could have used it the last time Giles fought you and this time."

"I like to save it for special occasions. And you're special."

Norris growled again. "I don't believe you. We know you have spies in our organisation, hence how you found our location here in the mountains. But we also have our own spies. And I know full well you can't do this transformation again. It was a one-off, a lucky shot. You can't bluff me. If you do transform into a dragon, then don't worry, I will run as fast as I can."

I tried to circle around, but he blocked off each move, mirroring my own, so I just ended up pacing left and right in front of him.

"Maybe or maybe not. But it will be too late to run by the time I turn into a dragon. But if you're willing to take the risk and face certain death, then who am I to argue?" I said, but it was a complete bluff. However, I hoped to buy some time so that Thorn and company may have tracked down my GPS signal.

"Well, let's find out," Norris said and paced towards me, his body transforming into the werewolf monster, rearing up on his hind legs, transforming back to huge jaws and his hands turning into claws.

I took a few steps back and lifted my arms into a fighting stance. I pictured my magic and sent it firing out across my body to generate supernatural power. He swiped his claws at my face, and I dodged out of the way. I blocked his back swinging arm with my two forearms and then slipped a punch across into his throat. But his jaw snapped and caught the edge of my hand, cutting it open across the knuckles.

I snatched my hand back and darted around the side to buy myself some time. He spun around and attacked from the other side, his giant clawed hands lashing out at me. I ducked and dodged, then punched him in the ribs. He buckled but kicked out and whacked me onto my backside into the pine needles, his claws having cut down my leg. I was bleeding again, and I had to use my magic to aid the healing rather than fuel my attacks.

I didn't know how to fight Norris in his werewolf monster state. I had only been trained to fight Giles in his standard wolf shape. I had to think of my own strategy. What would Rip say? What would Thorn do?

I tried to picture Rip in my mind, drinking his red wine while parting words of wisdom to me, but Norris was relentless in his attack and jumped forward again. I rolled under his outstretched claws and got behind him, but Norris swung around, catching me with a backhanded fist, which sent me sprawling across the forest floor, skidding through the dirt and fallen pine needles sticking into my flesh.

If I'd been quicker, I could have hit him in the back. Rip told me that my speed, agility and brains were my strengths. And that the werewolf's rage and slowness were its weaknesses. It seemed the same, whether it was a wolf or a werewolf monster.

"Is that all you've got? You are probably the worst werewolf I've ever met. No wonder your only friends are the Turned," I shouted.

"You know nothing about me. The Turned and the Hunters looked after me. No Dragan or werewolf ever came to help me when my transformations started. I was alone. The Turned and the Hunters offered something to belong to."

"They were just using you. Just as you have used Giles."

"No. I have not used Giles. I offered him a future. A chance to take revenge. However, is it any different to you teaming up with the Dragans? I've read your file, and you only hooked up with Thorn to take revenge and protect yourself. How is this any different to what Giles and I have done?"

"Thorn doesn't beat me if I fail."

"But she shot you in the warehouse. That could have killed you."

"It was the formula she shot me with. It was a calculated risk," I said.

However, I realised he had a point. Thorn had killed me before when we first met, only to save my life by injecting me with the formula. Giles was being used by them, but I could never be sure if Thorn wasn't just using me as well. Regardless of the arguments' truth, keeping him busy gave me a chance to think and hope that help was on its way.

As I was thinking of my next move, Norris rushed back in, swiping his claws at me. I fired off my magic, blocked his claws with both hands, twisted his arm over and sent him to the ground. He rolled through it and sprung out, snatching his hands out of my grip. He jumped back into the battle, swiping both claws at me at once. I fell to my knees to avoid the blow and caught both of his claws in each hand.

My hands gripped his giant claws, holding them above my head, my arms fully stretched out. Then his foot swung in and kicked me into the stomach. I stayed steady. Claws jutted out on his foot and slashed towards me. I pushed both his clawed hands away and rolled to the side, his foot missing by centimetres.

Each movement pulled my wounds further open, seeping blood. I was finding it difficult to concentrate on healing and fighting at the same time. Every time I attacked, I used my magic and my wounds opened up again. I was running out of time. This game of cat and mouse could only end badly for me. The mouse never wins. I decided to change the rules.

I summoned up all my magic in one enormous ball and blasted into an attack. I stepped inside his guard, flung in a volley of stabs with my clawed hands. The blood spurted out of his chest and drenched my face. He staggered back, and his hand grabbed my throat, picked me up, spun me around and pinned me against a tree. I pulled my legs up and kicked him in the face and slashed my claws down his arm, releasing his grip.

I jumped up, placing a foot on his leg, sprung up and over him so I was holding onto his back. I sank my fangs into the back of his neck and sucked his blood. The bite immediately sent him screaming in pain and sent him rolling back to the ground, slamming on top of me. The blood seeped into my mouth, and I forgot that the wolf's DNA was toxic to me until it started burning inside my mouth. I was supposed to just bite.

He rolled off me. I moved to one side and threw up the blood onto the floor. He grabbed the back of my neck and flung me into a tree. He raced over and pinned me to the floor with his giant claws. The big wolf's jaws snapping over my face. I strained against his grip but couldn't breakthrough. I tried to pull my legs underneath to kick him off, but his hind legs had pinned mine down as well. Saliva drooled off his jaw onto my face. He took a moment to transform his mouth back to speak. "This is the end."

Over his shoulder, a large rock loomed into sight.

"You're right," I said and grabbed his jaws and held his head still. The rock soared out of the night sky and smashed onto the top of his head. It knocked him sideways, enough for me to push him off. Giles slumped to the floor from the effort of smashing the rock into Norris.

The sight of Giles coming to my rescue filled me with overwhelming joy. We were friends again. We were there for each other.

A surge of emotion filled me up, and I directed it to my magic burning inside me, channelling it all into my right hand. I sprang up and kneeled on Norris's chest. He was just coming to and stared up at me. My right hand sucked up the magic, dragon scales rippling up it and talons forming. I plunged my dragon claw straight into his throat, ripping through his flesh. I coiled it back and slammed it down again, cutting into his throat and ripping it open, blood spilling out and spluttering from his jaws.

I leaned back to get a clear sight of him. I slammed my talons down, hit after hit, cracking through his chest, banging above his heart, ripping into the flesh and digging through bones. My talons gripped his beating heart and wrenched it out of his chest.

There was one last scream. His body went limp and transformed back to his human state.

I held his beating heart aloft, blood spurting out. I tossed his heart into the forest and collapsed on the pine-needle coated ground. Giles dragged himself over and slumped next to me.

"Friends," Giles said, and laid his hand on my chest.

"Friends," I replied and took his hand in my talons as they transformed back to normal.

Chapter Twenty

We lay broken and battered on the floor. I was happy, even although in a great deal of pain. We smiled at each other. No words required. But a rotten stink and breaking branches broke the peace.

"I hear and smell them coming. It's your crew," I said to Giles as I looked deep into the forest, waiting for the first sight.

He sniffed the air. "It is the Turned, but they aren't my crew anymore. I am coming with you."

I dragged myself to my knees and saw the first shape move between the tree trunks.

"For now, you must still be one of them," I said as figures flashed on both sides. "We don't have the strength to escape. Just follow my lead."

I balled my hand into a fist and shoved Giles into the dirt as he rose. I swung my fist back and punched down, narrowly missing his face and hitting the ground. Giles pretended to struggle out of my grip as I repeated the blows.

The decaying Turned broke through the tree line and surrounded us from all sides, with claws and fangs at the ready. Some of them gripped swords and others aimed machine guns. I held Giles by the throat and sat on his chest with claws pointing down to his vulnerable body.

"Don't come any closer, or I will kill him," I shouted out.

From behind the Turned, Bramel stepped out, clothed in his normal gothic black gear and piercings. Over the shoulders of the Turned, rifles aimed from the Hunters dressed in green camouflage gear.

"Leave the boy alone, or are you afraid to face me again?" Bramel said and sneered down at me, with hands tucked together behind his back.

I jumped off Giles and straighten myself up as best as possible. My body was battered, bleeding and bruised, but I still liked the idea of taking on Bramel now I was a Dragan.

"Question is, are you ready to face me? I am a proper Dragan this time," I said and flashed my claws, fangs and red eyes at him.

He looked me up and down and walked around me as I stood over Giles. "Maybe you are, but you don't look in particularly good shape. But I am surprised you got the better of Norris and his trainee," he said as he stepped over Norris's dead, naked body. "Beating a werewolf at full moon is good. But it appears to have considerably weakened you. Those wounds won't heal over, and the toxic werewolf DNA will bring you down. Plus, I have an entire army, whereas yours ran away into the night, abandoning you, just as you once abandoned this pathetic creature. But it is only you that I am after. Thorn and her subjects can hide away and lick their wounds for as long as they like," he said and looked down at Giles, who was spitting up blood.

I tightened my fists and blood poured down them. There was no point in struggling. This was a battle I couldn't win, and it may only worsen my condition if I struggled too hard. The smart thing was to let them take me and hope Thorn was on her way or that Giles would stick to his new path and break me out. However, I had to make it look good.

"Enough," I shouted and jumped at Bramel. I threw in a punch and caught him by surprise. He staggered back and tripped over a rock onto his backside. He snarled and sprung back up and then raised his fists. I swung a laboured punch, but he blocked and hit back. I rocked back but pushed forward again on weak legs. He blocked my next blow and kicked across my thighs, chopping me to the floor. I slumped down onto all fours to catch my breath.

"Useless," he said and laughed. "Is that the best the mighty Dragans can provide?" Bramel said and faced the Turned. "Look at him. He is nothing to be afraid of. He is no dragon. Now tie him up and bring him back to the base," he said and walked off. The Turned shuffled around me in a circle, all looking at one another to make the first move.

The first one pounced in and jumped on my back. I spun around to dislodge him, then others grabbed my limbs and pinned me down while another two lay across my body. I didn't struggle anymore, as Bramel wasn't watching, and I didn't want them to rip my watch off by accident.

The Turned's hands grabbed me from all sides, their rotten flesh and stinking breath smothering my senses. They tied ropes around my wrists and ankles, and then around my knees, holding my legs together and wrapping ropes around my arms, pinning them to my side.

They dragged my bound body away from Giles while a team of Hunters rushed over to him. One of them removed a large bottle of water from a rucksack and cleaned out all the bloody wounds. Another wrapped him in a blanket and injected him with three different needles. A third one set up a line into his arm and attached it to a bag of blood that he held up in the air.

A black bag smothered my head and fastened around my neckline.

Many Turned hands lifted me up and claws cut deep into my skin. They walked off and bumped me through the forest.

Behind us, they were carrying down Giles as well, and in front, Bramel led the way. As we walked, my wounds were bleeding out, and my consciousness fading. I couldn't even be bothered to scream when they pushed their claws in too far. But something must have alerted Bramel to my pain.

"He's bleeding too much. I don't want our grand prize to be dead by the time we get back. Keep him alive, wash out the wounds and bandage him. There will still be enough of the werewolf toxin in him to measure his response when we get back to base. And put your claws away."

The Turned lowered me to the floor, and then other people grabbed my clothes, ripped them open and poured water upon the wounds. I yelled out a few times when they caught the cuts as they cleaned them out.

"Stop complaining. It's for your own good. I need you alive for a while," Bramel said.

After they finished cleaning and bandaging me, they picked me up to continue our descent. After a long march through the forest, I heard engines, and then doors opened and slammed shut. "Put him in the back of the van and take him to the base. The doctors will want to perform some experiments while in his Dragan state. And then once human, we will have further tests," Bramel said. The van doors opened, and then I was placed inside with a couple of people sat beside me.

The van doors slammed shut, but I could hear conversations going on outside. "Take Giles back to the base and get him back on his feet. Once he is well enough, I want a full report from him. As a werewolf on a full moon, he should have won. Unless Harper has rediscovered his dragon form again, in which case we need to test it, record it, and work out how to replicate it."

The van moved away and I heard no more of the conversation. We bumped along in the van for about an hour, and then I was taken out and carried and dumped onto a cold floor. They left me with the hood still over my head.

I wriggled along the floor until I found the wall and push myself up into a seating position. I flicked out a claw and tried to arch back my hand to cut the ropes. But without seeing what I was doing, I just kept catching my arm and hitting thin air. I pulled against the ropes, but they were incredibly thick and strong. They had practice at capturing Dragans; hence, how I met Thorn in the first place. I decided to save my strength and wait for them to make the next move.

After about an hour, someone came in and swiped off the hood. Two men stood in front of me, one with an assault rifle pointed directly at my head and another with a needle in his hand.

"I just wanted to check we had the right person. But now it's time for you to go to sleep," the man said, and stabbed the needle into my arm and pushed down the plunger. After a few moments, I felt drowsy, but I tried to fight it, fearful of what they might do while I was asleep. I focused my magic on trying to accelerate the healing and burning off the sedative. I looked up at the doctor, burning my eyes red, keeping the anger inside at boiling point to drive my healing powers.

The man turned around, squatted down and rummaged around in a bag. He turned back again with another needle. "Eventually, young man, even you won't be to fight the number of drugs I will pump into you."

He moved the needle towards me, and I tried to squirm out of the way but received a rifle butt to my head. While I was disorientated, the needle stabbed into my skin and they pushed the drugs into my bloodstream.

I woke with my hands bound and hooked to a chain that was fastened to the ceiling. My feet were off the floor and I was dangling in the middle of a cold dark grey cell. I shouldn't have expected anything else. The last time the Turned and Hunters captured me, I was in the same predicament. I looked at my wrist to see my GPS watch had gone.

I tried to shake myself free, jerking my body up to break the chains, but it was no good. All I did was rattle them around and alert the guards outside to my recovery. They radioed through and within ten minutes, the door opened to the man who had injected me, Bramel, and two armed guards.

Upon seeing the man who had injected me again, I realised he was the doctor from my first set of tortures back in Leeds. He wore the same white coat and small round spectacles and had shaven white hair. He was back to finish the job he had started.

Bramel walked in front of me, and the two armed guards split either side of him and aimed. Behind, the doctor placed a box on the floor and opened it up, the light from the doorway providing enough illumination for them to work.

"We've a few more tests to run," Bramel said and smiled.

"You mean you want to torture me again?"

"Well, they may be torture for you, but for us, they are vital experiments."

"Like seeing how much you can hurt me before I pass out."

"That is one such useful experiment. Suppose that ability to control your pain can be replicated. In that case, we can develop formulas and create stronger soldiers and stronger Turned. Even if we can't completely duplicate the vampire formula, we can at least develop some beneficial effects. Speaking of which, I understand you appear to be immune to silver and daylight in your Dragan form. Our doctor would just like to confirm."

The doctor stepped to the side of Bramel, holding a knife and a torch. "This won't hurt too much."

I went to shake loose of the chains to fight my way out, even though I knew it was impossible. The soldiers pushed the barrels of their guns at me. "Keep still. Be a shame for my guards to shoot you. Won't kill you, of course, being a Dragan, but it will hurt a lot," Bramel said.

I stopped my struggle and gritted my teeth in preparation. The doctor flicked on the flashlight and pointed it at my bare skin. Of course, nothing happened because of my immunity. The doctor checked a couple of times on different parts of my skin. Bramel then held out his hand. "Just to double-check, light my hand."

The doctor flashed the light briefly across Bramel's palm and smoke rose up. Bramel snatched it back and placed it under his arm and gritted his teeth.

"Try the knife on him next. Might as well test it on me first," Bramel said, and stretched out his hand.

"Are you sure?" the doctor asked.

"Just get on with it."

The doctor slowly placed the knife's tip against one of Bramel's fingers and smoke rose up, and Bramel snatched his hand back again.

"That seems fine. Now test it on Harper."

The doctor placed it up against my jawline and looked me directly in the eye as he pushed the blade against my throat. No smoke rose, but I could feel its sharpness cutting into my skin. He then pulled the knife down an inch, scraping my flesh. No smoke rose from my skin and it rapidly healed itself from the cut.

"I can confirm that he is immune to both UV and silver. And from the healing of his skin, he is still in his Dragan form as well. So we have our confirmation that the formula transforms him into a Dragan. Also, it has given him immunity to what is normally the Dragan's weaknesses. He is the best of both worlds."

"We will continue with the tests, as discussed," Bramel said.

"So more tortures then. I see you want more answers from me. I will not sell out my friends again," I shouted.

Bramel laughed. "You should be so lucky. There is no Carmella here to protect you this time. It was her idea to bring you over to our side. She wanted a little pet of her own and enjoyed the idea of turning you away from Thorn. I could have cared less about your defection. This time I'm not even interested in you answering questions. I know everything I need to know. Only your human body has the answers I now seek."

"You're going to take more samples until you get what you need."

Bramel shook his head, and the doctor packed away his things and stood next to him. "Unfortunately for you, we no longer need any samples of skin tissue and blood," the doctor said.

I sighed and relaxed my muscles, and then I thought about what he meant by 'unfortunately'. "Then what do you have planned?"

The doctor looked at Bramel, and Bramel nodded back at him. "Surface samples are no good. I need to open you up and find out how your body really works."

I tensed up and gritted my teeth. "I won't give in, no matter what you threaten me with. I won't reveal the secret."

"So you know the secret to your transformation?"

I looked away and kept my mouth shut.

"I doubt if you do. We already know they encoded the formula to your DNA. We have tried to replicate the idea and encode it to our soldiers' DNA. But once again, we were left with a pile of dead bubbling bones and flesh."

I stared up at him. "What! You mean there is something else?"

"There is another secret to your uniqueness. One that alludes us all. We have everything we need from your living tissue, and we have run all the experiments we can. I need to do a full internal examination to discover the key to your transformation. We can't perform the examination on your Dragan body as it would heal too quickly. Plus, we know how Dragan's bodies work. What we need to understand is how your hybrid body works with both Dragan and human DNA. Once you become human again, then your time is up," the doctor said and walked out of the room. The two armed guards followed him, leaving Bramel stood in front of me.

I only hoped that Thorn was on her way, or else once I became human again, they were going to cut me into little pieces.

Bramel glared at me. "It is a shame. I would like to fight again when you were fully fit. But orders are orders."

"So you take orders from someone else?"

"I shouldn't have said that. But never mind, your body will go under the knife soon enough. Which I understand will be in the next 24 to 36 hours."

I tried to keep the image out of my mind of my body being cut apart, so I focused on keeping Bramel talking. Maybe I could get to the truth.

"So it was your boss that ordered Scarlett's murder?"

"That order never came from us. I would admit it if we had done it out of revenge, else there would be no point in killing her. My boss ordered your capture and your torture back in England. Even insisted we filmed the fight so they could watch it. Somebody else wanted Scarlett murdered and made it look like us."

"Who would want Scarlett murdered?"

Bramel sighed. "Is the truth really that hard to see? Who would gain from Scarlett being out of the picture? Who has never liked her? Who has the resources?"

"You mean Thorn had Scarlett murdered? Made it look like the Turned, to get Scarlett out of the picture and away from me forever."

"Of course. And before you say Thorn would never do such a thing, remember I have known her for much longer than you. She created me, and she created you, even if it was different. Her blood is in me as I am created from it. You have been created from her blood in this guise of the vampire formula. We are blood brothers."

I lunged forward but the chains held me back. "We are not brothers!"

"But we both have Thorn's blood."

"You desire her, don't you? But she has never repaid that affection."

"Who says she never repaid that affection? Did she ever outright say there has never been anything between us?"

"You're lying."

"Why would I need to lie? You know full well the Dragans have had difficulty conceiving more children. It made perfect sense for them to conceive with a Turned. We are part of them."

I shook in anger. I knew what he said was likely to be true. Although Thorn hadn't told me about Bramel, she had said she had tried every possible way to reproduce their race.

I had no right to be angry, considering how long ago this occurred or any reason to be annoyed that she hadn't told me.

Bramel sniggered. "You know it to be true?"

"Yes, it must be true. But it makes no difference to me. She rejected you eventually."

"We, the Turned, have every right to be the equals of the Dragans. We were used by them for their petty war. We just want to have the same powers, to be treated equally. Once the Dragans had no more use for us, they killed us off. As a matter of survival, we went our own way and took control of our destiny."

"You haven't answered my question. Who is your boss? I thought you were the King of the Turned."

"I am the King of the Turned. Whoever said my boss was a Turned vampire?"

"Then who, or should I say what?"

"I will tell you this. Their name is South," Bramel said. "I will leave you in your last hours to think about it."

Bramel marched out of the room and pulled the door to, plunging me back into darkness.

My suspicions had been confirmed. There was somebody or something behind the Turned that even Bramel answered to. I remembered the last time they had captured me; I heard Bramel talking to someone on his phone. The conversation sounded like he was taking orders. But what good would this knowledge bring unless Thorn came to my rescue? As soon as I became human again, they would cut me open.

I waited in the dark for another hour, thinking through who could possibly be South and what they might be if not a Turned vampire. The door opened and two armed guards entered. One of them placed their gun against the wall, and the other one kept his aimed at me. The one without the gun walked up and pulled his fists up. He swung back and punched me in the face and then swung a left hook and a right hook. He took a step back and stared at me as my skin healed and the blood absorbed into my face.

I flashed my fangs and eyes and jumped at him, but the chains held me back.

"He is still Dragan," the guard said, clutching his hand.

"Let's go. We will be back in an hour, little man, for more," the guard with the gun said, and his colleague picked up his weapon, and they both left the cell and shut the door again.

I assumed they would be back every hour, testing me to see if my Dragan abilities still existed. As soon as my abilities disappeared, I would be prepped for surgery. Bramel said I had 24 to 36 hours before turning back to human again. I suspected it was closer to 48 hours from previous transformations, so I had longer than they realised. I gauged from the battle with Giles and the travelling to their base; it had been at least three hours. I had time to think of a plan or for Thorn to find me.

Hopefully, elsewhere in the base, Giles was recovering from our fight and coming to rescue me. In the meantime, I would have to put up with the hourly beatings and look for an opportunity to escape.

They continued to come every hour, often different guards, taking turns to punch the Dragan. I sensed the feelings of revenge before I even saw them enter the prison cell. They pushed open the door and hit me in the face enough to create some wounds and then watched to see if I healed. They always left clutching their bruised hands, which made me smile.

On the fifth occasion, one guard put his gun down, and another covered him by standing aside and pointing his rifle. The guard smirked, rolled up the sleeves of his jacket and walked over.

He coiled back his fist. "This one is for my friends you killed at the warehouse. Patrick was my mentor."

The memory of Patrick, the man who had tortured me many times, fired the anger, and my fangs snapped out and eyes burnt blood red.

"He is still Dragan. No need to hit him, save your strength," the covering guard said.

"Are you kidding? Everyone else's got to hit him. Let's just make sure," the guard said and swung in a left hook. It didn't hurt much, as my Dragan abilities absorbed the punch. The man shook his hand, feeling the impact of my supernatural strength. The bruising on my face healed, and the blood soaked back in, leaving no marks on my Dragan skin.

"Still Dragan," he said and turned around, picked up his gun and walked out of the cell. The other guard followed him and shut the door.

The guards arrived every hour and punched me in the face, kicked me in the ribs and waited for my body to heal, regardless if I showed them my Dragan features. They continued every hour, and I kept track of the time until my powers would run out.

On the twenty-first time, the guards followed the usual routine. One guard aimed his gun, and the other punched me in the face and kicked me in the ribs for good measure. I gritted my teeth and stared down at the floor. I looked up into the guard's face.

"He doesn't seem to be healing," he said to the other guard with the rifle.

"Give it a few minutes. Maybe a couple more punches for good measure."

"Good idea," the attacking guard said and pulled back his right fist, pivoted in his body and unleashed his fist into my face.

The guard examined my face, put his hand against my chin and removed it, blood trickling between his fingers. He held his damaged fist. "You must have a face of steel. It hurts even when you are a human."

The other guard sided over to him and looked at the blood and squinted down into my face. He pulled out a torch and shone it into my eyes.

"Looks like the transformation has finished. This is the end of the road for you, boy. I will tell Bramel that he can start his experiments."

Chapter Twenty-One

The guards left in search of Bramel to tell him I was bleeding and therefore human again. Footsteps clattered up and down the corridor, and about twenty minutes later a group arrived.

Bramel walked in with his hands behind his back, followed by five guards and the doctor. The guards stood on either side and shone their torches into my face. I blinked from the harsh light. Bramel bent down, grabbed my chin with his hand and twisted my head back to get a better look. The doctor walked to his side and stared at my face. Bramel flicked out one of his claws and scratched it down the side of my cheek. They both watched the blood flood out from my skin and not heal. Bramel then let go of my chin, and my head sagged.

"They are right. The boy's transformation has run its course. He can be prepped for surgery," the doctor said.

"You heard the man," Bramel said and looked at the guards and waved them forward.

"It's a bit earlier than I expected. I guess not bringing him back to full strength from his battle with the werewolves has foreshortened his transformation and weakened his hybrid abilities. You hoped this might happen," the doctor said to Bramel.

Three of the guards placed down their guns, and two provided covering fire. They unchained me and wrapped a zip tie around my wrists, which they had pulled behind my back. They then pushed me forward, with one of the armed guards at the front leading the way.

My legs were tired and un-used to walking after hanging in the cell for the last 24 hours. I stumbled a couple of times to my knees, but they hoisted me up and pushed me forward. The doctor and Bramel followed us through the white hospital corridors until we reached a shower block.

The white-tiled shower block was open planned with a row of six showers. The guards cut the zip tie and stripped my clothes. They switched on a shower and pushed me into the middle of the row. The water was warm and washed off the dirt and blood from the forest. One guard grabbed a brush and covered it in soap. He then set about scrubbing my body, forcing the dirt away and cleaning me up. The man was vigorous with the brush and it burnt my skin, leaving it red raw. All the while, two guards had guns aimed at me, and the doctor and Bramel watched uninterestedly.

"Don't get any crazy ideas that we've changed our mind. Just need you clean for the surgery. I don't want any unwanted bacteria spoiling my results," the doctor said.

"Turn around," the guard with the brush shouted. I complied and faced the wall, and he scrubbed down my back, pushing so hard my face was pressed into the white-tiled wall. I watched the blood and dirt drain off my body and swirl down the drain.

Eventually, they switched off the shower and dragged me out. Two of the guards grabbed towels and violently rubbed me down. A guard handed over a green paper hospital gown and white paper slippers. I put them on. Then they pushed me out of the shower block and down the clean white corridors. The paper nightgown rubbed against my red raw skin, and my slippers scraped along the lino floor as we walked.

We arrived in a white hospital room with a single bed. The room reeked of antiseptic cleaner. They laid me down on crisp white sheets. The guards pulled up chrome bars on either side, with beige straps attached. They placed my arms and legs into the leather straps and pulled them tight.

The doctor and Bramel stood on either side of the bed. There was a guard behind them and two posted outside the door. "You have a temporary stay of execution while I prep my team for surgery and prepare our equipment," the doctor said.

"Do I get a last meal? Or a last request?" I asked.

"No last meal. I need your system to be empty of food. I don't know about any last requests that'll be up to Bramel."

"And what do you have in mind as your last request?"

I stared at them. "How about you let me out of here and I kill you both?"

"How funny," the doctor said and then opened the door to walk out of the room. As he went to leave, Giles walked through, but the doctor pushed him back outside and shut the door. Through a small window in the door, I saw them talking. The doctor appeared to be asking how he was feeling and giving him a brief check over. The doctor walked away, and Giles opened the door. Bramel turned to Giles and nodded, and Giles returned the gesture and walked around to the side of the bed to look at me. His face was bruised and cut, but he had been cleaned up and dressed in jeans and a t-shirt.

"So he has transformed back to human? What happens next?" Giles asked.

"You know what happens next, as we have discussed this before. The plan hasn't changed. We cut him open to find the secrets. It can either make the Turned into proper Dragans, or we can make super soldiers."

"Just checking nothing had changed. So when do we finally kill this betrayer?"

"He has a few hours left. The doctor and his team have only just eaten, and they want their food to go down before cutting him open. Even with their experience, they would prefer to do it on an empty stomach."

"Sounds messy. I would love to watch but would settle for being the one that gave him the injection to put him under, knowing mine was the last face he ever got to see."

Bramel placed a hand on Giles's shoulder and laughed. "Sorry, but there is no anaesthetic injection. Any drugs in his system will ruin the results. Same reason we haven't given him any food or drink. We need the organs as intact and untainted as possible."

Giles glanced down at me and then back to Bramel. "You mean they will cut him open while he is still alive?"

Bramel loomed over me. "Yes, they will have to cut him open while he is still alive. And it will be a slow death. They want to keep him alive as long as possible. They will put him on machines to keep him going to remove all his organs or test them while in situ."

Giles put his hand to his mouth and stepped back. I pulled at the straps binding me to the bed. "I'm going to kill you," I shouted at Bramel.

"That seems highly unlikely, considering the circumstances. I suppose you're waiting for another rescue from Thorn. I would put that out of your mind if I were you. As soon as they could, they ran. They are not coming back for you this time, and they wouldn't know where to find you, anyway."

"Are we not at the base that Max was trying to scout out?" I asked.

Giles had recomposed himself and stood next to me, glaring down. "As if. Our real base is somewhere else."

I hoped Giles was just playing along and hadn't switched sides again.

"But how did the information get to us? How did you find us?"

"I can answer that question for you," Bramel said. "We have spies in your camp. And we know who the spies are in our camp. So we fed your spies false information and our spy told us where you really were."

"None of them would help you. They are Dragans. They are your mortal enemy," I said.

"Yes, but I gave you something to think about earlier. A name. South. Have you worked it out yet?"

Bramel had told me that South was the genuine leader of the Turned and Hunter alliance. The person who he answered to, but they weren't a Turned. They were something else.

"You're trying to tell me that the true leader of the Turned, the person you answer to, is a Dragan. And it was them who told you where we were."

"I'm not telling you anything. I'm just opening your eyes to the truth. Not that it makes any difference. You're going under the knife in a few hours and will suffer a long, lingering death. I suggest you save your strength and forget worrying about who's betraying who."

"This is just another trick, another torment for me to suffer, making me think my friends have betrayed me."

"You can believe whatever you like. Giles, let's discuss what happens next in your training."

Bramel walked towards the door, but Giles hadn't moved. "I want to have a last word with him," Giles said.

"You can come back later and talk to him just before they take him away."

Giles glared down at me and slapped the side of my face. "See you later, dead boy."

Giles and the guard followed Bramel out of the room, leaving the guard on duty outside the door.

I laid in the bed, hoping Giles was acting a part and would return within an hour to help me escape.

If I were lucky, Thorn would return before then, having followed the signal to the watch, assuming the watch was still in the base and working. I just hoped they had gotten away safely and put their differences behind them to mount a rescue. While waiting for Giles to come, I couldn't think of anything else to do. I pulled at the straps, trying to see if I could loosen my hands. But they were too strong and tight to get any movement to tear the material apart.

I thought maybe I could pull the bars out and strained my arms. The metal was welded onto the bed frame. This was no standard strapping on the bed; it had been specially made to take the strength of a Dragan. I slumped back into the bed and stared at the ceiling.

Instead of focusing on the imaginable tortures ahead, I thought about what I could do if Giles came back to rescue me. I tried to put a plan of action together if he freed me from my restraints or what to do if Thorn arrived. However, I was still weak from the fight with Giles, even though they cleaned up my wounds and gave me some blood, but it was only enough to keep me alive.

I lay in bed running through all the options of what could happen next, all except the one where I was cut open and systematically dissected while still alive. But I couldn't help keep going back to that picture of me screaming while my body was slowly taken apart. My stomach cut open and my intestines pulled out in front of me.

I watched the clock on the wall marking every second I moved closer to my death. Back in school, that clock seemed to drag by as I waited for the end of each day, but now it was on fast forward. But despite the tortures and my impending death, I felt a sense of relief at rescuing Giles. I had repaid my debt of guilt.

The clock sapped my strength with every tick, and I tried to stay positive and stared at the walls instead. I still had a chance to survive. Thorn or Giles could make it, and I had my own plan already set in motion.

When Giles returned an hour later, I was relieved to see him. He walked around to the side of the bed and stared down at me. His eyes narrowed, and he glared and gripped the sidebar of the bed.

"You're going to get everything you deserve for betraying me," Giles said.

My heart sank. I couldn't think of what to say. Giles smiled and winked and then glanced over to the side of the room. I followed his eyes to a camera in the top corner.

I guessed this was all part of the act, as they could see and hear everything.

"My betrayal is nothing compared to this. You're sick and crazy to hook up with these idiots. After they cut me open, it will be you next."

Giles shuffled around the side of the bed, so his back was to the camera, concealing his hands around the straps on my arm.

"They respect me. They have helped me and I help them. You Dragans do nothing but take take take." Giles undid the strap on my arm, and as the vision of the camera was obscured, I leant across and unstrapped my other hand.

"Let me tell you a little secret. Let me whisper into your ear how I'm going to kill your girlfriend."

Giles leant over me and whispered into my ear. "We need to lull the guard in. While he is busy checking your wrists. I will knock him out. But then we will have to make a run for it. I'm not sure how far we can get."

"Don't worry about that. Just get the guard in and stand well back. I have a plan."

Giles frowned but nodded in agreement and shouted, "Guard, guard. There is a problem. Can you come and look at this?"

The guard walked through with his machine gun slung across his chest, Giles stepped back, and the guard stood by the side of my bed and saw my left wrist was unstrapped. "What on earth is going on?"

I launched bolt upright in bed. My skin healed, eyes burnt red, fangs jutted out, and claws ripped through my finger ends. I twisted his head to one side and bit into his neck. Giles jolted backwards and stumbled into a table of medical equipment, sending it flying. The guard tried to fight my grip, but I was far too strong.

The blood rocketed into my stomach and absorbed into my body, giving it the strength it so craved. My magic sphere blossomed with the exhilaration of feeding and the guard helpless in my grip. I gulped the blood down, and Giles watched on in astonishment. I held the guard in my grasp as his life force drained. As my strength increased, my psychic powers connected into his fear and eventual death. I finished and let the guard go, and he crumpled to the floor.

"What the hell just happened?" Giles said as he wrenched the machine gun off the guard.

"Just a little trick I picked up over a bottle of wine in the South of France."

Giles aimed the gun at the exit. I undid the straps on my feet and sprung out of bed. I undid the guard's clothes and pulled them on. Giles handed me the machine gun. "But I thought you were human again?"

"I was taught how to hide my Dragan powers. How to prevent my healing so I could appear to be human still. My mentor thought it may give me an advantage. I think I owe him a large bottle of wine."

I finished getting dressed and put the radio clip onto my belt buckle when it hissed into life.

"The patrolling guards have picked up our expected visitors. They have engaged the enemy. Everyone into your position as briefed by Bramel. We will kill these Dragans once and for all."

"Sounds like the guards are occupied already," I said and smashed the CCTV camera, just to be sure. We walked to the door, and I peeked through the window. With the sounds of gunfire in the distance, groups of guards stormed up and down the corridors as red alarm lights flashed.

"I know a back way out. Follow me," Giles said.

"I can't. I have to help Thorn. Sounds like she has walked into a trap. They knew she was coming."

"We have them surrounded. It's just a matter of time," the radio crackled.

Giles spun back. "This is your friends?"

"Who else? On my watch, there was a GPS tracker. I knew Thorn would never give up on me, but someone knew she was coming. South must have told them. The informant is real. Let's head towards the gunfire. Our only way out is to help my friends."

I ran down the corridor, listening out with my superior hearing for the sound of gunfire and battle. A couple of guards came tearing around the corner, trying to escape.

"It's one of them," the guard shouted. I responded with a bullet into his forehead and then shot the other one through the heart.

I knew Thorn would hear the gunshots but so would everyone else. I threw the gun to Giles. "Do you know how to use this thing?"

"Yes, Norris ensured I had extensive training in martial arts and firearms."

"It appears we have a lot in common. Can you use the gun, as I need to see if I can contact Thorn?"

Giles held it into his shoulder. "Do you think she has one of the radios?"

I tapped the side of my head with my finger. "No need for radios."

I reached out with my thoughts, but the environment was cluttered with the soldiers' fear. But I could sense where that fear was coming from. Then I could detect another thought of pure rage. I knew who that was coming from. Giles kept watch while I focused on those thoughts. I tuned into those emotions and then cast my thoughts to her. *'We are alive and coming to you.'*

'We?'

'Giles and I.'

'We will hold our position, but we can't hold them off forever or make our way further into the base. Engage the enemy from the rear. It will break their attack. Rip will ensure the exit remains clear.'

'On our way.'

"Okay, Giles. You ready to meet the Queen of the Dragans. Let's go."

As we ran down the corridor, I scooped up one of the machine guns from the dead guards. Giles ran to the corner and crouched down and peeked around, and then signalled me to move. I ran to the corner to provide cover for him to move out and down the corridor. He stopped halfway and crouched down again and waved me on. I ran past to the next corner, where I checked around the side and signalled Giles to take up the covering position in the far corner.

Giles and I instinctively work together as a team, checking the corners and working around the blind spots. He was well trained. In fact, he was better than me with the gun and his movements.

He covered all the doors and checked all the entrances and exits. He signalled me to move up and hold when necessary. I had been trained in single combat rather than working in a squad. Giles could teach our group a few things.

We worked our way along the corridor towards the sounds of increasing gunfire and the strength of psychic thoughts. A group of guards ran around the corner, looking back over their shoulders. I unleashed the machine gun and mowed them down. We rounded the corner to see a group of Hunters in a firefight. They turned to us.

"Thank God, reinforcements." One guard said, then took a double-take at my Dragan features. He levelled the gun around to face us, and Giles fired in a burst, sprawling him backwards into the other guards huddled around the corner of the corridor.

His momentum knocked the other soldiers into the open, where they were shredded by bullets. I followed up with my own shots, finishing them off in between the crossfire. We jumped over the dead bodies and around the corner.

Thorn walked out into the middle of the corridor, gun slung across her body. She smiled and gave me a flash of her fangs. "You won't even let me rescue you properly. You were already halfway out, I reckon."

"Giles had already sprung me from the hospital room, and we were going out the back exit when we heard gunfire and that you were in trouble. I had to come back through the hard route to rescue you. I heard on the radio that they were expecting you."

"I think I may have survived. But let's not hang around too long. Rip is keeping the exit clear. Let's go." She then threw a metal object at me. I caught my watch and strapped it back onto my hand and turned off the GPS tracker. "I think you lost something," she said.

She ran back up the corridor and we followed. Max was waiting around the other side, holding a gun across his chest. Standing next to him were six other men, all dressed in black and carrying machine guns. Immediately, I recognised them as the MI5 units that worked for Mary. I looked to Thorn.

"We have some new allies," she said. "I will explain it all back at the base. The Hunters may have been expecting us but not in these numbers. We would have been okay."

"Yes, lots of new allies. Thorn, this is Giles. He is my best friend." I put my hand on Giles's shoulder as I spoke.

"Good to have you on board. Glad you two have made up."

"Thank you. Just glad we had the chance," Giles said.

We sprinted through the base, twisting through the bloodied corridors, jumping over dead bodies. I jumped over the body of a man with his hand cut off. I guessed he must have been wearing my watch. Big mistake.

Chapter Twenty-Two

As we left the building through a fire exit, I looked back to a two-level flat roof building with multiple sections angled out into the forest. The lights from the building cast out into the night, providing a dim light into the dark. Ahead of us, the MI5 soldiers positioned themselves behind trees and rocks.

Thorn led the way to the fence line. The soldiers fired back into the building, smashing the windows, hitting the doorway from which we escaped. The bullets smash the lights inside, cutting off the dim light casting outside.

The wire fence circling the hospital had been cut, and a soldier lifted up a flap of the fence for us to duck under. Cassius had to crawl underneath. I ducked through, followed by Giles, and then Thorn, Max and Rip. The soldiers continued with the heavy suppression fire into the building, smashing glass and peppering brickwork while we escaped through the woods.

The MI5 soldiers retreated from the hospital grounds, following us back through the fence line and laying down suppressing fire. They took it in turns to move, take cover, and shoot in bursts at the chasing Hunter army. The Hunters tried to fan out and encircle us, but the heavy gunfire forced them to take cover. Screams echoed through the trees as a couple of Hunters crashed to the ground in a hail of bullets.

We chased after Thorn as she led the way. The soldiers provided a shield from the pursuing army. Thorn held up a fist and we stopped. I crouched next to her.

"Up ahead, three snipers in the woods. I can detect their thoughts," she said.

Giles sniffed the air. "I can detect their scent. Even in my human form."

"V, go left. Stay light on your feet and curl around the side. I will take the one on the right. Giles, once you hear the screams, I want you to aim straight ahead and give it a good spray," Thorn said and ran off into the woods.

I sprinted off to the left, reaching out with my senses to pinpoint the sniper. I darted through the woods, curling around to get to the sniper from the side. Behind a tree, I paused for a moment to soak in the environment. Around to my left, I could smell something. I opened my mind and detected the nervousness of the person lying down in the woods. They hadn't had time to fully blend in. Hence, why we could smell them. I rested against a tree and poked my head around. A hundred meters ahead, a shape glowed in my Dragan eyesight. The heat signature of the sniper.

The sniper rifle was pointing towards the building still. I had made it around without alerting them. I crouched on one knee and put the crosshairs onto their prone body. I squeezed the trigger and fired off a burst of shots. The sniper's body burst in blood and screamed for a moment. I ran over, kicked their rifle away and flipped them onto their back. A woman stared back. She had hands on her sides to stop the blood flow and was taking quick breaths. She gritted her teeth and lashed out with a foot.

I kicked the foot away and knelt at her side. I wasn't expecting the sniper to be a woman, but it didn't matter.

"Keep the pressure on the wound. They will be here soon," I said.

"It's too late. I've been hit too many times. I am going to die. I hope they catch you and gut you open, scum," she said.

I stood up and fired a shot into her head. I heard other gunfire coming from the woods. Two sets of shots. One followed by another scream and the final one a spray of gunfire up the middle. Thorn had eliminated her target, and Giles had set down some covering fire. I ran across the woods, searching for the final sniper. The sniper had already turned in the other direction, firing into the woods as a dark shape dashed between the trees. I ran across to get a clear shot. The sniper had stood up to shoot. I aimed, fired, and the target's head exploded. I didn't bother to look this time.

Thorn walked out of the trees.

"Good clean shot," she said. "I will radio back that it's okay to move on."

Thorn radioed Cassius, and soon we sensed their approach. Giles ran past the dead sniper, glancing at the body.

"Any more?" he asked.

"Not sure, but V and I will go first, just in case," Thorn replied.

We headed off again with the MI5 soldiers bringing up the rear, continuing their suppressing fire back to the pursuing Hunters and Turned.

We ran through the forest for another fifteen minutes. All the while, the MI5 soldiers were firing backwards and keeping any Turned or Hunters from gaining on us.

We ran down a slope and jumped down onto a road. Waiting for us were four black range rovers with tinted windows. Thorn rushed straight over, yanked open the door and ushered me in. The driver started the engine. I climbed in with Giles right behind me. Thorn jumped in next to us, and Max jumped into the front passenger seat.

"Okay, driver. Let's not hang around," Thorn said.

The driver pressed the button on his radio. "Package received, bringing them in."

He pushed it into first gear and drove away. Cassius and Rip clambered into the Range Rover behind us, with some armed soldiers. The last guards laid down a blanket of fire and threw in a couple of grenades.

As we drove off down the dirt lane away from the mayhem, the second range Rover followed us. The last MI5 soldiers jumped into their Range Rover and sped off, firing out the back windows as they went to discourage any further chasing.

The lights on the range rovers flicked on. We bounced down the roads, twisting and turning the way out of the forest and off the hillside. I sat in the middle between Thorn and Giles, bouncing about. Giles gripped onto the side of the car and Thorn strapped herself in. I followed suit, and so did Giles and Max.

"Where are we going?" I asked.

"MI5 has an agreement with the Spanish authorities to use one of their army bases near the mountains. All governments know of the Turned and the Dragans and the impending war. There is a secret international network that is helping us to compile information and share it. As part of that network, we are also sharing resources."

"So you did a deal with MI5."

"I am not sure I trust them, as it was their info that led us into the trap, but I had no choice if I wanted to rescue you. Once the Turned had taken you, I didn't have the resources and capabilities to spring a rescue and secure your safety, although I knew where you were. The Hunters were a government agency with vast reach and capability, and it seems they have made some alliances in other countries with their peer organisations. Hence why I had to join up with MI5. We need the resources and authority that a government agency can bring us, and the help of their international allies."

"And when all this is finished, do you trust them to keep their word?"

Thorn stared at the driver in the mirror and flashed her fangs. "Of course not."

The driver looked back at the road and then accelerated harder, trying to get us out of his car as soon as possible.

Thorn grabbed my hand and looked into my eyes. "So what happened in there? You can tell me."

"What you would expect to happen? They wanted to experiment on me again. But I don't want to discuss it right now. I learnt something in that place, which I can only share with everyone at once."

"But you can tell me first?"

"I would prefer it if I said it only once. I learnt important information about our struggle with the Turned. Also, Giles has information that he can share with us."

Giles looked over at Thorn. "I'm not sure how much I know is of any use, but you're welcome to any information I have. I know where my loyalties lie," Giles said.

"You will have your chance, Giles, to get your revenge on them. I promise there will be plenty of battles ahead."

"Thank you," Giles replied and went back to looking out the window and gripping on tight to the door frame.

Thorn grabbed my other hand and held them both and twisted herself around to look at me. "There are no secrets between us, remember? You need to tell me what happened in there."

I squeezed her hands and rubbed my thumb across her fingers. I looked straight into her eyes. "I will tell you this now and then the rest once with the group. And finally, something else, which is private between the two of us. For now, Giles rescued me. They wanted to cut me open while I was still alive to experiment on my organs to discover the secret behind the transformation. They know of the encoded formula to my DNA, but this isn't the secret to why it works only for me. There is another secret. It would have been a slow lingering death while they tested each part of my body. But with Rip's training and Giles's help, we escaped."

"But how did you end up there? I assumed the werewolves captured you and took you back, but then why would he rescue you," Thorn said and looked over at Giles.

I shook my head and remained silent, as I didn't want to brag about beating Giles and Norris, while he was sitting next to us.

Giles twisted around in his seat. "Jon is obviously too humble a person to tell you the truth. We fought and Jon won. He was leaving to find his way back to you. But he returned to rescue me from Norris, who was going to beat me to death for disappointing him. Norris is a powerful werewolf and it is a full moon. Jon held his own, but he was already weakened from our fight. However, Jon beat Norris."

Thorn smiled at me and squeezed my hand. "That's my, V."

"Giles does himself an injustice. Norris had pinned me down. I wasn't sure how I would survive when Giles smashed a rock over his head and distracted him long enough for me to attack and finish him off."

"I am sure you would have thought of something. I only hit him on the head with a rock. It wasn't enough to seriously hurt him. It is what you did with your hand that killed him."

"What did you do?" she asked.

"I was in a rage and the dragon was coming out. Instead of letting it take over completely, I focused it on my hands. I used the extra strength and talons to smash through his chest and rip out his beating heart."

"Wow. That is some party trick," she said and reached across me and placed a hand on Giles's shoulder. "Thank you. I will be forever grateful. I will ensure you are rewarded."

"No reward is necessary. Jon is my best friend. We have saved each other."

I leaned over to Giles and whispered in his ear. "Giles, don't be silly. She's fabulously rich. You really should ask for a reward."

"I can hear you," Thorn said

"I know," I replied and laughed.

Max twisted around in the front seat to look back at us. "Giles, if I were you, I would take the money now. She's never offered me a reward."

Thorn glared at him for a moment. "I didn't realise you are in it just for the money."

"I'm not. But it wouldn't hurt," Max said and then stretched out his hand to Giles and held it open. "My name is Max, by the way. I am a werewolf in case you didn't realise."

Giles looked at me sideways but didn't really move out of his chair to acknowledge Max and shake his hand.

"Giles, Max is a good guy. He's not like Norris. It was Max that helped train me to fight werewolves."

"Oh, great. So it's you I have to thank for Jon beating me."

Max shrugged. "Sorry about that. But it seems to have all worked out," Max said, and stretched his hand out again.

Giles leaned forward and shook his hand. "Maybe you can show me what I did wrong. Next time I can beat him."

"Of course. Werewolves stick together."

We carried on in the car for another hour until we finally pulled up outside the Spanish military base. The entrance had a red barrier and green metal gates behind it. From the barrier, the Spanish military guards stepped out and levelled machine guns at us. The driver wound down his window and showed him a pass, and then the red barrier lifted and green gates rolled opened.

We drove in a convoy of three vehicles, through the dark base and round the back, pulling into an airport hangar at the end. Inside, a few black vans and a Mercedes sports car were parked at the side. The aircraft hangar's big door scrolled down once we were inside, and we climbed out of the vehicles.

Mary waited for us, surrounded by another group of soldiers. And behind the group soldiers, Cyrus stood with his arms crossed and a scowl on his face. It was only then I realised he hadn't come on the rescue but stayed back here in safety. Mary walked over to me and put her hands on both of my arms. She looked up into my face and smiled and squeezed her hands on my muscles. "They got you out safely, then. I was worried."

I raised my eyebrows at her. "You don't have to pretend anymore, Mary."

She let go of my arms and gave me a hug instead. "Just because I was playing a part when we were at college together doesn't mean I never cared for you. You were my friend, and I hope we can still be friends. I did nothing to hurt you back then. In fact, I remember helping you on quite a few occasions."

I sensed no dishonesty from her and remembered the past with affection. I had Mary to thank for getting Scarlett and me together. And I remembered all the good times we had together as a group, Mary, Scarlett and I.

"I'm sorry. Just hard to know who is my friend and who is my enemy these days." I said and looked over at Cyrus and then back at Giles.

Thorn, Max, Rip and Cassius walked over, and Thorn waved a hand over to Cyrus to beckon him across. "V has something to tell us. He has learnt something while in the Turned base that apparently he can only tell us all together, as we must hear it as one. We can do the rest of the introductions and debriefing later. But I think what V has to say is important."

Thorn put a hand on my back and then pushed me into the centre of the circle surrounded by Mary, Max, Rip, Cassius, Giles, Cyrus and Thorn, and an outer envelope of MI5 guards and behind them, the Spanish military.

I cleared my throat while thinking of where to start. All of them were staring at me, and I knew what I was about to say would cause chaos. However, the truth had to be told. We had to find out who was betraying us.

"Let's start with what happened to me. I fought Giles and Norris, but Bramel and his army captured me. They took me back to their base, which appears to be an old military field hospital."

"I knew you couldn't beat them. It was a waste of time all that training with Rip and Max. It just goes to prove you can't be our king," Cyrus interrupted.

Giles stepped forward and put his hand on my shoulder. "No, you are wrong. Jon beat us all. He won his fight against me and then returned to save my life, as Norris was going to kill me for losing the battle. Jon defeated Norris but got injured. By which time we were completely surrounded by the Turned with Bramel at its lead. Jon beat two werewolves at a full moon. I was told that was impossible."

Cyrus fell silent and then took a step back and looked away.

I allowed a moment of silence and scanned around the circle. "He had me chained up in the cell, constantly testing me to see if the transformation had finished. Because once it had, they were going to cut me open and test my body to find the secrets to the transformation or use this knowledge to create super soldiers. While they were testing me, Bramel would visit. On one occasion, he let slip he was taking orders from somebody else. When I asked him that I thought he was the King of the Turned, he said he was. I asked then who was possibly giving him orders. He said it wasn't a Turned vampire, but something else, someone else. He told me their name was South."

I looked around the circle to gauge the reaction. Cassius and Rip were smiling, and Thorn sighed and shook her head as she walked to my side and leaned into my ear. "You should have told me this before we arrived. I could have saved you from embarrassing yourself."

"Pardon. Am I missing something here? Do you already all know who South is?"

Thorn nodded. "South is supposedly a Dragan. They are the equivalent of the bogeyman. The rumour of South has been around ever since the Turned rebelled against us. None of us takes that seriously. It was just another Turned and Hunter lie to set us against one another."

"Are you sure? When I was captured before, I definitely heard Bramel talking to someone on the phone and taking orders. And today he said orders are orders. He seemed pretty adamant that he was being directed by another person. The fact that the decision seemed to come after any calls or any action from elsewhere indicates another power is controlling them."

"But you have no actual proof. It's just Bramel's word for it and you could have overheard conversations that may have been faked. He was playing with you."

"He told me that South was responsible for giving away our location in the forest hillside, and they knew you were coming to rescue me."

"There could be another explanation for that."

Behind us, Mary coughed and everyone spun around to look at her as the MI5 guards held up their rifles for protection. "I believe what Jon says is true. Our intelligence shows that there seems to be an outside force guiding them. All movements and actions seem to come shortly after phone calls or messages to them. Although we can't monitor their activities in real-time, we can analyse their behaviours and messages afterwards once we know where they have been. And often, like the other day when they attacked, they received a call shortly before they set off. I am afraid to say that yesterday's call appears to have emanated from your group. I wasn't going to say anything just yet. We were waiting to catch them out. But Jon has already uncovered the truth. So maybe you should tell us about who South could be."

The Dragans tensed up, arms folded and stared suspiciously at each other.

I stared at Cyrus. "Well, I have my suspicions who South could be. Someone who created a Turned army before to overthrow the Dragan throne. Someone who only joined the group recently. Someone who has a history of betrayal. Someone who didn't come on the rescue. Someone who has already tried to kill me."

The rest of the group all stared at Cyrus, who snapped out his fangs and eyes burnt red.

"I am not South. What happened with the Turned was in the past. I came here to work with you all to put that wrong right. Just because I don't agree with you being king doesn't mean I am against the Dragans and betraying you all."

"Seems a massive coincidence of your arrival and our betrayal. Your history with the Turned, using them to build an army to kill the Dragans doesn't look too good either. You still want to be the king and would allow your fellow Dragans to suffer for your ambitions."

"You are a liar. This is just a way of taking revenge. You invented this whole thing. You will not force me out. I think you are South, or you have become South. After all, you did side with the Turned and betray Thorn last time."

Thorn intervened between us. "Cyrus, you know he was being tortured. He told them what he needed in order to survive. How could he have been South? He has never heard of him before."

"Bramel told him of South the last time he was captured and recruited. He willingly went to that base and came back with this lie about South to disrupt us. How else did he escape and come back with the werewolf apprentice? And supposedly beat a mature werewolf on a full moon? It's all too unbelievable. He has been on their side the whole time."

"He beat Norris, and I released him from his restraints because we are still friends. He came back to save my life when it would have been easier for him to run the other way. Anyway, we escaped because he tricked them. He made them think he was human again when, in fact, he was a Dragan still," Giles said.

Cassius and Cyrus looked surprised. Rip grinned. "Well done. You remembered your training."

"How on earth did you do that? I guess this is your doing, Rip," Cyrus said.

"Yes," Rip replied and took delight in it.

"So, are you going to share the secret?"

"Of course. With those I can trust."

Cyrus growled. "So you all believe I am actually South? I have done all this to claim the throne. We can settle this once and for all. Let me and the boy finish our fight. He is a Dragan now, so it will be fair according to your rules. If I lose, then I know I can't be king. If I win and become king, if I am South, then the war will be over. But I can tell you now I am not South."

"There is no way I'm letting you fight V. This would not settle anything. It would not prove if you are South or not."

"Regardless, the boy has made accusations. My honour has been tainted.

I deserve the right to clear my name and take my revenge."

Thorn shook her head, walked towards Cyrus and pushed him back. "This is just an excuse. You've already attacked him once and tried to start a fight with him before. If we hadn't been battling each other, maybe we would have stood a better chance against the Turned when they attacked."

"You're scared he will lose. And you will see the truth that he is nothing but a pathetic human. Even with the formula, he doesn't have the true spirit of a Dragan. He is not our blood. He is nothing but a human in Dragan clothing."

"He's more of a Dragan than you will ever be. Being Dragan is also a mindset, it's an attitude. Not what you're born into, but how you behave. I don't think you are a proper Dragan."

Cyrus shoved Thorn backwards and bared his fangs, ready to attack, and Thorn responded. It filled my heart with great pride to see Thorn fight for me.

"Thorn, leave him. This is my battle. I accept your challenge, Cyrus," I said.

Thorn spun around. "No. It tarnishes my honour and my rule as well. I have every right to defend my name, and as Queen of the Dragans, I reserve the right to fight first."

"Thorn, that is probably true. But Cyrus and I are technically still in the middle of a fight from earlier. We should finish this first. Then he is all yours."

Thorn looked at Cassius and Rip.

Rip nodded. "He is right. Our laws allow the first challenge to be completed before the next one can start. If V wants to fight, then he must be allowed to continue without interruptions."

"I am sorry, Thorn. I have to agree with Rip. V must finish his fight first," Cassius said.

Cyrus laughed and stepped around Thorn. "Thank you, my Dragan friends. You understand the truth of what I say. New leadership is required. This woman has gone weak in the head from her time with this human."

Rip wagged his finger back and forth. "No, I believe V will beat you. He has just defeated two werewolves on a full moon."

"As do I," Cassius added.

Cyrus growled back. "What do I care? You will soon see he is not worthy of our name. He is not a proper Dragan. He is a pretender, and I will prove it."

Max walked to Thorn's side and placed his hand on her arm and escorted her back to the edge of the circle, leaving Cyrus and I facing off against one another. Thorn shook off his hand and stomped back to the sidelines. "Thorn, don't worry. You know how well V can fight."

Cyrus stared into my eyes, his eyes burning red, and fangs and claws already out. "Are you ready to die?"

"Ready? I have died so many times before; it will be like greeting an old friend. But are you ready?"

Cyrus' muscles tensed and he held his claws up. I switched on my Dragan transformation, my claws and fangs cut through my flesh, and my eyes hazed in a blood rage. I held my claws up in front of my face to mimic Cyrus' battle stance.

Cyrus flung his claws down, cutting through the air and launched forward, covering the space between us in a couple of steps and slicing up his right claw towards my face. I skipped to the side, and the claw whistled past my ear.

I danced backwards and to the side. Cyrus spun around to keep me front on. I stopped and then slid back the other way, making him chase after me. He fainted to the left, getting to me to move to my right and then switched to attack to the right, lashing a backhanded fist. I swung both hands up to block and took the blow across my forearms.

His hand slid off and scraped his claws across my skin, cutting them in four lines across both arms. I snatched back from the stinging claws and focused my magic on healing them. The lines quickly dissipated back into my Dragan flesh, the blood on top soaking in.

I jumped back to gain breathing room, but Cyrus gave me no quarter, following up with a swinging left. I swayed out of the way, it slashing past my face. I went to counter-attack, but Cyrus had already spun around, pirouetting to hit back with his left elbow into my jaw. He caught me square on the chin and knocked me to the floor. He jumped after me, slamming his foot down. I rolled out of the way as the heel of his boots tried to stamp onto my ribs.

I twisted onto my hands and then vaulted back onto my feet. I immediately front kicked him back in the stomach, sending him flying backwards into Cassius and Rip, who pushed him back into the fight. We circled around each other, fainting attacks and dancing out the way.

I had my magic stored up as a glowing purple sphere in the pit of my stomach. But it wasn't big and strong enough to turbocharge my powers enough to beat him. I needed more emotion to fuel it, something I felt drained of after my ordeal with the Turned. I was just relieved to be away from them and back with Thorn. Having to face Cyrus again just made me feel depressed and desperate rather than angry, which would have helped.

However, it was clear this battle meant everything to Cyrus. And even though he didn't understand how the magic and the Dragan powers work together, this emotion was enough to fuel his abilities and attacks. I needed to get angry; I needed to feel something. Depression and desperation weren't strong enough to feed the magic.

Cyrus attacked again, even quicker than before, as if he sensed my desperation. He had retracted his claws and attacked with his fists, a quick couple of jabs, a right and a roundhouse into my lower right thigh. Then he launched a kick into my ribs, which I blocked, but I took a nasty smack on my shins to stop it.

The bruising subsided, but the sight of his success drove on his frenzied attack. His fists swung in fast. I covered up, blocking the hits across my arms but underneath, an uppercut snuck through. My head jolted backwards. I tripped up over my own feet and slammed to the floor.

Cyrus flung his hands in the air. "And in the first round, our favourite Dragan is dominating the ring," Cyrus said, smiled and punched the air in victory and walked around my prone body.

He was arrogant, which I realised was fuelling his power but was also his weakness. The sight of him bragging and the look of fear on Thorn's face snapped me out of my desperation and depression, and I felt a tingle of anger brewing inside.

I jumped back onto my feet. "But he hasn't taken the count yet and our underdog is back in the match," I said.

Cyrus stopped smirking and coiled back his fists. He was lightning fast again, but I didn't bother to duck too much. I took one to the chin, one in the ribs and one across the face. I allowed my legs to go, and I fell to the floor again.

He kicked me in the ribs a couple of times. I curled into a ball as he kicked my back and shins. The blows rained in, and with it, his laughter echoed around the air hangar. "Pathetic boy. Beaten so easily. Whoever said you could be one of us," he shouted.

The event triggered memories of other beatings at the hands of the Hunters when they fought against me as an experiment. And at the hands of Barry's gang when they beat me up when I moved to London. With every kick and every taunt, my rage grew exponentially from my memories. His arrogance grew, which would make him sloppy and would weaken his own anger.

The next kick came in, and I caught it and shoved him backwards and staggered to my feet. I held my magic back from healing me, letting it build up to an unstoppable torrent to launch my attack.

All the while, blood dripped off my face, and the bruises on my body swelled and pulsated in agony. But the pain fuelled my magic.

I rocked on my feet and pulled my hands up into a boxing guard.

"Are you joking?" Cyrus said. "You've got guts, I will give you that. But it looks like you're broken. Your body can't keep up with the damage."

I said nothing but just waved him forward, my magic at bursting point. I just needed to direct it and unleash my fury upon him. He swiped out his claws again and jutted out his fangs.

"I am going to rip your throat out and then spill your guts all over the floor," he shouted.

He ran forward, but Thorn jumped in between us and pushed him back. "No, that is enough."

"You are conceding for him. Throwing in the towel?"

"No," I said and stepped around Thorn to continue the fight. He swung a claw, and I went to block, but Thorn had grabbed hold of my arm to pull me back, accidentally preventing me from defending myself. Cyrus' claw slammed straight into my throat, and Thorn yanked me back, unplugging the wound and blood poured out.

I crashed to the floor and slapped my hand over my throat to stem the bleeding. I had no choice but to focus all my magic on healing, else I would bleed to death. The purple sphere evaporated as its energy fuelled my healing powers. The flesh around my throat reassembled and stopped the blood from pouring out. I was empty. I had no magic left to fix the rest of my beaten body. And nothing left to fight with.

Thorn crouched over me and held her hand up to prevent Cyrus from pressing his advantage. Thorn looked down, her eyes swelling with tears. "I'm sorry. That wasn't supposed to happen. But stay down. Let me take care of this."

Thorn turned to Cyrus, keeping her body between him and me. "Leave him. You win."

"You concede. You recognise me as the King of the Dragans?"

Thorn cast her eyes down. "If I must, so I can save him. But you don't realise how important he is."

"Because of his genetics. Because of the DNA secret his body holds and the fact he can become Dragan. I understand it completely. I just don't believe we need any more Dragans. So our race cannot reproduce, so what. Maybe there shouldn't be too many of us. I prefer to remain unique and immortal. The best thing we can do is to end this experimental monstrosity, taking away the chances of the Turned and the Hunters getting their hands on the secret."

"You're not going to kill him. Do you not want there to be more Dragans? Do not want to continue our race? Do you not want to be king of a great number of people?"

"More Dragans, more competition for the throne. We are immortal. We don't need to worry about the survival of our race. I will enjoy my life while it lasts, which will be a very long time. The less of those like us, the less I have to worry about someone trying to steal my throne. This is our uniqueness, this is our strength. If there's an entire planet of Dragans, then we are no longer special."

"Do what you want, King of the Dragans. But please don't kill him. Let him go," Thorn said, crouched next to me.

I tugged on her arm to show her that I was okay, but she just placed a reassuring hand on my shoulder and squeezed it while still looking at Cyrus.

"Why would I let him go? What will you give me in return?"

"I will be your Queen. Isn't that enough?"

"Nearly. You can remain with me but not as my Queen, but as my concubine. I will choose my own Queen or Queens. You can merely serve me."

"No, he means the Twins. Don't agree to it, Thorn. Let me finish the fight," I said.

Thorn spun back to me, red tears running down her cheeks. She shook her head and placed a hand on my face and stroked my bruises. "He will kill you. I cannot let you die. While you're still alive, there is always hope for us."

My own tears stung the back of my eyes. She was willing to give it all up, all of her dreams and ambitions, all of her authority and power. She would sell herself into servitude to this arrogant Dragan to save my life. If

I ever questioned if she loved me, now I had my answer. My magic was empty from healing the critical wound to my throat. But her love was like emotions on steroids, and my purple sphere of magic erupted back into life.

Cyrus stepped forward. "Now get out of the way, wench. Let me dump this monstrosity in the trash."

Thorn looked back up as Cyrus swung down a backhanded fist across her face. She stumbled across to the side. Her tears were streaming down her face and cheek was swelling up. She spat out blood and pulled herself onto her knees. Cyrus pointed at her to stay down.

I stared at her in total shock. He had hurt my Queen. He would continue to beat her throughout eternity. My magic was charging again from her expression of love for me, but this last action triggered a red rage that I couldn't channel or hold.

My core of purple magic exploded like a nuclear bomb. I tried to direct it the best I could, but it overwhelmed me and incinerated through every muscle and limb. The remaining bruises and cuts healed within an instant, my strength renewed, and an extra power flooded my body. I rolled onto my back and flicked myself on to my feet.

A roar grew from my guts and exploded out. "Leave her alone."

Cyrus stared and clenched his fists, ready to attack. My magic burnt as I looked down at her crying and bruised figure. My arms and legs spasmed as they filled with power. Dragon scales rose across my flesh. I knew it was a bad idea to allow myself to become a full Dragon, so I focused on redirecting the energy to pure Dragan power instead. The muscles warped, growing stronger and bigger across my body. My claws thickened and eyes burnt so fiercely I saw everything tinted red. So violent was the change that my head shook and my arms jerked around trying to contain the influx of power.

As my body went into overdrive, Cyrus' face slumped, his hands released to his sides and eyes widened. He turned and ran, but Rip and Cassius propelled him back into the circle. I strode across the gap between us. Thorn's face was in shock. The blood from her tears absorbing back into her pale cheeks. The bruise on her face shrinking.

I swung a left claw and Cyrus tried to block it, but it smashed through and cut into his shoulder. He twisted in pain and spun away from me. He turned and placed his hand on the blood and inspected it. The sight of his own blood fuelled his power, and he unsheathed his claws and leapt back and swung down with a right claw.

His attack was wild but full of rage. My arm blocked it, but his claws pierced through my flesh and stuck into it. I tensed up the muscles and activated the dragon scales around it, preventing him from retracting his claws. I swiped down with my free hand and broke off his claws embedded in my forearm.

He yelled and stumbled back into Max and Giles, who pushed him back into the fight. He retracted his other claws and swung with wild fists. I released my power into a straight left and hit him before his wide punch came full swing. My fist slammed into his nose, blood spraying down his face, and he crashed to the floor. He wiped the blood from his face and scrambled to his feet.

He looked around the edge of the circle, looking for an escape, but everyone held firm and glared back with satisfied smiles. He twisted back and charged at me. I focused my power and slid out of the way, sending him crashing to the floor at the feet of Thorn, who had stood back up.

He went to grab her leg to pull himself up, and she backhanded him across the face. "I owed you that one."

I stomped over, grabbed him by his waist, hoisted him over my head and then dropped him down onto my outstretched knee, his back cracking on impact. Then I tossed him to the floor like a piece of junk.

He tried to stand, but his back was broken. He crawled away towards the hangar doors, where the MI5 agents stood in the circle.

As he crawled, his bones snapped back into place, followed by his screams of agony. He pushed himself onto all fours as the last of his back repaired. I waited for his body to recover, and then walked around and kicked him in the ribs, spinning him over onto his back. I knelt across his chest and place my new massive hand across his jaw to open it wide.

"You don't deserve these," I said and reached in with my free hand and gripped his left fang and twisted and pulled it out. He screamed with arms and legs thrashing around. I pinched his other fang and tore it out, throwing them both into Thorn's hands. His screams drowned out as the blood from his gums poured into his throat. I stood up and loomed over him. "We finished here, South."

Chapter Twenty-Three

Cyrus lay beaten at my feet. Thorn walked over to my side and held my hand.

"Mary, can your team take care of this thing?" she said, gesturing down to Cyrus.

"Of course, we have the facilities," she replied, and the MI5 agents moved in and rolled him onto his front and cuffed his hands and legs together. They picked him up and flung him into the back of a black van.

"We will take him to a safe facility, and I will be in touch with the latest intel to create a joint strategy. We will see if he talks. But I doubt it," Mary said.

"We will stick to the plan as agreed. Hopefully, there will be no more betrayals with him gone," Thorn replied.

Mary looked at me and smiled, and then joined the guards in the range rovers and drove off.

I let go of my hold over my magic, and it buzzed through my body, leaving me on a new high. My psychic sense heightened for a moment, and I read Cyrus revengeful thoughts. I summoned up the last of my energy to deliver a psychic punch into his mind as they drove away. From the back of the van, a scream burst out. I grinned and turned back to my friends.

Rip walked over and placed his hands on my shoulders. "Your training is complete. You even had me fooled with your beaten act for a while."

"You will have to tell us that works," Cassius said to us both.

Giles shook my hand. "I never doubted you. Not after what we went through together. I knew there was more in the tank."

Finally, I turned to Thorn, who slapped me across the face.

"You deceitful little bastard. I was out of my mind, ready to give up everything for you. This was just an act, a game. I should knock your head off."

The rest of the gang backed away and looked elsewhere. "I needed to get him off balance, build my emotions and channel it the right way, as Rip and you had taught me. But it was no act after he pierced my throat. I had nothing left. Your rescue didn't help. I had to use all my energy up to repair my throat. But your offer to Cyrus and your tears and pain gave me plenty of fuel."

"Oh. I'm glad my tears and pain were of use to you. You get a good feed off my heartbreak? I thought I lost you."

I nodded, daring not to speak. The anger in her eyes diffused and she smiled. "Good. Because Rip told me to cry to get you going. I thought he was crazy," Thorn said.

"What? It was an act?" I asked.

Rip turned back. "Thorn, I never..."

"Shh, no need to say anything else. Your insight was instrumental," she replied and waved a hand in front of herself, cutting off their conversation. There was no need to challenge her statement. We all knew the truth.

She grabbed my hand and led me out the back of the hangars, towards a door. "Morning everyone, get some sleep and see you at dusk."

I allowed myself to follow on, checking that Giles was alright before I left. I saw Max wave him over and start talking. They probably had a lot to discuss, and I knew Max would take care of him.

We walked through a series of small grey corridors until we reached some air force personnel rooms. She opened the door into a small grey room with two single beds pushed together in the centre of the room. The beds had white cotton sheets with grey blankets over the top. There was a cupboard in one corner and a small desk in the other. It was a basic military personnel bedroom, nothing fancy, just practical.

Thorn stood at the bottom of the bed, and I shut the door behind me.

I smiled and approached her with my arms held out to give her a hug. "I always look forward to this part. Being back together and making up."

She held out her hands and halted me in my tracks. "Are you kidding? After that little stunt you pulled. There will be nothing going on tonight."

"I had it all under control. You nearly ruined it with that intervention. But it all worked out. Let's not argue now."

"But you could have ruined everything. Surely you would expect me to protect you. You shouldn't have put me in that position. We could have lost everything. Anyway, before we carry on, you said there was something you needed to tell me in private."

I scratched my head for a moment, trying to remember after the haze of the fight. "That's right. When I was talking to Bramel, he denied they killed Scarlett. He said if it was purely for revenge, he would admit it, as that would have been the point of the revenge to upset me."

"Do you not think they're capable of senseless acts of revenge and then lie about it to cause more confusion? Who knows what is really happening in that organisation? If Cyrus is South, he hates you enough to have killed her. They may have hoped it would destabilise you for when he came to fight for the throne."

"We hadn't even met Cyrus at that point. Bramel said it definitely wasn't them. He also suggested other people would benefit from Scarlett's death and they made it look like the Turned killed her."

Thorn's eyes narrowed at me. "So who would that be, or should I take a wild guess?"

"Bramel said, you would gain the most from her being out of the way? You never liked her. I asked him whether he believed it to be you. And he said yes, it is the type of thing you are capable of."

Thorn crossed her arms. "Bramel is right. It is the type of thing I am capable of. But in this case, it was nothing to do with me. We have made a Union." She held up her ring finger with the gold ring of Thorns I gave her. "That was enough for me to know she was no longer a rival."

"There is more. He also said that you and he were once an item."

She shook her head. "This again? You accuse me of jealousy and being unable to let go of the past. At least everything I did was before we were together. In fact, it was before you were even born. And the answer is yes, there were several times we were together. As I said before, I was trying to find a way of reproducing our race. If no Dragan male was capable, I wondered whether a Turned male would be able. The issue may not be of female Dragan fertility, but male Dragan fertility. So I wondered whether Bramel, being removed from the Dragan bloodline but being close enough in magic as a first-generation Turned, might be capable. But it wasn't to be."

"I am not jealous. I had a moment when he told me. But I realise this was before our time together. I remembered what you told me about trying to continue the Dragan race. I just wanted to know if it was the truth."

"I am not lying to you about Scarlett. And I have told you the truth about Bramel and me."

"Okay. Sorry to have asked. And you realise why I had to ask this alone."

"Yes. It's not a question for the general public."

"So, are we all good?" I asked and smiled.

"Well, if there were a couch in this room, I would make you sleep on it. As there isn't, you will have to share the bed with me tonight."

I was disappointed. "Okay, I understand. It's been a long day and I'm tired, and I would like to get some sleep then."

"Yes. Daylight approaches and we need a rest," Thorn replied and started getting changed for bed.

I went around the other side of the bed and removed my clothes. Thorn climbed into the bed and pulled the covers over herself and turned her back on me. I turned off the light by the door and shuffled around to my side of the bed. I climbed in and looked at the back of her head. It's not how I imagined the end of my night once reunited with her, but I could do with the sleep, and I was sure she would forgive me, eventually. I closed my eyes and let the exhaustion of the battles take over and the randomness of my thoughts was drifting me into sleep.

My lips tingled, and I opened my eyes to Thorn's smiling face. "You don't try very hard, do you? Of course I want to make up before we sleep."

My tiredness evaporated in an instant. I leaned forward and kissed her. I put my arms around her waist, and then rolled her onto her back. She kissed back and placed her hands on my back. I stopped kissing for a moment and smiled, and she beamed back. "I still have a lot to learn," I said.

She stroked her hand down my back. "Don't worry. I'm happy to teach you, starting from now." She kissed me again and rolled me over, so she was on top.

Afterwards, we slept the whole day through and partway into the next night. I guess I needed sleep. When I woke at about 10 PM, I was human again, or should I say not fully Dragan anymore. Thorn woke with me. She wrapped her arms around me and pulled me over to her and kissed me again. "So another transformation and another step to becoming a full Dragan. You won't be Human for much longer. I will miss it. I have grown to like you in this more vulnerable state."

I didn't know what to say to her comments. I hadn't noticed a change of being less vulnerable when Dragan. Physically, yes. I was obviously stronger, but it was still me. Still full of the same emotional insecurities, whether Human or Dragan.

She ran her hand across my cheek, and then wrapped her hands around my back, and pulled me on top of her. "I want to make sure we remember these times together."

I understood and kissed her.

We made love again, but this time it was more tender than when we were both Dragans. I think she worried about hurting me. It gave her an excuse to behave differently.

Thorn got up and headed to the shower block while I lay in bed and regained my breath. After a few minutes, I decided I needed a shower as well. I headed out the door and found a pile of green army clothes by the wall. I took them and headed to the showers.

I showered and changed into the new clothes. I stood in front of the mirrors over the sinks, taking in my altered body: another injection and another physical change. The change wasn't as pronounced as the first few, but my forearms and hands were bigger from where I had pushed the dragon energy into them. I required a few more injections to be fully transformed. I doubted I would physically change much more, but the genetics would improve and my abilities grow. Dressed and hungry, I headed back down the corridor to find the rest of the gang.

I wandered down the grey, soulless corridors, listening for them. Further down, voices echoed down the corridor, and I followed them around the corners until an open double doorway led into a large room with several round tables in the middle and long tables against the wall with hot metal containers and jugs of drink.

The smell of bacon, sausages, and eggs steamed out of the metal. The thought of hot food lifted my spirits. At the circular tables closest to the food, the gang all sat together. Giles and Max were talking, and Rip was in deep conversation with Thorn and Cassius.

Thorn looked up as I entered the room and winked. Rip jumped out of his chair and walked over. "Come in and grab a seat. I have got us a bottle of red wine. We must keep up with our training."

He opened his arms up, hugged me and kissed either side of my cheeks. All that time in France must have rubbed off on him.

"Good to see you as well. But I will pass on the red wine for once."

"Okay, more for me then. You are my star pupil, after all. But don't forget to keep up your training."

Giles and Max rose out of their seats as well. Cassius walked over and shook my hand. "Good to see you back with us, little man. Thorn dragged you off last night before I welcomed you back."

"Thanks, Cassius. It was great to see you all came for me."

Max walked over, followed by Giles, who hung back a little. Max slapped me on the shoulder. "I knew you would be okay. I have seen you fight before."

"Thanks, Max. I can always rely on you."

Max stepped to one side to leave Giles standing alone. Max walked over to Rip and Cassius. "Guys, we are taking in the night air for a while. Stretch our legs a bit. It's only one night after the full moon, so it's good for me to burn off any transformation energy. And I promised these guys a race to answer the age-old question, Dragan vs Werewolf. I will give them a head start," Max said, and followed Rip and Cassius out of the room, leaving me with Giles and Thorn.

Thorn's phone rang. "Hi, Mary. Just give me a minute to go somewhere quiet." She waved to us both and walked out of the room, leaving Giles and me alone.

Giles smiled. "I think they have left us alone to talk."

"Okay. Is there a problem? I thought we were all good or at least on the road to amends."

"We are all good. Best friends again. But I need to tell you something. Let's sit down," he said and returned to the table.

I followed him over and pulled out a chair to sit next to him. He pulled out his chair, so we were face to face.

"Well, best spit it out, old friend," I said.

Giles took his cup of coffee and drunk it down. "I am leaving with Max."

I sat upright in my chair. "Okay. Why? I thought you would stick around and help us fight, get your revenge. Your knowledge of the Turned and Hunters will be invaluable to us."

"I know. But I can still help, even if not with you guys. I need time to come to terms with what happened. Max is the best person to help with it, as he understands everything about being a werewolf. I'm not as strong as you. I am only human again once the transformation is over."

"But you've changed. You're bigger and stronger as well."

"Yes. The werewolf transformation alters every person physically, so I am stronger and more powerful than the average human, just as Max is, but in human form it's not enough to fight against the Turned. Max is worried you guys will get me killed."

"Max is a worrier. But he may have a point. I would like to have you about, but I don't want to put your life at risk either."

"Max is going to tell me the truth about being a werewolf, and if I want to change permanently, he will do it."

"You want to change for good?"

"Maybe. Do you want to be a Dragan for good?"

"Yes. But it's different."

"Why?"

"Being a Dragan is like being human regarding my body, it's just more powerful. But being a werewolf is a complete change."

"I get what you are saying, but the feeling of being a wolf is amazing. Being one with the wild is a feeling of total uninhibited freedom. But it comes at a cost, the change is horrifically painful, and it is easy to get lost in the animal instinct."

"Giles, it's your choice, my friend. Whatever you decide, I'll understand. I will always have your back from now on. I am so sorry for what happened to you and your family. It's my fault. It was me they wanted on that day at school. Then I abandoned you and never came back for the trial, which would have saved your mum."

"I know and I understand you had your own problems. It is clear to me now. And when you could, you took revenge for me. Thorn and Mary will pull some strings and get my mum out. You have already taken revenge on the O'Keefe family for me. Just Kieran left to deal with. We can sort that one out together."

"Okay, but no killing. I also think we should pay a little visit to Mr May and give him a fright. He could have protected us, as our teacher it was his job."

"I agree. The time will come when we can tie up all the loose ends."

Both Giles and I stood up. I stretched out my hand, and he shook his head and put his arms around me. I hugged him back. It was good to have my best friend again.

Thorn walked back into the room, putting her phone into her pocket. "Good. You've spoken?"

"Yeah, it's all sorted. What did Mary want?"

"Mary has a proposition for us."

"Cool. We have a plan then on how to fight the Hunters and Turned."

"Yeah. Pack your bags. We are flying back to England."

"Cool. Then what?"

"We are going back to school."

Thank you for reading

Did you enjoy it? Did you love it?
Reviews are the life blood of books.
They are quick and easy. It's fangtastic to get them.
I would greatly appreciate a review to spread the word.

You only need to click your number of stars, write a sentence on why you liked it and add a quick couple of words for a title. It will only take you as long as sending a tweet or posting a quick message on facebook.

Want to know how it ends?

The War of Vengeance - Vampire Formula 4

The final book in the Vampire Formula series.

Bramel frees Cyrus and forms an unholy alliance, forcing V and Thorn to seek the powerful Dragan Twins.

Both sides draw together their most powerful allies and draw up their battle strategies. The Dragans and MI5-S must work together, as war against the Turned and Hunters is inevitable.

To survive, V (Jon Harper) needs to complete his training and fully transform into a Dragan if he is to fight Cyrus and Bramel. Only the heat of battle can decide the future and reveal the past.

In the explosive last book, everyone is gathered together for the final battle. When the dust settles, nothing as it appears.

Printed in Great Britain
by Amazon